ANCIENT SHADOWS

The Ancient Secrets Novels

ANCIENT ECHOES

ANCIENT SHADOWS

ANCIENT ILLUSIONS

The Rebecca Mayfield Mysteries

ONE O'CLOCK HUSTLE

TWO O'CLOCK HEIST

THREE O'CLOCK SÉANCE

FOUR O'CLOCK SIZZLE

FIVE O'CLOCK TWIST

SIX O'CLOCK SILENCE

THE THIRTEENTH SANTA (Novella)

The Angie & Friends Food & Spirits Mysteries

COOKING SPIRITS

ADD A PINCH OF MURDER

COOK'S BIG DAY

MURDER BY DEVIL'S FOOD

COOK'S CURIOUS CHRISTMAS (A Fantasy EXTRA)

Plus...

DANCE WITH A GUNFIGHTER

THE DRAGON'S LADY

SEEMS LIKE OLD TIMES

THE GHOST OF SQUIRE HOUSE

DANGEROUS JOURNEY

ANCIENT SHADOWS

JOANNE PENCE

QUAIL HILL PUBLISHING

ANCIENT SHADOWS

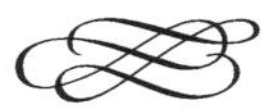

PART I

The Visitor

CHAPTER 1

"The demon does not physically inhabit the body; it possesses the person's will. We have to compel the thing to reveal itself and its purpose. It can be slow and difficult, with the demon taunting, scorning, abusing you - speaking through the mouth of the possessed, but not in his or her Voice. In the end, though, it does come out - and when that happens you experience the sensation we call 'presence'. At that moment you know you are in the company of the purest evil."

—Father Malachi Martin
"An Article on Exorcism"

Florence, Italy

Michael Rempart pulled the collar of his jacket tight against his neck and side-stepped black, grit-filled rain puddles. The rain had stopped, but the air was damp and cold. He hurried along the narrow city streets unable to shake the feeling of being watched, of being followed.

A high forehead over intense brown eyes and jutting, angular cheekbones gave him a severe demeanor, while jet-black hair without a single strand of gray despite his forty-one years swirled and slapped against his face in the blustering wind. Murky yellow lights from street lamps shimmered on the wet cobblestone. Florence was colorful and charming in sunlight, but in rain it became dank and shadow-filled. Michael first arrived here in the spring to recuperate after badly injuring his left arm and shoulder in a bizarre incident in Idaho. Florence suited his mood then, colorful, green, and lush with flowers, light showers and gentle mists. The summer was brutal with heat and wall-to-wall tourists. He nearly left, but the locals encouraged him to stay, saying the gaggling crowds would soon be gone.

Autumn wrapped itself around his heart, with its waning warm days, cool night breezes, and opulent harvests—fresh fruit, vegetables, cheese and wine, the abundance of Tuscany in all its glory. But far too soon the bone-slicing winds of the approaching winter would hit. He wasn't sure how much longer he would stay in Florence. But if not here, where? He was an American, but no one waited for him back in the U.S. No one particularly cared what he did, or where he went. Nor did he.

He was a solitary figure, friendly but a mystery to his neighbors who were quick to notice that he seemed to have no close friends or companions, male or female, and spent most of his time pouring over books. That night he had gone, alone as usual, to a lecture at the Uffizi Museum given by an archeologist who had recently unearthed a sealed Etruscan tomb not far from Florence. Although Michael's Italian wasn't very good, he found the slides interesting. He, too, was an archeologist—or had been. Currently, nothing captured his interest sufficiently for him to pursue a new dig. He wondered if anything ever would. He had become almost a hermit, burying himself in studies of the Middle Ages and Renaissance. Instead of the tanned, well-toned, outdoor-loving traveler he had once been, he hardly recognized the pale, gaunt figure that looked back at him when he shaved.

The hour was late, and this part of the city still and quiet. A dark, covered walkway off a side street led to the dimly lit courtyard of the nineteenth century building where he rented an apartment. He walked up three steps to his front door, unlocked it, and switched on the light. As he turned to shut the door he was startled to see an elderly stranger standing in the courtyard just a few feet away. He was small of stature, with olive skin, long salt and pepper hair and a scraggly gray beard that reached his chest. Dressed completely in black, his unbuttoned overcoat revealed a large silver crucifix on a heavy chain over his heart.

"C'è qualche problema?" Is there some problem? Michael asked.

"We must speak." The stranger's deep, raspy voice sounded harsh and determined. He spoke English with an accent Michael couldn't readily identify. As the man stepped closer, the light from inside the apartment showed a cadaverous face with a waxy, yellowish cast, and thin, painfully tight skin. His brows, a thick mixture of wiry white and gray hairs, shadowed dark, red-rimmed eyes that never left Michael's. "My name is Yosip Berosus. I am a Chaldean priest. Time is running out for me."

A dark chill rippled through Michael at the priest's odd statement. He was familiar with the Chaldeans, one of the ancient Eastern rites of the Catholic Church, found mainly in Iraq, northwestern Iran, and southeastern Turkey. Their leader was the Patriarch of the diocese of Baghdad. The priest sounded desperate, but not dangerous. Michael nodded and stepped back, opening the door wider by way of invitation.

As the priest entered the dimly lit apartment, he rested an emaciated, pale hand against the burnt ochre wall and took several deep breaths to steady himself.

Michael moved closer to help him. The old man reeked. Not the usual stink of sweat and filth, but a sour, musky odor, one of rot. An odor that reminded Michael of death. He gripped the priest's arm, so fragile it felt like no more than bone, and led him to a chair at the wooden dining table. Shelves overflowing with books and research papers lined the wall behind the table. A desk, sofa, coffee table, and television on a stand made up the remaining furniture. The tiny bedroom was upstairs.

Michael crossed to the alcove that served as a kitchen, its appliances old but sufficient for his solitary purpose, and poured one glass of Chianti and another of water and set them before the priest. He drank the water first, then reached for the wine. "I've heard about you," Berosus said. "Everything. I know you have been to Mongolia, and what you discovered there."

Michael had wondered why the old man sought him out, but hearing those words, the door to any sympathy he might have felt for the priest slammed shut. A year earlier he had opened the two-thousand year old tomb of a Chinese governor and his wife who had died in Western Mongolia. The wife had been a practitioner of alchemy, and finding her led to a change in Michael's life from which he still hadn't recovered, and most likely never would. He didn't like it that this stranger referred to those unnerving events. "Anything I may have discovered in Mongolia is now lost to the world."

"So be it." The priest's gaze was hard and flat. "You remain the only person I dare give this to." With a shaking hand he reached into his coat pocket. The edges of the sleeves were frayed, the elbows worn thin, and one of the buttons on the cuff hung by a thread. In his hand he held a wadded up cloth, yellow with age.

Placing the cloth on the table, he unfolded it. Michael gaped at the object revealed. Berosus gestured for Michael to pick it up and inspect it.

The bronze vessel was small, with a lid, and stood on three legs. Michael had spent a great deal of time in the Orient with archeological projects and had more than a passing familiarity with China's past. The bronze appeared genuinely old and cast with a monster design that the Chinese call *t'ao t'ieh,* a mask with large round eyes, c-shaped horns and an s-shaped mouth. The design had been prevalent in the late Shang dynasty but its meaning was no longer known.

Only tests could determine the exact age of the piece. The workmanship was primitive, but it seemed far too well preserved to be from the Shang, a dynasty so ancient that for centuries Westerners believed it was mythological. Archeological finds proved it did exist, however, from about 1600 B.C. to 1050 B.C.

Michael tried to lift off the lid, but it seemed to be stuck. Gnarled, brown fingers snatched the vessel away.

"You must not open it." Berosus scowled. "Inside is a pearl, a red pearl. Were you to look upon it, you might think it beautiful and harmless, but it is not. It is evil. It will look back at you and know you. From that time, you will be under attack. It has the power to do irreparable harm to you, to destroy your life."

Michael fought the urge to laugh at the irony of the words, considering what a mess he'd made of it. "I don't need a red pearl for that." He would have thought a priest was above such superstitious claptrap. That many significant archeological findings contained "something evil," yet none were ever said to contain "something good" was nothing but an irritating publicity stunt in hopes that the resulting attention would translate into more funding. Not one of the warnings stood up to serious scrutiny. The red pearl wouldn't either.

Berosus frowned. "The pearl was guarded by Nestorian Christians when Marco Polo stole it from them and brought it to Venice. It has been a curse to the Western world ever since. I, alone, have saved the world from its wickedness. Now it is your turn."

"Did you say Marco Polo?" Michael all but spit out the name. *This old priest thinks he saved the world? If so, he's done a piss-poor job of it.*

He wished this visit was a sick joke, but he knew no such jokesters. His onetime assistant, Li Jianjun, Michael's last remaining link to his past, worried about his increasing melancholia and withdrawal from people. He could almost see Jianjun coming up with something like this. Almost, but not quite. This priest was no actor, and Jianjun was currently home with his wife in Vancouver, Canada. "You don't really expect me to believe any of this, do you? What do you want? Money? Do you expect to sell this to me? Where did you get it? If it's truly as old as it appears, it should be in a museum, dated and catalogued."

Berosus' face tightened with anger. The light over the dining table and the one in the kitchen area flickered. The storm, Michael thought, must have gotten much worse. "I am trying to warn you!" Berosus shouted. "I don't want your money. I have no use for it. And you cannot give this to anyone, especially not to some fool at a museum."

He breathed deeply, trying to calm himself. "I've spent my life, every waking hour, controlling it, fighting it. But now, my time is short. I came to you because I believed you would not only understand, but if anyone could do what must be done, it is you. Others want the pearl for its power, but they must not get it. You must keep it from them. The red pearl is the only means to control certain demons loosed upon us."

"Demons?"

"Yes! The pearl must not be destroyed or the demons will be set free. The way to stop them is to return the pearl to the Nestorian monastery on the Silk Road, the monastery from which Marco Polo stole it. Only there will the demons be stopped. I tried to get it there, but I failed. You must not."

Michael shook his head. Demons, what rubbish. The old priest was not only sick, but delusional. Perhaps insane. "I've spent a lot of time in China, Father, and studying its history, so I know a bit about the Nestorians—that they went to China after their split with Rome, but were eventually thrown out of the country. It's said they no longer exist anywhere." As he spoke, he sensed the turmoil in the old man, his fear and anguish, and Michael was softened by them. Even if his story was no more than a feverish delusion, the priest's desperation and sorrow were real. Michael's voice turned gentle as he added almost pleadingly, "Even if I wanted to take up the task, Father, it's impossible. I'm sorry."

"The most learned among us are often the least willing to listen. I know what I speak of." Instead of responding to Michael's sympathy, Berosus sounded bitter, his gaze more desperate, fiercer. "You must do as I say. I pray my faith in you was not unfounded."

The priest's black eyes bored into Michael and seemed to look into his very soul. It bothered him; he had buried too much there to be easy with its revelation to the padre.

Berosus began to tremble. He sipped some wine and when he spoke his words came slowly, his voice thinner and more quavering with each syllable. "For years I attempted to return the pearl to the place where it would do no further harm. I left my order and tried to travel deep into Central Asia, but I was always turned away. I took to hiding, trying to sneak through the area to search for the monastery that most people believe no longer exists. I lived in shadows, a figment of the darkness the pearl cast on the earth. Ultimately, I failed." Increasingly agitated, he added, "An evil lurks about the pearl. Remember, it can read your thoughts. You must hide any thoughts from it. Don't forget. Don't ..."

Berosus shut his eyes, needing to catch his breath after saying so much. "I am too tired to fight it any longer, and I cannot give this burden to one of my fellow priests, not when there are too few priests and the people desperately need each one of them. And sadly, I cannot think of a single priest who would believe my tale. I fear what will happen upon my death, the evil that will walk the earth. As I weaken, it grows stronger each day, each hour. I believe you feel it as well."

A hacking cough interrupted him.

The air became heavy. Michael's skin prickled. He had walled himself off from others, from emotion, from passion, ever since he learned what he was capable of doing. And now, this old priest threatened the peace he had found here. "What if I refuse? What if I say you're crazy and I want nothing to do with you or with this false Shang dynasty container?"

"You are not as foolish or skeptical a man as such words would have me believe," Berosus said. "I sense your ability. Your power is stronger than my own. I was right to come to you if only you can be made to see, to believe, what your heart tells you is true. You have seen things most men would never believe. But I believe them. You must take up my task, I beg you. Return the pearl."

"But if there is no monastery," Michael insisted, stopping when the old priest's color turned even more ashen.

Berosus stood up, his eyes wide as he faced the window. "There! Begone! Leave me in peace!"

"Calm down, Father." Michael stepped to the priest's side and placed a hand on his back to steady him.

Berosus groaned, raising his fist towards the sky, bending over, his arms tight around his stomach.

"What's wrong?" Michael asked. "Is there someone I can call? A doctor?"

"No, no. I don't need anyone," Berosus said. His hands gripped the tabletop for support. "Not anymore. But I warn you—"

"Sit, please." Michael took the priest's arm. "You aren't well."

"They are stronger now. They must not find me here."

"Who must not find you?"

Berosus clutched Michael's sleeve. "Think! Why did you come to Florence? You knew no one here, yet you remained. Alone. Restless. Waiting. For what?"

Berosus let go and walked shakily to the door. Michael opened it, and as he watched the priest cautiously descend the front steps, a black disquiet crawled from the pit of his stomach up to his brain. The priest's words echoed the questions he'd asked himself. Why had he stayed in Florence? Something held him here, something he had never been able to articulate.

The old man's gait steadied as he crossed the courtyard. Michael abruptly shut the door, relieved to see the man's back. But in the living area he saw the bronze vessel sitting on the dining table, its monster-design S-shaped mouth mocking him. He grabbed it and ran out to return it to the priest.

The priest was no longer in the courtyard. Michael hurried to the street where the rain now fell in heavy sheets, but didn't see him there either. Berosus must have fallen, perhaps was lying in a doorway. Michael rushed up one side and down the other.

Berosus had vanished.

The words the priest had said to him reverberated as he went back indoors, drenched and chilled. Was this the reason he had been drawn to Florence? He grabbed a towel to dry his hair and wipe his face. He glanced at the clock. It was midnight.

He should go to bed and forget the strange visitor, but he couldn't The Chinese bronze called to him.

The priest had warned him against opening it. As an archeologist, he had often been warned not to open tombs, chests, sarcophagi. The popularity of "the curse of King Tut's tomb" only added to common perceptions of the dangers of tampering with ancient objects, despite the fact that all the men who opened King Tut's tomb had died of natural or easily explained causes.

He picked up the bronze, took hold of the lid, and tried twisting it, but it refused to open.

Michael held it up close to the light. It was tiny for a bronze, no larger than a ripe apricot. The three legs, he saw, had been cast separately. He fiddled with them and found that he could twist them. But still, nothing happened.

Then, quite by accident, he simultaneously twisted two of the legs, and with that, the lid began to rotate. It split into five leaves that separated much like a shutter opens over a camera lens. The opening grew larger as he continued to turn. He had never seen such a mechanism in any early Chinese craft. A tiny pillow of black silk lay directly under the opening. He lifted it by its black tassel. Beneath it, nestled in more black silk was what looked and smelled like soil, like earth. He lightly brushed some aside with the tip of his finger, and buried within it, he found a small red stone.

He placed the stone in the palm of his hand and held it under the desk lamp. It was the shape of a perfectly round pearl, but that was where the similarity ended.

He knew what it was.

He had seen a stone similar to this once before, a red philosopher's stone, the source of alchemy, the prime agent needed to perform an alchemical transformation. He had seen it in Idaho … before his life went to hell.

Now he understood why the old priest had sought him out. But how did the priest know?

The blood of alchemists flowed in Michael's veins going back to Edward Kelley, a 16th century Irishman who claimed to be able to transmute cheap metals into gold. He was popular in Elizabeth I's court, but was later imprisoned by the Emperor of Bohemia when he failed to enrich the empire's wealth. Kelley died trying to escape, but his bastard son seemed to have inherited his abilities, as did a grandson. Those abilities could be traced through historical records, from one generation to another, down to Michael himself.

If alchemists did nothing but turn lead into gold, Michael could easily live with that. But alchemy in its purest state was about power, including power over life and death.

Michael had seen men do terrible things because of it, and he didn't want it back in his life.

But it seemed he had no choice.

As he held the pearl, it began to glow. The lights died in the apartment. All turned black around him except for a faint radiance from the small orb in his hand. Despite the darkness he saw a mist, a black mist, swirling around him. His breathing quickened, and his head began to spin.

The priest's words that when you looked at the pearl it looked back at you filled his mind before he fell, unconscious, to the floor.

CHAPTER 2

MALIBU, California

Gene Oliveros stood on the deck of his multi-million dollar, contemporary Malibu home atop a cliff overlooking the ocean, and watched his daughter play with her birthday presents. The sun was shining, the temperature warm, but the air was absolutely still. Californians called days like this earthquake weather. His nerves tightened. He glanced out at the Pacific. No seagulls, no pelicans, not even a pigeon scavenging for food.

It was a bad omen. The thought came unbidden. He believed in omens, although he wouldn't let anyone know that. Gene paid close attention to the hurricanes, typhoons, volcanoes, earthquakes, to any strange natural phenomena that could potentially be dangerous. Maybe that was because of his work. Producing horror movies, where everyday objects turned into deadly missiles to dispatch people to their eternal reward in the most gruesome ways possible, had to have some effect on a person's psyche. Or so Gene liked to tell himself.

Now, he tried to tell himself the weather was, in fact, a good omen. Good because it made him appreciate all he had, and to appreciate it even more than he normally did. That was the trouble with omens, who knew what they meant? Who cared? The day was gorgeous, and he wanted it to be gorgeous, just like his little girl. His princess.

She was five today, the apple of his eye, which was saying a lot given the beauties that buzzed around his studio every day in Hollywood. Not that his films would ever be nominated for an Academy Award. They weren't that kind. They were moneymakers, the kind of movies kids went to on a Friday night. Special effects, blood, and gore.

Amberly, his "third-time's-the-charm wife" as he called her behind her back, was looking young and radiant today, as always. The rumors about her … he tried to shake them from his mind. He didn't believe any of them. They were jealous, those bastards who went running to the gossip pages with any little thing. Let her go to the dentist, and they'd say she was having an affair. Gene didn't go for any of that crap.

She was devoted to him, and his age didn't matter to her. He was thirty years older than she was. So what? He gave her their daughter, didn't he? Besides, those who didn't know his age and didn't know his filmography always took him for a good ten to fifteen years younger than he really was. His peers wanted to know where he got his Botox and facelifts, but he never used any of that shit. Didn't believe in it. Didn't need it. He smiled. Didn't even need to touch up the gray. Good genes, he'd say. Gene of the good genes.

But he shouldn't think of all that here; not now on his baby's birthday.

His chest swelled with pride as he looked around at all that his money had bought. Who would have thought a nobody like him, who used to pick grapes in the fields as a kid with his father and uncles, would now have so much? It was a miracle, no doubt about it.

His daughter's birthday party, held on the deck, had just ended. The house had been built atop a cliff, and the deck hung out over a rocky beach far below. Ocean waves rolled onto the beach under their feet. It was magical, as if one were on a ship. Of course, ever since the baby was born, the walls of the deck had been built higher, and there was even a little ledge around the outside of them so that if she ever did crawl over, she would fall onto the ledge which was also railed. Gene tried to think of everything.

The ocean had served as a glimmering backdrop to balloons, glitter, cake, candy, and clowns who had made Lake's birthday perfect. Lake Oliveros—yeah, weird name. Sounded like a place to him, not a person. He was almost used to it. Amberly had insisted on a "different" name, a name she thought had 'class.' Class was important to Amberly, maybe the most important thing. He didn't see how giving his kid a name that sounded like a pond was classy, but he loved both his girls, so he agreed. What the hell.

He heard a woman's voice inside the house. "I'm sorry I'm so late." The voice was breathless, but mellifluous, the kind that sounded good in movies, and Gene found himself listening. "Verity couldn't make it to the party, but I wanted to be sure your daughter received a present from her. Something special. I'm sure Lake will enjoy it."

"How nice," Amberly said. "Verity is a lovely girl. I'm sorry you and I haven't met before."

"Me, too. My name is Dana. I've got to hurry now, but maybe we can have lunch one day soon. Where is Lake?"

"On the deck, I'll show you."

The two women joined Lake.

Gene watched. There was something oddly familiar about the stranger. She must be connected with the film industry, he thought, and if she wasn't, she should be. Her hair was long and thick, a luscious brown with auburn highlights. After a few moments with Lake, she turned to leave. As the family's housekeeper showed her to the door, she glanced over at him and smiled.

Her eyes, he noticed, were fabulous—a sparkling, brilliant green, the color of emeralds.

He, who prided himself in never forgetting a face, was perplexed as he smiled back and nodded in response.

She tilted her head and then mouthed a word.

He stared, stunned for a moment, he was no lip-reader, for cryin' out loud ... but then he understood. The word was "Egypt."

Everything rushed back at him.

It had been long ago, another time, another world. The smile he wore vanished into horror, and under his perpetual Hollywood tan, his skin paled to ash. "No. This can't be."

His gaze fixed on the wrapped present Lake was about to open.

The sounds of war broke out all around him. An aircraft carrier's shrill whistle blasted, warning all hands to take cover, to prepare for attack. He looked up. The putt-putt of a decades-old Army helicopter sounded, coming closer. It was a movie, he told himself. That's all. A movie suddenly playing in his brain. He covered his ears as he gaped in horror at his daughter. *"Noooooo!"*

"Gene," his wife called, alarmed by his cry, his expression. "What's wrong?"

He didn't hear a word she said as he began to run towards Lake.

She glanced up and gave him one of her darling smiles.

He felt as if his legs wouldn't move, as if he were in a dream where he was trying to run, but couldn't. His legs were numb, his throat so tight he could no longer speak, couldn't cry out a warning as his little daughter reached for the ribbon wrapped around the gift. He saw her pull on it.

When the box exploded, the force of the blast tore the deck from its moorings and shoved it away from the house. Then, like a car that careens off a mountainside, it hung suspended out over the water a long moment before it dropped like a stone, falling hard onto the rocks and waves below.

CHAPTER 3

FLORENCE, Italy

Michael awoke hot and sweaty at seven to the sound of matin bells from the Basilica Santa Maria Novella, a thirteenth-century cathedral that would be famous were it anywhere but Florence where more magnificent structures overshadowed it.

He sat up, oddly dazed and disoriented, his pillow on the floor and the bed covers twisted and yanked out from the mattress.

The night before, he saw four a.m. before he was able to quiet his mind enough to sleep. He was troubled by the way he had passed out. Nothing like that had ever happened to him before.

When he finally did go to bed, he slept fitfully with anxiety-filled, terrible dreams.

He headed for the shower. An old memory came to him of Magda, his nanny after his mother's untimely death. She was Romanian, and he used to believe she was a gypsy. She told him to beware and to never invite a witch, warlock, devil or demon into his home. That if he did, it could possess him.

He felt better as he dried off. Renewed. Clearly, the strange old priest with his absurd stories of an evil pearl and Marco Polo, and seeing what looked like a philosopher's stone, had triggered memories and fears deep in his psyche. In turn, they, along with an overzealous imagination, and probably a bad clam or two in his dinner, caused him to imagine flickering lights, dark swirling mists, and to briefly black out. Now, he was fine.

Surely, the bronze wasn't from the Shang dynasty, but was a very clever fake. And the pearl wasn't a philosopher's stone, but just an amalgam produced in some laboratory—and probably filled with plastics and phosphorescent materials so it seemed to glow in the dark. He should laugh about it.

Marco Polo, indeed!

That the old priest mentioned Marco Polo at all was either a lucky guess on his part, or came about thanks to someone who knew Michael well. Michael's fascination with Polo began at an early age. In fact, he often suspected learning about Polo's adventures in China was one of several reasons he became an archeologist. The mere mention of the "Old Silk Road" sent him into a reverie of the stories he had read in *The Travels of Marco Polo*. He wanted to have similar adventures in his own life. He was living proof of the old saw, "be careful what you wish for."

Several of his archeological travels had taken him to portions of the Silk Road around the Central Asian cities of Tashkent and Samarkand. Most of the road was gone now and warring governments and fierce tribal peoples made what little remained difficult to traverse.

One of the recurring themes in history was how other nations would ignore that part of the world until its inhabitants rose up in unstoppable fury and mercilessly attacked rival states—states they regarded as soft, degenerate, and arrogant in believing themselves immune to falling. The Huns, whose origin is disputed to this day, when led by Attila hastened the Roman Empire's final collapse. Centuries later, again out of seemingly nowhere, the Mongols under Genghis Khan rose up, crossed the steppes, and extended their empire to the gates of Vienna. Even today, Michael thought, much unrest in the world traced its roots to that same rugged area, fingering into ethnic conclaves from around the Caspian Sea eastward to the deserts of Western China.

He walked to his combination living and dining room. The bronze receptacle still sat on the dining table, the bulging eyes of its monster design seemed to follow him, as if to say it would not be ignored. Maddeningly, to his trained eye it looked like the real thing. An uneasy feeling crept through him once more. He had hoped that moving to Italy would free him of these "feelings." It hadn't happened.

He paced back and forth, running thin fingers through his black hair, pushing it back off his forehead, all the while trying to rid himself of a horrible feeling of relentless, approaching doom. He had come to Italy to study, and if he were being completely honest, to hide amidst the antiquity here and lose himself in its museums and universities. He wanted nothing to do with anything else.

That damned bronze was the problem. He needed to find the priest and return it. He could not, would not, take this on. Too much danger lurked along that path. A lesson he had learned well.

The rain had stopped, but dark clouds covered the sky as he left his apartment. Cold morning air cut through his jacket, and he hunched his shoulders, hands in his pockets as he took long-legged strides to the corner café. He bought the morning paper, *La Nazione,* and ordered a cappuccino, paying extra to sit at a table rather than stand at the counter to drink his coffee, a common requirement in many Italian cafés. His smattering of Italian plus a lot of Latin—which he had studied along with classical Greek and Syriac for his archeological pursuits—helped him understand the gist of the news stories he read.

He flipped to the last page of the news section, about to sip his cappuccino, when he jolted, sloshing some coffee onto the paper. A photo of Father Berosus peered up at him. The headline read *"Who is this man?"* It went on to say that "this stranger" was at the Santa Maria Nuova Hospital, and the administrators asked that any relative, friend, or other person who had information on him, to contact them.

There wouldn't have been time since last evening for the hospital to have put the request for information into the newspaper, so the news story had to have been placed a day or so earlier. Most likely, the priest had recovered and was released.

Once Michael got over the shock, he realized this was a break. The hospital would know how to contact the man.

He gulped down the rest of his cappuccino, rushed back to his apartment, put the bronze in his pocket, and then rode his Vespa motor scooter through the chilly streets to the hospital.

Santa Maria Nuova was the oldest active hospital in Florence, dating back to 1288. At one time it had housed beautiful frescos, paintings, and statues, most of which had been moved to museums. Leonardo da Vinci was said to have learned anatomy there by dissecting corpses. At the reception counter, Michael pointed at the newspaper article and said he had some information.

The reception nurse raised her eyebrows. "The doctor who attended him last night is still on duty. I'll page him for you."

"Last night?" Michael asked, confused. Ah! She must mean the doctor who released him. He took a seat and waited.

After some fifteen minutes, a harried physician ran to the nurse. She pointed at Michael. The doctor wore a peculiar expression as he approached. Michael stood.

"I am Doctor Orrecchino," the man said in Italian as he held out his hand. Up close, Michael could see he was younger than he seemed at first glance. Weariness and dark circles below his eyes aged him.

They shook hands. "Michael Rempart."

"I understand you know something about our mysterious patient." The doctor switched to English.

"His name is Yosip Berosus, and he's a Chaldean priest, although I assume you've learned who he is by now. In any event, he gave me something valuable to hold, and I need to return it." Michael decided not to tell them he knew the priest had been released. "It's very important that I give it back to him."

The doctor's expression turned grave. "Are you family?"

Something was very wrong here. "I'm a friend."

"Would you be able to identify him?"

The question jarred. "Are you saying Father Berosus came back here last night and died? Is that what happened?"

The doctor's lips tightened. "He came to us three days ago, *signore*. He was catatonic, unmoving, unaware. In the end, he slipped into a coma. Last night, he passed away very quietly without ever regaining consciousness."

Michael told himself it couldn't be the man he saw. The two looked alike, that was all. Or perhaps the hospital or newspaper had mixed up the photos.

"Tell me, Doctor, what was the cause of death?"

The doctor looked uncomfortable. "He was an old man."

"And?"

"His heart stopped. He died."

"Why the coma?" Michael asked.

"I don't know. We found no trauma. No signs of a stroke. But, at his age ..."

"So you don't know."

The doctor frowned, clearly not liking being questioned this way. His tone was abrupt. "As I said, he was very old. Sometimes, that's the only reason a person dies."

"Will there be an autopsy?"

"There is no need," he said sternly. "In any case, if you could identify the body to be sure it's the man you named, that would be helpful. He was taken to a mortuary for indigents since he died with, apparently, no family and no money. The nurse will give you the address. Perhaps, with your help, someone will claim the body."

"Certainly." Michael nodded. "But before you go, could you tell me the time he died?"

The doctor's gaze was cold. "A few minutes before midnight. Why do you ask?"

Michael couldn't reply. He had looked at a clock shortly after the priest left his apartment. It had been midnight. "It's nothing," he said, in a voice barely more than a whisper.

CHAPTER 4

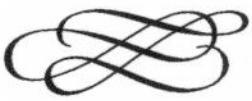

Idaho

"Berosus is dead."

"Damn!" Hank Bennett's hand tightened on the satellite phone at the private eye's news. Bennett, founder and onetime owner of the most advanced internet security program in existence, had spent years searching for Berosus. Just that morning he found a photo of the old priest in an Italian newspaper online. He immediately contacted a private investigator he knew in Italy, Lorenzo Fermi, and told him to find Berosus and the pearl. "What about the pearl?" he asked.

"I don't know. It wasn't in his room at the hospital, and we can't find where he was living. Frankly, we suspect he slept on the streets or homeless shelters."

"Not good enough!" Bennett fumed. He stood in his cabin high on a mountain side in an unprotected area in central Idaho. It was called "unprotected" mainly because the feds, who controlled most of the forest and wilderness lands, never bothered to formally decide if it belonged to the eastern Bitterroot forest, or the western Nez Perce forest. As a result, no one watched the hundreds of thousands of acres of no-man's-land, with no phone lines or cell towers, and no electricity beyond what could be supplied by a generator.

"*Signore*, the priest didn't have what you want." Fermi kept his tone calm. "The man had nothing."

"Do I have to come there myself to investigate?" Bennett raged. "I've paid you good money, more than good. And now he's dead. Where could he have hidden it? Have you done anything at all to earn the money I sent you?"

"*Sì, sì!* I heard that someone, an American, went to the hospital asking about him. I'm trying to track him down, but if he's asking, most likely he doesn't have it either."

"An American? That's bad, extremely bad. Find out everything you can about him," Bennett insisted. "In the meantime, the priest was Chaldean. There can't be that many of them in Florence. Someone's got to know him. Find whoever knows him, and find where he was living, where his possessions are. Do I have to do your thinking for you?" Bennett yelled. "And do whatever it takes, do you hear me? If you want to see the bonus I promised, you'll get some answers for me —useful answers."

"Yes, Mr. Bennett. I will not disappoint you."

"You had better not."

Bennett ended the call and walked to the window, planning his next step. He was in his mid-sixties, but would have looked much younger if he trimmed his light brown hair and bushy beard so that the few frizzy strands of gray wouldn't stand out, giving him the appearance of an aging hippy. A thin man, his face seemed concave from his cheekbones to his jawline, and his eyes were two small, gray-blue circles surrounded by pale lashes.

He looked out on a western branch of the Rockies, broad, rugged mountains, sliced by glaciers into jagged monoliths, many of which had ever known a human footstep. People who opined from their small, crowded urban residences that creatures like Bigfoot couldn't possibly exist or some authoritative person would have sighted and photographed them, had never seen an expanse of mountains like this. Some considered it the most rugged land in the continental U.S.—roadless, impregnable, and threatening.

As much as he cherished the solitude of the area, the land had a sameness to it despite its beauty, and a loneliness that could drive a man mad.

People who knew Bennett would swear he'd gone crazy long before moving there, however. Madness was the only explanation they could give for Bennett leaving the world of information technology ten years earlier. Some of his colleagues swore that if he hadn't sold his company, his fortune one day might have neared a billion dollars.

But Bennett had walked away from all he knew and sold all he owned. He owed no explanation and gave none. Why should he? Those authoritative know-it-alls thought the item he had spent his adult life tracking did not exist.

They were wrong.

His gray tabby leaped onto the window sill and then let out a loud squawk followed by a strange chattering noise at a squirrel on the opposite side of the window, the kind of clicking sound that told him every sinew in the feline's body wanted nothing so much as to sink its teeth into the furry little critter's neck.

He understood the feeling perfectly.

CHAPTER 5

Los Angeles, California

At precisely 5:18 a.m., a loud rumble and violent shaking of the earth woke clinical psychologist, Dr. Kira Holt, from a deep slumber. Dogs in the neighborhood barked in fear of the quivering ground. As she sat upright, the earth stilled. She waited a moment, ready to stand in a doorway or run out of the townhouse if the trembler began again. It didn't.

She switched on her clock-radio to listen for news reports. They would begin to come in almost immediately, and sure enough, a disgustingly cheery-voiced radio announcer let everyone know they weren't feeling whips and jangles or having nightmares. The Los Angeles area had just experienced what he called "a beaut of a shake."

Kira took a quick shower and had just finished drying off when the first report hit from the seismology lab at U.C. Berkeley. The quake rated a 5.9. So far, there were no reports of serious damage. More would become known after the sun came up.

Kira made coffee, glad to have been awakened from a disturbing dream, even if by an earthquake. It was one of those strangely recurring dreams, but she had no idea why she kept dreaming it, or what triggered it. In the dream, she was still married to Ben Simmons.

Remarkably, she was happy, which was rarely the state of her short, ill-conceived marriage. But then, everything turned fuzzy and tinged with red, including the eyes of some strange black creatures. They weren't dogs, and she guessed from their tails they might be foxes, although she had never seen a fox except in pictures, and she couldn't remember ever seeing one completely black. Whatever they were, they frightened her, and she screamed for Ben to run—to run and not look back, to run and be safe.

As a psychologist, she knew if she could connect the bizarre images to real life, she would understand the dream, rationalize it, and overcome it. A tried-and-true formula. But so far, she couldn't find the link.

After yogurt and half a bagel for breakfast, she dried her long red hair and pulled it straight back into a pony tail. She hated the bright color and found that keeping it tight against her head was the best way to stop people from commenting on its color or speculating on whether her temperament matched the fiery locks. It didn't, most of the time.

She dressed in a business-oriented gray pants suit with a silk blouse that matched the sky-blue color of her eyes. She didn't consider herself especially attractive, but she had often been told that her large, penetrating eyes were an effective asset in her line of work. She routinely did all she could to highlight them.

Her nerves were still raw as she reached the Federal Building, a massive, white modern structure on Wilshire Boulevard near Veteran Ave. She showed her badge to get past security. Although her degree was in clinical psychology, she worked increasingly often in criminal profiling. The FBI's criminal profilers were back in Quantico, but the Special Agent in Charge of the Criminal Division of the Los Angeles field office found the practice useful and set aside funds to hire consultants. After she helped successfully track down a child pornography ring, the FBI called for her services so often she found it difficult to maintain a private practice. She had to admit, however, the scope of the FBI job was far more interesting than holding one-on-one sessions, and capturing criminals was more personally rewarding than listening to wealthy people lament about their low self-esteem.

She stepped onto an elevator filled with government workers and pressed the button for the seventeenth floor. The morning's earthquake made her nervous about going so high, but she tried to put it out of her mind by thinking about her current case, one that involved a potential serial killer. Five young women had been murdered, three in California, one in southern Nevada, and one in Arizona. Several odd similarities made it appear the same killer could be involved, but she wasn't one to jump on the "serial killer" bandwagon without hard evidence. They weren't nearly as common as books and movies portrayed, and that line of pursuit could mean that up to four murderers were getting a pass while all of law enforcement concentrated on only one.

Understanding the criminal mind came easily to her, growing up as she did with a father who worked as a district attorney and a judge. Throughout her childhood, Judge Daniel Holt, now on the Federal Ninth Circuit Court of Appeals and rumored to be the top prospect for the next Supreme Court opening, would often muse aloud about his cases, not particularly directing his thoughts towards her, but she was often the only other person nearby. He would ponder what could make a criminal do some of the outlandish, cold-blooded or downright stupid things he saw in his courtroom day after day.

As she progressed in her study of psychology, she realized the workings of the criminal mind weren't exactly the sort of thing one should discuss with a child. But if her father hadn't thought out loud in her presence, he wouldn't have talked to her at all. He never asked her anything as mundane as whether or not she liked her teacher, or her school, or even what she enjoyed reading or watching on television. He had no idea of her best friend's name. But she had listened and learned, and that upbringing served her well in taking on the most interesting cases of her career.

On the seventeenth floor, she crossed the large open floor filled with FBI agents' desks. Hers was in a dark but quiet corner. Only supervisors had private offices.

Someone had placed a couple dozen Krispy Kreme doughnuts beside the staff coffee pot. Kira guessed she wasn't the only one shaken by the earthquake. She poured herself a cup of coffee and grabbed a glazed doughnut, then sat at her desk and picked up the papers in her "in-tray" eager to inspect the latest evidence from Arizona. She had just begun to read them when Special Agent in Charge Edward Lungren approached.

"Something's come up, Dr. Holt," he said. He was tall but rotund, with a fleshy, lined and sagging face that reminded her of a bloodhound. His tie was loose and the top button of his shirt was open. "I have to ask you to put aside your current case for a day or two. I don't think this will take you long, but it's high profile, and I want to be sure all the bases are covered."

He dragged a nearby chair to the side of her desk and sat as he told her about the death of Hollywood horror movie producer Gene Oliveros and his family. "We need a psych profile from you. There's talk it might be a murder-suicide, but from what we've heard so far, he had no reason to do what he did, and was supposedly in love with his wife and kid. Still, the kind of movies he produced showed a warped mind … maybe. Or, he could have made them simply because that was the kind of movie that made him rich. We're only speculating. We need you to find out for sure."

He handed her photos from the crime scene. They were horrifying.

"I'll be glad to help," she said. "But why is this an FBI case?"

He looked sheepish. "It isn't yet. It might never be, but right now, you're our in. The LAPD will do what they can, and that's plenty, but they don't have a criminal profiler so we're happy to assist—with you. If the local police screw-up, or if Washington gets interested given how palsy-walsy they are with Hollywood contributors, we might be asked to help. If so, I want to be on top of things."

"Got it." She threw on her jacket and then picked up her handbag and notepad. She was happy to get out of the high rise.

CHAPTER 6

FLORENCE, Italy

Michael dashed out of the hospital to the sidewalk then stopped and took a deep breath. The air felt crisp but clean after the rain. Sunshine. Pigeons flew. Car horns honked. Crowds of people bustled through the streets lined with shops and cafes. Here, life was normal.

He wanted to get away from the hospital and quickly reached his Vespa. Clearly, the man who died wasn't the elderly priest who had visited him. Maybe the two were relatives. He had no idea, but told himself all would become clear once he reached the mortuary.

First, however, he had the problem of the bronze and the pearl. He traveled as if on autopilot to his bank and placed the bronze and pearl in his safe deposit box, then continued to the place he was dreading to go.

At the mortuary, he was directed to a chillingly sterile, small room. Before long a man, older, balding, and wearing a white uniform wheeled a gurney into the room.

Michael steeled himself. He had seen dead bodies before, but a body without the spark of life was a sad thing to behold.

Please don't let it be Berosus. Please ...

The mortuary assistant quietly watched him, waiting. Michael nodded, and the assistant pulled back the sheet covering the face.

Michael drew in his breath. "Well, he does look like the man I met. But according to the hospital, he was in a coma during the time I spoke with him, so ..."

"Sometimes hospitals are off by a few hours," the assistant said, trying to be helpful. "If he looks like the man you know, I suspect it's him."

Michael stared at the body. It was definitely Berosus. "I'm not sure," he said. "May I see his clothes?"

"No problem." The assistant put the sheet back in place, wheeled the body from the room, and soon returned with a large, black plastic bag. His mouth wrinkled with disgust as he handed it over. "Be careful. Everything's filthy."

Michael opened the bag. It contained the black clothes Berosus had worn and the silver crucifix. He went through the pockets, looking for identification that the hospital might have missed. He found a five euro note, a few coins, several holy medals, and a small photograph of a group of American sailors folded in half. Badly faded, it was the size and shape of a photo taken with an old Polaroid camera. When the assistant looked away, Michael slid the photo into his jacket pocket.

"It's him," Michael admitted, handing back the clothes bag.

After signing some papers to positively identify the body as that of Father Yosip Berosus, he left the mortuary, glad to get the scent of chemicals and flowers out of his nose.

He shivered, but not from cold as he walked to his parking place. He had heard more than once that when the body died the soul sometimes remained on earth for several hours to finish its work or to assure loved ones. He had never experienced that phenomenon, and tended to believe it was said only as a means to comfort the bereaved, but it was the best explanation for what had happened.

He couldn't help but think of how ironic it was that he'd moved to Italy to get away from paranormal weirdness, and now a ghostly spirit may have arrived at his doorstep. But Berosus hadn't been a ghost.

Whatever had come to his apartment was alive and real. He had drunk wine and water, and handed over an object of some weight.

How was it possible? Michael got on his scooter and started it up. It was late afternoon now, and the streets more crowded as they filled with people shopping and going to restaurants.

At the first intersection, a Fiat sedan cut him off. He swerved and nearly ran into a wall. The driver jumped out of the car, followed by another man, and they headed towards Michael.

From their expressions, he knew they were trouble.

The driver swung first. Michael sidestepped the blow, then grabbed the fist that flew by and used the attacker's own thrust to pull him forward and downward. He then struck a Shaolin blow to the back of the man's neck. The attacker dropped like a stone.

But the quick, powerful movement caused pain to shoot from Michael's bad shoulder down his arm to his fingertips. He gasped, unable to move for a moment, and then turned to look for the second man.

He heard a whoosh just before something struck the back of his head and all went black.

Michael opened his eyes to see concerned faces of strangers peering down at him, women's as well as men's. He slowly stood, trying to get his bearings and shake the fuzziness from his brain.

The Fiat and its passengers were gone. One person had picked up his motor scooter, another handed him his wallet, while others tossed a barrage of Italian at him. He didn't understand the words or the situation, and kept repeating *"grazie"* and smiling like some doofus, while inside he was furious. What the hell was going on?

He felt in his pockets and found everything, including his passport, except his keys. He searched the ground, but they were gone. A sinking feeling hit, especially when his wallet still had money and credit cards.

This was no typical mugging. He gingerly touched the back of his head and felt a lump forming. Last night, he'd passed out for no reason, and now some strangers knocked him out. If Florence was trying to tell him he was no longer welcome here, he was getting the message. All he wanted to do, now, was get back to his apartment.

An English speaker offered to help him report the attack to the police or go to a hospital to be checked for a concussion. Sure, and spend hours trying to explain the inexplicable while his apartment was being cleaned out. He thanked the man, but declined, wanting no part of cops, hospitals, doctors or anything else disrupting what had been, until midnight last night, a quiet life.

Without his keys, he couldn't even drive his scooter. A couple of men pushed it to a parking space. Michael caught a taxi home. Anxiety over what he might find there, along with the bump on his head, made him slightly nauseous.

Luckily, his landlady, Mrs. Silvestri, was home. She was in her fifties, rotund, usually jolly, but looked horrified when he told her what had happened, and that his apartment key had been stolen. He once overheard her calling him her "quiet, lonely tenant," and she had even introduced him to a couple of women who immediately became overly shy, and couldn't say much more than hello. Those experiences had been even more painful to him than the whack on the head. Now, Mrs. Silvestri's brown eyes showed her worry as they walked to his apartment and she tried to persuade him to see a doctor. He refused and said he'd be fine. She shook her head as she unlocked his door.

Stepping inside, he saw he'd been right to worry. The apartment had been ransacked, everything overturned and scattered, including his books and papers. Whoever had done this had worked fast, but still managed to open up the back of his computer. It meant whatever was being sought was small. Perhaps the size of a bronze vessel. Or a red pearl.

The landlady entered behind him. He had a spare key, but asked her to have his lock changed as soon as possible, adding he would pay. She soon left, glad to be of some help.

He walked into the living room and sat on the sofa, his head throbbing. If this had been a normal mugging and robbery, they would have taken his watch and cell phone, and once inside the apartment, his laptop, tablet, TV, and cameras. But they took nothing of that, which left him assuming the attack had to be related to the dead priest's strange gift. The attackers probably watched him go to the hospital or the mortuary and when they didn't find the bronze and pearl on him, they'd come to his apartment. His driver's license gave them the address.

Three ibuprofens later, Michael straightened up his apartment, re-shelved books and papers, and put his computer back together. He wanted everything the way it had been. An inner voice laughed at him —*ain't gonna happen, fella.* Any normal person would have dismissed the priest's conjecture of demonic forces at work. But "normal" wasn't in his lexicon.

Because of his ancestors, he had studied quite a bit about alchemy. Modern man dismissed it as a sham, but for over five thousand years, people from China to Europe had practiced it. Men who weren't exactly stupid or gullible, such as Leonardo da Vinci and Sir Isaac Newton, believed in alchemy and its spiritual tenets, including its path to immortality.

And, if alchemy could deal with spirituality and immortality, it could also deal with demons.

Maybe the blow to his head was worse than he first thought? He took his spare motor scooter key to retrieve his Vespa.

By the time he returned, despite his head and shoulder vying for attention as to which ached worse, he took out the photo of the American sailors he had found among Berosus' clothes. Seven young men wearing Navy whites and caps smiled into the camera. He saw no medals or badges to indicate they were anything more than young seamen, probably second or third class. Directly behind them loomed the Great Pyramid of Egypt—Egypt, the birthplace of Western and Arabian alchemy.

He assumed one of the men in the photo must have been the padre's close friend or relative. He found a magnifying glass and used it to study the features of each man. He didn't know why, but as he studied it, he felt a presence. He put down the glass.

When he was young, he managed to ignore the peculiar sensations that afflicted him. And afflicted was the right word. Unwanted, they washed over him like an illness. In fact, he had become quite adept at discounting feelings of any kind until the situation in Idaho forced him to listen to them.

Going to the hospital to find the priest had been a mistake. He should have known better. The last thing he wanted was that sort of trouble in his life again.

He couldn't stop studying the photo. None of the men seemed to have features similar to Berosus, but the priest was old, the men were young, and the photo was grainy. If he could find out who those men were, that might lead to knowing who should inherit the bronze Berosus entrusted to him. And move it from his life to theirs. Lucky devils!

He scanned the photo at high resolution, and emailed it to his assistant, Li Jianjun.

Jianjun had been born thirty-six years earlier in Beijing, China, and left at the age of eight when his family moved to Hong Kong. At fourteen, the family immigrated to Vancouver. He landed a good job with Microsoft in Seattle and married the woman his parents chose for him.

Michael met him after Jianjun discovered he enjoyed recreational hacking far more than his programming job with Microsoft in Seattle. For some reason, they clicked, and Michael offered him a new kind of job and a life of constant change. Michael didn't do typical, university-supported archeological digs where masses of students were sent out with tiny brushes to clean the dust off of pottery shards from some ancient civilization. Instead, he followed legends. Using a combination of history, migration patterns, ancient tales, and Jianjun's clever computer skills, he had found buried treasure, hidden tombs and, once, a sunken galleon.

Someday, Michael hoped to return to such archeological adventures. But for now—or at least until last night—he had found peace in Florence and had sent Jianjun home with a generous stipend. After Idaho, Michael was hesitant to plunge into a new endeavor. Fear of the unknown filled him—exactly the sort of fear that was anathema to someone whose career was built on excavations and venturing into dark and mysterious areas.

He hated the idea of delving into Father Berosus' life and the people in this photo, but at the same time, he felt obligated to return a potentially valuable old bronze to its true owner.

He phoned Jianjun.

The time difference was nine hours, with Florence being nine hours ahead of Vancouver. Although it was 11:00 a.m. there, Jianjun was still sleeping. Like Michael, he preferred to stay up late into the night, and to sleep in the morning. Michael's call woke him up.

Michael told him about the photo he had emailed and asked him to find out who the sailors in it were.

"You're asking me to hack into old U.S. Navy records?" Jianjun asked, his voice thick with grogginess.

"Why else would I be bothering you at this ungodly hour?" Michael quipped. Jianjun could be nervous, whining, and at times a royal pain, but he was also extremely smart, and as true and loyal a friend as anyone could hope for.

"Good question, boss. But what you want is easy. Anyone can do it. You don't need someone with my skills."

"In that case do it for fun. And, by the way, good morning." Michael hung up and poured himself two fingers of single malt Scotch. He usually drank wine, but the day he'd had called for something a lot stronger. He stepped out his back door and sat on the stoop.

A few steps led down to the garden he shared with four neighbors. It sat barren now, but in summer it thrived with herbs and vegetables.

He listened to the night sounds of Florence: cars, scooters, buses, people calling to each other, arguing, singing, children playing, babies crying, and nearly constant peals of laughter. He had come to love Florence and yet felt as if his time here was coming to an end. Berosus and his accursed pearl threatened to take him away. He took a sip of Scotch as he continued to listen to the cacophony all around him. He found it strange that after traveling and living alone in some of the most remote corners of the world, it was here in this crowded city, filled with people entwined in each other's lives, that he felt the most alone.

His drink finished, he headed back into his apartment, but then stopped in the doorway. The night had gone stone silent, as if all of Florence had simply vanished.

A flicker of a shadow overhead caught his attention.

On the moonlit roof of his building he glimpsed the silhouette of a dog or a jackal. He viewed it only for a second before it disappeared into the night.

Somehow, he knew it was evil.

CHAPTER 7

ANYANG, China 1150 B.C.—during the Shang dynasty

"I have not traveled all this way to simply turn around and return to the palace." Zhou Xin felt good about the raucous reception the people of Shendao had given him in his first visit as their new king. He was young and arrogant, filled with his own self-importance. The old king had recently died, and although Zhou Xin was the third son, the former king's counselors had chosen him over his brothers because of his strength and daring. Now, he needed to convince his people that he was worthy of their love. The day's festivities were an excellent start.

He wore heavy silk clothes in bright colors and was surrounded by a group of aging ministers. They expected the king to climb into his carriage to return home, but instead, he continued to walk along the town's main street.

"I understand the Snail Goddess loves and protects this area above all others," King Zhou Xin said when he reached a stone wall surrounding a holy place. "I wish to see the temple of this so-called goddess."

His ministers dared not deny him anything, and so King Zhou Xin and his retinue entered the temple of the goddess Nüwa.

It was large and beautiful with meticulously tended gardens. The statue of the goddess was kept behind a drape, it being said that mere mortals should not look upon one such as she. Zhou Xin walked deep into the grounds, and as he neared the statue, a breeze caught the drape and blew it to one side, revealing Goddess Nüwa to the king.

"Ah! Look at her!" He gasped with awe. "She is no snail; she's beautiful! I have never seen such perfection in a woman. In fact, she is"—he chuckled —"fit for a king."

"Please, King Zhou Xin," the chief counselor said as he bobbed his head several times. "You must not speak such thoughts."

"Oh?" Zhou sneered at the old man. "I am above all other men, and no one can tell me what I can and cannot do." He smiled as an idea came to him. "Bring me ink and a writing brush."

His servants scrambled to do as he commanded. When he received the supplies, he proceeded to write a poem on the wall of the temple for all to see. In his poem, he not only spoke of Nüwa's beauty, but that she should come alive and join him in his palace, in his bed, and that she would greatly enjoy becoming the lucky recipient of his kingly favors.

His advisors were horrified. They said it was blasphemy to write such a thing, and when the people saw it, they would believe that their king was without virtue.

Zhou Xin refused to listen. He announced that his poem not only praised the goddess' beauty and female charms, but that he would be admired for writing it. He insisted it be left on the temple wall.

Later, when the Goddess Nüwa walked through her temple grounds and came upon the poem, she was shocked and insulted. Never had any human shown such vile disrespect towards her.

Outrage, complete and boundless, surged through her. Her first thought was to strike down the lecherous king, but then, a better idea came to her.

"Death is too easy for him. I will make his lust a thing of complete derision, something that will cause the name Zhou Xin to be reviled until the end of time. Only then, will I feel vindicated!"

She immediately called for three demons to attend her. The first, the leader, was known as the Thousand-Year Vixen. It was a black, female, green-eyed fox. Next was the Nine-Headed Pheasant, and the weakest of the demons was called the Jade Pipa—a pipa being an ancient lute-shaped instrument much beloved by Nüwa. "You three will go to earth. There, you will form yourselves into women to tempt and seduce the too lustful king.

Once he is in your power, you will pervert and defile him, make him depraved, and after that, you will cause his complete and total destruction."

And then she added. "Beware that, in doing this, you do not harm anyone else."

The three demons bowed and nodded, promising to do as she wished.

"If you follow my orders, I will give you the one thing you, and all specters, most long for—to be reincarnated as humans."

The Thousand-Year Vixen fell to her knees. "We will obey you, Goddess Nüwa. The Shang dynasty will come to an ugly end, and will be destroyed so completely that it will vanish into the mists of time."

CHAPTER 8

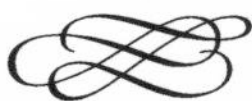

Los Angeles, California

A shudder ran through Kira as she stood at the sliding glass door of Oliveros' large family room and looked out. The area beyond had once been a deck and was now a horrifying drop to the ocean. Far below, the wooden planks and pillars ripped from the house lay in a jumbled, burned heap in the water.

The bulk of Kira's job involved talking to people who knew the victims of a crime as well as the potential suspects. When the situation allowed, she also went through victims' and suspects' homes and belongings to make some psychological assessments. Once, diaries were a great source of behavioral clues, but fewer people kept them. Now, the online "social media" du jour and e-mails to friends were the most common passages to a person's inner thoughts. Even looking at TV viewing history for anyone with cable or satellite internet could be helpful in finding a pathology.

She put on rubber gloves and went into Oliveros' den. Her search began at his desk. It contained amazingly little personal information. An accountant handled his business and household finances, and a personal assistant took care of his business paperwork, publicity, and fan correspondence. He also paid a cadre of others. Exactly what all of them did was a mystery to Kira.

She wasn't searching for anything involving the crime or potential crime—that was being handled by the LAPD's homicide and crime scene investigators. Her job was to look for clues that might lead to a psychological understanding of Gene Oliveros.

When she reached the desk's bottom left drawer, it was locked. A quick search didn't turn up the key.

She turned on his computer. It opened without a password and she quickly read through his email and saved files. Nothing worrisome jumped out.

Facebook opened onto Gene Oliveros' personal page. She scrolled through his postings and those of his friends. He most likely paid someone to post for him since the majority of postings were promotional. A few, however, were personal.

She discovered him to be a man with a strong sense of self-worth. He had achieved fame and fortune, was proud of it, and thought he deserved every bit of it. Also, he was extremely vain about his looks and his youthfulness. She smirked—her father was the same way.

When Oliveros wrote about his wife, he focused on her physical appearance—figure and jewelry—to the extent she had no personality. He treated his daughter differently and seemed to post every gurgle she ever made. Although he had two prior wives, Lake was his first child. He had been too busy for children in the past and, until he became a father, couldn't tolerate the little darlings.

She could understand such sentiments. In her own life, she had pretty much accepted that she would never have children. She actually would have liked kids, and even thought she'd be a good mother, despite her own strange upbringing—or because she'd learned, first hand, what not to do. But after her unhappy marriage to Ben, and now in her mid-thirties, motherhood was very likely not on her agenda. No potential father was in the picture nor likely to be given how busy her work life had become. She loved criminal profiling, and the more she became involved with the FBI, the better the cases she was given, and the more all-consuming the job became. Ironically, a major part of her work came about because her clients had miserable childhoods and even worse parents. Tell me about it, she thought, and found it all kind of sad.

Finding nothing interesting anywhere else, her attention returned to the locked desk drawer. She hunted through the den for a key, but couldn't find one.

She searched the house. In the nightstand, she found a small one typical of the type used in a desk. She carried it to the den, and sure enough, it fit.

In the drawer were a number of newspaper clippings.

The first was about an electrical and mining company called Powermore Industries, second only to General Electric in size. Several articles about Powermore successes followed, and then the announcement of the retirement of Powermore's founder and CEO, Stuart Eliot. She flipped through the stack to find more articles about energy sources, as well as about the success of JV Global Energy hedge fund. She guessed Oliveros was an investor.

The next item in the drawer stunned her. She stared a long moment at it: a news article announcing that her father, Daniel Holt, had been selected as a judge for the 9th Circuit Federal Court of Appeals. Why in the world would Oliveros care about her father?

She dug deeper.

After her father's announcement came an article from years ago about the new U.S. Senator from California, Kevin Wilson. Kira was surprised at the date of the article. She had no idea Wilson was old enough to have been a senator for over twenty-four years now.

Another article announced the purchase of the *Los Angeles Post* by its managing editor, Scott Jones.

And finally, a news article on the sale of VaultGuard, the top internet security company in the world whose security systems were used by the U.S. government. It was sold by its founder and company president, Hank Bennett. More than ten news clippings followed, discussing the disappearance of Hank Bennett, followed by an announcement that he was alive, but wanted no contact with the world.

At that, Kira reached the bottom of the desk drawer. This was a strange collection of news clippings, but she saw nothing here that needed to be locked up. And why, in particular, was her father's judgeship appointment included? He had never mentioned that he knew Oliveros.

But then, he never talked about any acquaintances outside of his work. Dan Holt was completely defined by his profession, much as she was. A family trait, she supposed. In fact, he never mentioned friends at all. All the people he talked about were colleagues at best.

In that, too, she thought wryly, she and her father were alike. She had plenty of people she liked, but no one she felt really close to—which had been a reason her marriage failed and a second try was pretty unlikely.

Kira stacked the news clippings neatly and was about to put them back in the drawer when she stopped. Again the troubling question: why the lock? What was Oliveros hiding? She put the clippings on top of the desk, knelt down and pulled the drawer all the way out, and then peered into the opening. Nothing.

She turned the drawer upside down. An envelope was taped to the underside. She removed and opened it.

Inside was an old snapshot, a group of seven young American sailors smiling at the camera, their arms around each other's shoulders. Behind them was a pyramid.

As she scanned the grainy, fading faces to see if Gene Oliveros was among them, her gaze froze at that of one man. Her father.

She knew he had been in the Navy sometime in the 1970s—"after Vietnam" was how he put it—but he never mentioned going to Egypt. The most he had ever said about those days was that after high school he took a job working as an apprentice to an auto mechanic, but when he found that the economy was terrible and no good jobs were available, he joined the Navy. After he got back from serving, he got serious about his studies. He met his future wife while in school. She was independently wealthy, and his life became much easier after they married. He went on to law school and became a prosecuting attorney.

Looking at the photo, it was almost startling to see what a fresh-faced, handsome young man her father had once been. She wished he would talk to her about those days. Not only was he close-mouthed about his time in the Navy, he was close-mouthed about himself, period. He was her father, but she hardly knew him. Here, he looked relaxed with his fellow sailors, boyish, and happy. Remarkably—no, sadly—she had never seen him that way. She was going to have to ask him about this photo and why Oliveros kept it hidden.

She searched the faces of other men in the photo, found a young Oliveros, but then her jaw dropped. One of the men looked exactly like Kevin Wilson, the U.S. Senator from California. Could it possibly be him? Her father never mentioned that they knew each other. She had never imagined Wilson was old enough to have served in the 1970s, but clearly, he was.

The connection between the odd news clippings about energy companies and hedge funds, and the photo struck her. Could the men in the photos be the ones in the news?

She asked the police to bag and log in all of the material and photos as evidence and then deliver copies to her office. Something wasn't right here.

She hadn't talked to her father since a short, obligatory phone call on his birthday two months earlier. She called his number.

He didn't answer.

CHAPTER 9

Rome, Italy

Michael always liked walking through Trastevere on the west bank of the Tiber River, an area of old buildings and narrow, cobbled streets heavily populated by the famous cats of Rome.

Early that morning, he located a small group of Chaldeans in Florence, but they had only recently arrived in Italy and didn't know Father Berosus. They directed him to Rome. He had the address, but the streets were winding and poorly marked. The sky was overcast, and a light rain began to fall before he found the building. It was an old, two-story stone house with no indication on the outside of who lived within. A man in a monk's habit answered the door, and Michael asked to speak to the leader of the community. He was left to wait in a dark hallway.

A man, one side of his face badly scarred and his black eyes sad and world-weary, approached. He wore a casual dark blue pullover shirt and dark gray slacks.

His name was Brother Ashur Hasani. Michael asked him if he knew Father Yosip Berosus.

"I don't know him well," Hasani replied, "but our paths crossed years ago." His gaze was wary, his voice hushed.

"I'm sorry to say he recently passed away," Michael said.

Hasani shut his eyes a moment. "May he rest in peace with God."

"I'm here because of a conversation I had with Father Berosus," Michael said. "I don't know if I should believe what he told me or not. His words were strange and troubling. He came to me right before his death and asked that I help him. I would like to speak with someone who knew him, who could tell me if he was a man who took to strange flights of fancy, or if his words could be believed."

Hasani invited Michael into a small parlor directly across the hall from the front door. The walls were dark paneled wood on the bottom and faded cabbage rose wallpaper on top. The furniture was outdated, stained, and threadbare. Hasani waved his hand in the direction of a carafe of wine on a side table and offered Michael glass. He turned it down.

Hasani sat on an overstuffed side chair, and Michael took the high-backed dark maroon sofa. Hasani cast his gaze downward a moment, then said, "I am not surprised to hear any of your words, but I am puzzled that Father Berosus would confide something troubling to you rather than to another priest. His story, the little I know of it, is quite strange."

Michael placed his hands on his knees in an attempt to seem less nervous about this visit. "Anything you can tell me ..."

Hasani seemed to be debating with himself whether to help or not. "Father Berosus was a young, enthusiastic priest in Mosul, Iraq early in the 1970s. He was a scholar, profoundly intelligent, and many of the older priests who knew him were certain he would become a bishop, perhaps even our Patriarch. But then something happened in the course of his studies, and everything about him changed as he became intrigued with the nature of evil. With ... demonic things. I dare say, is that why you're here?"

Michael nodded. "Yes."

Hasani sighed, then said, "I am sorry to tell you, he became a little mad. He wouldn't tell people what caused this sudden unholy interest, and his confessor apparently spent long hours with him, warning him that the study of demonic creatures could open a door that the devil might enter—a door to one's own soul. But Father Berosus ignored all warnings, saying he had no choice, that this pursuit was his mission."

"Excuse me," Michael interrupted. "Do you know what area, or which aspect of evil and demons he was studying?"

Hasani shook his head. "All I've heard is that it was about Genghis Khan and Marco Polo. I'll admit, what they have to do with demons makes no sense to me."

"I see," Michael said.

Hasani continued. "One day, Berosus left his church without permission and traveled to Egypt. We don't know what happened to him there, but he never returned to us. We tried to find him, but could not. We didn't know if he was alive or dead until one of our monks encountered him on a visit to Medjugorje in Bosnia-Herzegovina, where the Virgin Mary is said to appear. The brother scarcely recognized Berosus. The madness we once feared within him had become complete. His hair was long and unwashed, his clothes ragged. He lived alone and had stopped performing his priestly duties unless there was an emergency, such as anointing the dying, when no other priest was near. The monk asked him to return to the monastery, but Berosus said he dared not. He feared it would be destroyed if he returned, and that he held its means of destruction.

"A few years later, another of our brothers went to Medjugorje and looked for Father Berosus, but couldn't find him. Apparently, he had taken to living as a traveling holy man who relied on the charity of others and brought grace in his wake through nearly constant prayer to ward off evil. No one knew where he was."

Hasani had come to the end of his tale, and was silent a moment, contemplating what it all meant. His voice lowered to almost a whisper. "It is my observation that he was a sad man who had lost his way. He seemed to believe he carried something evil, something he must hide to protect the church he loved. I'm afraid nothing said about him made sense to me. In any case, I've heard nothing more about him until your news today."

Michael absorbed the tale a moment. "Father Berosus talked of the

Nestorian Church," he said. "I thought they had died out. Is there any connection between your church and that one?"

"In fact there is." Hasani folded his hands. "The priest, Nestorius, was a Syrian. He became Patriarch of Constantinople in 428 A.D. but soon found himself in trouble with the Bishop of Rome—the Pope—over the nature of Jesus. Nestorius preached that Christ had two natures: one of man and another of God, and that Mary was the mother of Christ the man, not God. That became a heresy. The Roman church believes Christ's natures are in union with each other, and refer to Mary as *theotokos,* mother of God."

Hasani must have noticed Michael's frown because he suddenly smiled and said, "Yes, yes, I realize it must sound like trying to count how many angels can dance on the head of a pin to non-believers, but to those of us who care, it is important."

Michael nodded. "You read my mind, I'm sorry to say. But please continue."

"By the end of the fifth century," Hasani said, "followers of Nestorius declared him a saint, completing the break with Rome. They headed eastward, traveling into Central Asia and China, to spread his teachings. In 735, they were given permission to build a church in the Chinese city of Ch'ang-an, the imperial capital of the T'ang dynasty, but as the T'ang dynasty became increasingly xenophobic, many Nestorians headed back towards the west and settled along the Silk Road."

"What happened to them?" Michael asked.

Brother Hasani shrugged. "In the nineteenth century, the few that were left gave up their idea of the dual nature of Christ, and made peace with Rome."

"Are there any pure Nestorians left anywhere?"

"No." Hasani raised his head, his gaze hard as he said, "The sect is no more."

Just then, they heard a ruckus in the outer hall. Hasani told Michael to wait as he headed for the door. Before he reached it, the door swung open and two armed men entered, each with a gun held to the head of a monk.

CHAPTER 10

PASADENA, California

For all his power, Judge Daniel Holt was a curiously solitary man. He chalked it up to being too intimidating to others. That was their problem, not his. A perk of being a judge for the Ninth Circuit Federal Court of Appeals was to have his pronouncements, both public and private, obeyed without question.

It was evening as he left his office in the Federal Courthouse, a tall building with a Spanish-colonial zigzag tiled dome, and headed for his personal parking space. His cell phone began to vibrate.

He wondered if his daughter was calling again. Kira had already tried to reach him a couple of times that day. She knew he didn't take personal calls at work. He would return her call tonight from home when he felt like talking to her. He found her impatience annoying and became doubly irritated by the phone's vibration. He pulled it from his pocket and was about to dismiss the call when he noticed the name of the caller.

He hesitated, then answered while getting into his silver Mercedes. "How many times do I have to say I don't want to hear from you?" he announced, without waiting to hear the caller's words. He slammed the car door shut.

"The old priest is dead." Hank Bennett spoke quickly, as if to be sure the judge didn't hang up on him.

"I know," Holt said. "Wilson already contacted me."

"The Senator? What the hell is wrong with you? You don't want the government putting its goddamned nose in any of this."

"The government is exactly what this is about. Wilson being on the Intelligence committee gives him needed resources. Once he has what we need, there's no stopping us. We have nowhere to go but up."

There was a brief silence, then Bennett asked, "Did you hear about Gene Oliveros?"

"Of course. The man was crazy. Everybody knows it. Calm down. I don't want to hear from you unless you know something I don't."

Holt not only ended the call, he turned off the phone. He didn't want anything more to do with the damned thing, or with the caller. Just because they had served together a lifetime ago on the U.S.S. *Saratoga* didn't mean he had to listen to the crack-pot today. The fellow was a loser. He had once amounted to something, but then tossed it all away.

Not like Holt. Half-way through his tour in the Navy, he discovered that he had a brain, and a good one. He made something out of himself.

And now, if he wanted a little help to ensure he got onto the Supreme Court, who could blame him? He had long known that California's junior senator, Kevin Wilson, saw himself as the next president. He smiled at the thought of the two of them together controlling Washington … with a little help from their friends, he thought … and then chuckled.

He drove from Pasadena to the hills above Laurel Canyon in Los Angeles. The trip took a little more than thirty minutes, traffic permitting, so it was dark as he neared home. From the hills, he looked down past the steep, tree-studded darkness to the lights of the city far below. Every day that view warmed his usually cold heart, reminding him of his magnificence in having accomplished so much. He expected that was why he chose to continue to live here rather than move to the more plebeian suburban city where his office was located.

As he pulled onto his driveway, the night was too dark and his attention too distracted to notice a dark, foxlike shape crouching on the roof, watching him. The garage door creaked as it opened. From the attached garage, he entered the kitchen.

Nothing sat in the warming oven awaited his arrival. Nothing simmered on the range top, or roasted in the oven. He was hungry when he got home, and his housekeeper knew that. She had an easy job, keeping house for a single man. Her chief duty was to prepare a healthy, tasty meal that was warm and waiting for him when he returned from work—and being out of the house so he didn't have to talk to her.

His dog ... where was Oscar? The Wheaton terrier was always waiting for him, spinning with joy. If the housekeeper let the dog run out of the house, unsupervised, and maybe lost, her days in his employ were over!

He shoved open the swinging door between the kitchen and dining room, bellowing Oscar's name.

From the dining room, he stormed into the living room.

A beautiful woman sat on the sofa, her long legs crossed at the knee.

She was petite and shapely, with straight black hair that flowed down her back to her waist. Her tight emerald green dress perfectly matched her eyes. As he stared, something about this woman niggled at his brain. And then, he remembered.

"I don't believe it," he whispered.

"I knew you would never forget me," she said.

Slowly, all the memories he had shut out for almost forty years flooded through him, stronger and stronger, until they frightened him with their intensity, then disgusted him over all that had happened. Somehow, he gathered himself together. He was a man in control, always in control, and then he smiled. "You're here to help me, aren't you?" he whispered.

She made no reply, but simply stood up.

"You know where the pearl is," he said. "You know what I want, and that I'm close, so very close!"

She lifted her arm and stretched it towards him with her forefinger pointed at his chest.

Holt looked confused at first, and then felt a stabbing pain in his heart. "What are you doing?" he shouted as the unseen jab cut into him. He covered his heart with his hands. "Stop!"

She laughed aloud, her laugh causing the hairs on the nape of his neck to stand.

He gasped for breath as the pain from his heart became crippling. "Please. You need me," he pleaded as he fell to one knee, near tears, his once-powerful voice little more than a simpering cry. He couldn't run, couldn't do anything to protect himself, but watched her with mounting terror.

She continued to smile as his face crumbled, as his lungs stopped working, and he could no longer breathe. Memories swirled. *A black fox.*

He was on his hands and knees now, unable to divert his eyes from the creature before him. His lungs were raw, empty, as he tore at his throat, trying to open it, needing air. His heart pounded harder, ever faster, until he feared it would burst through his chest.

He held his hand out to her. "Please, I'll do anything. Anything."

Her lips spread into a disgust-filled sneer as she shook her head.

Against his will, he crawled to the fireplace and took hold of the poker that stood on the hearth. He reared up on his knees as he turned the sharp end of the poker towards him and drove it hard into his throat, crushing his windpipe. He dropped it, bleeding, as his fingers clawed at his eyes, and his mind filled with the heat of the desert and the sounds of war.

CHAPTER 11

"WHO ARE YOU?" Brother Hasani faced the gunmen who stormed into the monastery. "What do you want here?"

Michael recognized them as the same two men who attacked him in Florence. One was middle-aged, stocky, and of medium height. His dark brown hair was combed straight back off his forehead, falling into a curly cluster in back. The other appeared younger and thinner, and wore his hair clipped short. The monks they held were young men, cowering with their hands raised. "We meet again," Michael said, moving closer. "Did you follow me here?"

"We aren't here to hurt you or them," the taller, heavier gunman said. "We just want the pearl."

"Pearl? What pearl?" Hasani cried. "We're monks. We have no riches."

"He's right," Michael said, facing the big man. "They don't have any riches and have no idea what you're talking about."

"No games, or you'll have a bloodbath here."

"Calm down! Maybe I do know what you want, but the old priest didn't tell me where he hid it."

"You're lying!"

The smaller gunman looped an arm around his captive's neck, and pulled him backwards, a gun to his temple. The monk cried out, struggling for breath.

"Why would I lie?" Michael raged. "Let these men go, and we can talk. Surely, one pearl isn't worth taking a life. Why are you doing this?"

"Why not?" The big spokesman gave a lazy grin.

"Who are you working for?" Michael asked.

"Someone with enough money to make all this worth our while."

Just then, the parlor door opened and a monk carrying a tray laden with cups of hot tea walked straight into the room, his gaze fixed on the tray as if to be sure the cups wouldn't slide off. He had far more cups than there were people, but before that registered, he threw the tray at the large gunman who jumped back and roared in rage and pain as the hot liquid hit his face.

The smaller gunman's eyes darted, shocked, at his partner. Michael sprang at him, knocking his arm upward, then grabbing it and twisting it in a way that caused the gun to drop, and the gunman to flip head-over-heels onto the floor. At the same time, Hasani and the tea-carrying monk wrested away the big man's gun as three more monks ran in to help.

The two gunmen, both disarmed, struggled to break free from the monks holding them down.

"Call the police," Michael said. "They should be arrested for this."

Hasani shook his head. "We don't want trouble here. No police. We had enough of them in Iraq, and no good ever came of it." He faced the two men. "We don't have what you want, and if you bother us again, more than hot tea will be used against you." He nodded at the monks. "Let them go."

The gunmen ran from the room.

Michael rubbed his bad shoulder and grimaced. "I'm sorry if those men followed me here. I never meant to bring you trouble."

Hasani's thick brows rose.

"Father Berosus told me dangerous people would want his pearl,"

Michael said. "But he never said who, or why. He said the pearl was evil and it could not fall into the wrong hands."

"In that case," Hasani said, holding a grim, steady gaze on Michael, "I'm glad we know nothing about it."

The night train brought Michael within a few blocks of his apartment.

The rain left the air heavy and humid, and only increased his foul mood. Now, on top of strange "feelings" he was being followed by gun-toting maniacs. At least they were fairly incompetent maniacs —so far.

A certain rhythmic pattern broke into his reverie, and he listened carefully. He knew that pattern; he'd heard it many times as a kid with pets: the trot of four legs, the click of claws over a hard surface.

He stopped, and the trotting stopped.

He turned around slowly, some part of him knowing what he would find. He was wrong about it being a dog or a jackal. It was a fox, its eyes glowing green and ominous in the moonlight. The image unsettled him and sent shivers up his spine, just as it had last night on his roof.

It stood less than a yard away.

He knew better than to stare back at a wild animal, but he couldn't avert his gaze. No foxes were believed to be in Florence's city center and those in the countryside ran when humans approached. They weren't animals to stand and fight, but this fox curled its lips in a snarl.

He saw a policeman at the corner, and shouted to him, pointing at the beast. The policeman gasped, and put his hand over his firearm, ready to pull it from the holster if needed, as he ran towards Michael.

The fox backed away from Michael, then ran in the opposite direction down the street.

"*Signore,* what was that?" the policeman asked Michael in Italian as he approached.

"A fox."

The policeman switched to English and said, "But there are no foxes in this city."

Michael eyed the now empty street. "So I understand."

CHAPTER 12

—He doesn't know it yet, but he's coming to us.

—I'm glad to see the end of that foolish old priest.

—So tedious, that constant praying.

—And no sex. This one should be much more interesting in that area.

—Watching is nothing. Killing him, that's where the fun comes in.

Michael's cell phone began to ring as he entered his apartment.

"I found out about the men in the photo," Jianjun said when Michael answered.

"I knew you would." Michael sat down at the table.

"Yeah, well it almost didn't happen. I had to darken and sharpen the image, but my equipment wasn't quite up to the task, so I had to go and buy some new, top of the line hardware and programs to get the image crisp enough to work on. The prices are ridiculous. China's jerking all our chains over rare earth elements."

"Rare what?" Michael asked.

"Earth elements. That's what they're called. They're metals, not alloys or amalgams, but pure metals from the ground that are now being used in all kinds of high tech equipment from computer chips to lasers to nuclear reactors. They're real big in smart phones, and—"

"Send me the bills," Michael said impatiently. "What did you—"

"Believe me, I will. But I want you to understand it's not me. It's China!"

"Why are you picking on your motherland again?"

"Not my fault where I was born, bro!" Jianjun cried. "Now, I'm a Canadian. It's just that China undercut the price of rare earth elements so mines in other countries couldn't compete and shut them all down. Now that China has a monopoly, the prices are skyrocketing. One went up from fifteen dollars per whatever, to five-hundred dollars!"

"Jianjun! Enough with the money already!"

"I know, I know. You archeology types only pay attention to what's old, you've got no idea about what's new in the world."

"And that's how I like it. So, tell me, what did you find out?"

"With my new equipment for restoring pixels, I could read a name tag on one of the duffle bags."

"You're shitting me!"

"I'm not, bro, which is why I had to buy—"

"Were you able to do anything with the name?"

"Need you ask? Of course! How many times have I hacked into the military database? Piece of cake!"

"And?"

"Once in, I learned the guys were on the U.S.S. *Saratoga*. They patrolled waters in the Indian Ocean, Arabian Sea, the South Atlantic, and they saw action in Lebanon and Angola. Not that any of it made the news, but what else is new? Anyway, in the photo, it looks like the sailors were on shore leave in Egypt—but I guess you already knew that with a pyramid behind them."

"Not a pyramid—the Great Pyramid."

"Whatever," Jianjun muttered. "Anyway, I tried a facial recognition scan against the Navy's data but their pictures weren't there, which means they never rose very high, probably left after their term was over. I'll have to check other databases one by one. But keep in mind, there's a good chance none of them have photos in any database. Most people don't. They simply go about their lives."

"True," Michael said, "but I know you'll give it a try."

There was a pause on the line before Jianjun said nervously. "I will, but … the last time we had anything to do with a pyramid, pyramid shape at least, it was in Idaho, and had to do with alchemy. We were nearly killed."

CHAPTER 13

THE CALL CAME into the FBI at 10:22 a.m. the next morning. Kira sat at her corner desk, looking over material from Gene Oliveros' home, and thinking of how furious she was that her father not only refused to answer her phone calls, but wouldn't even acknowledge her text or voice messages. A few other agents were at their desks in the big open office space, but most were already out of the office. A couple of young, attractive file clerks stood by the coffee pot, talking about their dating life.

When the phone rang, something made Kira look up at the clock, and then at the agent taking the call, the agent she most often rode with, Peter "Scoggs" Scoggins. He could have been an FBI agent poster boy with his short hair and well-toned physique covered by an inexpensive two-button suit, white shirt and tie. A wife and two kids in the suburbs rounded out the picture. He held the phone to his ear, but then his head snapped towards her with both shock and pity on his face. His look scared her.

He hung up the phone and stood. She stood as well, her heart pounding.

She couldn't believe his words. Her father had been found dead in his home. Because he was a Federal judge, the FBI had been immediately contacted.

"Dead?" she whispered. Her mind raced. When he hadn't returned her calls last evening that was par for the course. She hadn't worried. But now, grief and guilt surged through her. If she had gone to his house, had checked on him, could she have helped him, possibly saved him? "What happened to him?"

"They aren't saying, but they're treating the house as a crime scene."

The news rocked her. "My God! Why?"

Scoggins put his cell phone and badge in his pocket, then checked his gun. "I'll let you know as soon as I find out anything."

"I'm going with you," she said.

"I don't think—"

"He's my father," she interrupted.

He looked at her closely and she kept her shoulders firm, doing all she could to show him she wasn't about to fall apart even though, inside, she wanted to scream that it couldn't be true, that Daniel Holt could not be dead.

Scoggs nodded his consent.

She said nothing, her expression flat as she sat in the passenger seat while he drove up to Laurel Heights. He did most of the talking, as always. He made small talk about yesterday's earthquake, how fortunate it was that no serious damage had been done, and even gave a blow-by-blow of waking up to the quake and how his seven- and nine-year-olds were pissed off because they had slept through it.

Kira scarcely listened. She understood why he was chattering nonsense and felt glad she wasn't being asked to speak. She kept her gaze riveted on the sky as she tried her best not to think about her father and all the unhappiness between them. The day was bright and sunny, the kind of southern California day that made people who lived in the area congratulate themselves for putting up with all the usual crap just to experience weather like this.

She shivered.

She was the first one out of the car and up the few steps to the front door of the small but elegant home and then waited impatiently as Scoggs told the cops who had secured the crime scene that they were taking over the case. The police blustered and fumed for a while, but she could tell they were relieved. That worried her.

As soon as Scoggs gave the okay, she suited up, including gloves, booties, and a head covering. He told her to wait, that he should go in first, but she didn't listen and dashed into the familiar house, the house she had grown up in. She turned from the foyer directly into the living room. There, she froze, scarcely able to comprehend the sight before her.

Her eyes took in the entire scene in one quick movement. She had thought, working with the FBI, dealing with serial killers and other sickos, that she had hardened, that she could handle pretty much anything. But she was wrong.

His eyes had been ripped out; his throat torn open. A bloody fireplace poker lay beside the body. He seemed to have bled to death. But the strange thing, the unbelievable thing, was that not only were his hands bloody, but that one of them held an eyeball in its grasp.

The room began to swirl, to turn black and purple …

She felt sick and placed a gloved hand against a wall for support. The way the scene was staged, it could have been a macabre suicide. But her father could never have done that to himself. Never. Someone had done it to him and made it look like self-mutilation.

Scoggs' arm clamped tight around her waist. Her feet barely touched the floor as he whisked her out of the living room to the kitchen and had her sit, then handed her a glass of water.

"Who would do such a thing? Who could possibly hate him so much?" she whispered, staring at the floor, at the vinyl pattern from her childhood.

"I knew I shouldn't have let you come here," he said, standing over her.

She shook her head and then looked up at him. "I'll be all right."

"No, you won't. Not for a while, not after seeing … I'm sorry, Kira. I had no idea it would be that bad. I'll get a uniform to see you home."

"I'm not leaving." She took deep breaths. "I can help, and I will."

Her thoughts suddenly turned to the photo of her father at Gene Oliveros' house. The two deaths couldn't be connected, could they? Her father had never mentioned Oliveros and had never said anything to her about his days in the Navy. But two men in the same photo, both involved in suspicious, grisly deaths within one day of each other, were too much of a coincidence to be ignored.

She bent forward, burying her head in her hands. She couldn't coldly analyze this case and pick over the bones of the deceased's life as if he were no more than a carcass after Thanksgiving dinner. This was her father. The man she had both worshiped and loathed.

Her ex had once told her that no man, no mere mortal, could live up to her desire that he surpass her father in everything. Ben claimed Daniel Holt was the reason their marriage failed. She had denied it, but deep down, she knew Ben was right.

She always assumed that she and her father would have time to work out their differences, time to learn to understand each other. Time to tell him she loved him and time to hear him say he loved her. But now that dream was gone. Those words had never been spoken, and never would be.

CHAPTER 14

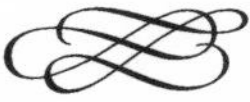

VANCOUVER, British Columbia

Jianjun gave himself a virtual pat-on-the-back as he sat in front of his computer and successfully hacked into the FBI's Next Generation Identification, NGI, the national facial recognition system. It felt good to be hacking again. He enjoyed the challenge, and he was able to concentrate hard enough to block out his wife's nagging and complaints that he didn't have a "real" job.

He made good money—far more than he ever had working for Microsoft, especially since some of the archeological finds included riches that the finders were able to legally possess and sell. But since he didn't have a nine-to-five job, nothing else mattered to her. They lived in a small, plain ranch-style house in a nondescript subdivision near downtown Vancouver. His wife wanted something bigger and newer, with all the latest conveniences, but Jianjun saw no reason to move. A fancier house wasn't going to fix the problems the two of them had.

He went back to work, took the scanned photo, separated out each sailor individually, and then ran them one-by-one through the NGI. It was a time-consuming process. None of the men was found in the criminal system.

Poking around the innards of the software as any good hacker enjoyed doing, he discovered that the photos-of-criminals section was the "public" portion of the system, but the database was far more extensive than that.

It had a "persons of interest" section, which seemed to consist of potential terrorists, suspected drug lords, mobsters in the making, and extremists or "potentially" extremist groups of any sort from environmentalists to neo-Nazis to PETA. Another section dealt with politicians, major campaign contributors, and heads of large corporations. A few small files grouped miscellaneous people—everyone from IRS cheats to scientists to university professors. Jianjun was stunned to find him and Michael in it. Knowing that any deletion of files might trigger some alerts, he simply rewrote them into candidates for citizen of the year awards.

All those paranoids who worried that the government was watching them were right.

This was the mother lode of spy data.

He ran the photos through the massive data bases, and then went into the kitchen to make himself some lunch, knowing it would take a while. After a tuna salad sandwich on Wonder Bread, some Cool Ranch Doritos and a Diet Coke, he hurried back to his den. To his surprise, every one of the men in the photo had a hit.

He read the search results with amazement, then muttered, "Holy shit."

Scoggs had sent Kira home less than fifteen minutes after she entered her father's house that morning. Back at her townhouse, she walked around in circles all afternoon, trying to get over the shock. She had no tears, though. And she wasn't even sure why.

By nightfall, however, she needed to return to her father's house. She wanted to look it over carefully. She pleaded, and Scoggs eventually consented. She knew the routine with the gloves, booties, and all, and he realized that she, more than anyone else, would know if something was out of place or had been taken. Her father hadn't changed anything in the house for years. It remained the same as when she lived there, the same as when her mother lived there before the divorce.

One of the police officers standing watch over the crime scene accompanied Kira as she entered the house. Walking through her father's home, his body gone, memories flooded over her.

She knew her parents hadn't been happy, but as a teenager, she had blamed her mother for their divorce. To hear her father tell it, Darlene Holt hadn't bothered to keep up her looks. But as Kira thought back, she remembered her mother constantly dieting, tanning—natural or otherwise, and dying her hair to hide the gray. Moisturizers made her look like she had bathed in a vat of baby oil, Botox left her expressionless, while tummy tucks and breast firmings were painful. But no matter what she did, how hard she tried, her body sagged, her skin wrinkled, and she couldn't prevent herself from looking years older than her husband.

During the last ten years of their marriage, Darlene refused to have her picture taken with the Judge. She had been a beauty in her day, yet Kira remembered once going to a fancy party with her parents when her father was elevated to an appellate court judge. A couple of people mistook Kira for Holt's younger sister, and Darlene for a cougar who managed to get him to marry her. Darlene nearly died of embarrassment. Dan, however, was well pleased.

Eventually, Dan, too, acted as if he was too young for Darlene, even though he was two years older.

Kira hadn't really paid that much attention to Dan's looks—after all, he was her father—but he did appear young for his age. At the time of his divorce, in his mid-forties, he looked to be in his early thirties at most. And at sixty-two, he was as slim, trim, and spry as someone in his forties.

Since Kira was fifteen at the time of the divorce, her choice to live with her father carried much weight with the judge over the custody proceedings—a colleague of her father's.

Darlene visited her a few times, but her father had poisoned Kira so much against "the mother who didn't want her" that the visits grew increasingly strained, with Kira being as nasty and cruel as only a teenage girl could be. Eventually, her mother stopped visiting altogether.

Back then, Kira wore a youthful "righteous indignation" over her parents' divorce as a badge of honor, but now she felt nothing but sadness and disgust over the way she had treated mother, and their resulting alienation.

Now, in this empty house where she had experienced such joy as a child, hatred and disharmony as a teen, and indifference as an adult, Kira never felt more alone.

Kira entered her father's den. Accolades for Holt as a DA and judge filled the book-lined room.

Nothing seemed to be missing from it, or anywhere else in the house, except for Oscar, her father's terrier. If the poor little thing ran away because he was scared, he probably became a coyote's meal. These hills were crawling with the predators. But how he had gotten out of the house troubled her.

She called Scoggs. He had already contacted the housekeeper who claimed that in the morning of the day the judge died, she had received a text message from the judge telling her that her services would not be needed that day. When he checked her phone records, he found that the message, although signed with the judge's name, had been sent from a burner phone.

That piece of information told Kira her father's death had been premeditated murder.

She went into his bedroom, looked around a bit, and then checked the closet. In the back, on the floor, she found a cardboard box. She took it out, and inside found paperwork, medals, and badges from her father's time in the Navy. At the bottom was a photo.

It was the same photo as she had found hidden in Gene Oliveros' house.

She sat on the floor and looked at her father and wondered what had happened that made him so different from the happy young man in the picture.

And more importantly, perhaps, why had two men in this photo been killed? Were the others in danger? And was one of them the killer?

CHAPTER 15

Florence, Italy

Michael felt uneasy about calling one of the people who had been with him in Idaho last year, wondering if those awful events would cause her to simply hang up on him. But Charlotte Reed was such a treasure trove of information about Middle Eastern antiquity, he decided to try. He didn't have her cell phone number, but he suspected the sheriff of Lemhi County, Idaho knew how to reach her.

He had Sheriff Jake Sullivan's office, home, and cell phone numbers. He rang the number of Jake's home first and wasn't completely surprised when Charlotte answered. As soon as he said his name, Charlotte warmly greeted him, and they quickly fell into the easy rapport they had once shared. Charlotte was relieved to learn that Michael's arm and shoulder had healed well, and with physical therapy his shoulder was slowly regaining strength and mobility. He didn't mention the pain his recent fights caused so he wouldn't have to explain why he had been fighting—not yet, anyway. Of course, she asked about women in his life. Beneath an academic, brainy exterior, Charlotte was an incurable romantic and wanted to see Michael find someone to break through the walls he had built around himself. She understood his connection to the supernatural, and specifically alchemy—once, it nearly killed her—and his fear of ever inflicting that kind of danger on anyone else. But she thought he was wrong, that women were stronger than he gave them credit for being, and that he was a good man who deserved more than to hide away because of what might turn up next in his strange life.

He learned that she was quite happy living with the sheriff and kept busy using her knowledge of antiquity to study Indian artifacts found in the Bitterroot Mountain area. She was also becoming quite a Lewis and Clark scholar and was pursuing an investigation of the secret expedition that had followed Lewis and Clark across the continent. Of course, she could never say what actually became of them, but thought the story of their heroism and disappearance was fascinating, even if it was only half of the story. She believed it was something the country deserved to know.

Michael then broached the subject of his call. He told her about the strange visit he had from the Chaldean priest, and Father Berosus' tale of Marco Polo stealing a red pearl from the Nestorians and bringing it to Venice. "One more thing," Michael said. "You may now decide I'm officially crazy, but while Berosus was here giving me the pearl and telling me the whole, unbelievable tale, he was supposedly in a hospital dying."

"Maybe he left the hospital for a while, knowing he had to give you the pearl," she suggested.

"He was in a coma for three days before his death."

"Oh."

Michael waited, but Charlotte was quiet. He could picture her brow furrowed with concentration as she pondered his words. "So tell me," she said finally, "what does this mean? Why are you involved?"

"Berosus suggested I find the Nestorians and give them back the pearl, that they would know how to stop it from continuing to cause evil deeds."

"I thought there were no more Nestorians," she mused. "But aside from that, I guess I know why the priest went to you. A red stone, or a red pearl, is often used as a description of a philosopher's stone."

"Could be," he confessed.

"Yeah, right." He could all but see her mouth wrinkle. "Your family background doesn't mean a thing."

"Okay, I'll admit that it isn't a real pearl," he said. "It's an amalgam of some kind. Since the old priest called it a pearl that might be its historical identity."

"A pearl …" Charlotte murmured. After a moment her voice turned bright. "Since the pearl came to you from a Chaldean, I can think of one story from that general part of the world. It has to do with King Herod of Biblical fame. The legend says he had a secret amulet—a red pearl—that he believed brought him wealth and great power. While he praised the good it did for him, others saw something quite different. They believed it drove him mad. As he aged, he became increasingly evil. Everyone knows the story of how he insisted all newborns in the vicinity of Bethlehem be murdered because he was so fearful of the birth of a new king. The rottenness of his personality became so bad it eventually turned into a physical malady as well as mental and spiritual one. Some called it 'Herod's Evil.' Finally, he became so filled with pestilence, it's said that his body burst open and all manner of worms, putrefaction, vermin, maggots, and flies spewed out, killing him."

"Gross," Michael said.

"Isn't it? The amulet was supposedly destroyed so that no other man would come under its evil influence."

"That does sound much the way the red pearl was described by Berosus. But if it was destroyed, it wouldn't be the one that was hidden in China with the Nestorians."

"Unless it wasn't destroyed. If it went instead to Chaldea, in what is now Iraq, the followers of Nestor living there might have taken the pearl with them when they were driven out of the area and headed for China."

"Maybe." Michael was dubious.

"You're right. Forget it." Charlotte agreed. "In fact, many scholars now believe Herod most likely died from some combination of kidney disease and gangrene. I'll do some research and call you back as soon as I find anything. But isn't the story of Herod's exploding stomach fun?"

"Kaboom," Michael deadpanned. "Thank you, Charlotte. I appreciate your help." He was heartened by how happy she sounded—a far cry from the dour woman he'd first met. "And give my best to Jake."

CHAPTER 16

Los Angeles, California

Kira sat at her desk in the FBI office and logged onto the agency network. She wanted to see what the LAPD had posted on its investigation of Oliveros' death. They hadn't yet officially requested the FBI's help in the case.

No explanation of where the bomb came from, or how it came to be at the house, had yet been uncovered. The housekeeper had survived the blast thanks to the thickness of the glass and walls of the house. She confirmed that all the guests had left the party and only Oliveros, his wife, and child were on the deck. But she also told them about the guest who had arrived late. She gave a detailed description of the attractive woman who had brought a birthday gift. A sketch artist was brought in and created what the housekeeper called a very good likeness of the woman. The housekeeper was emphatic that all earlier presents had been opened before the party ended, so none of them could have caused the explosion.

The LAPD was attempting to locate that late arriving guest, but they were having no luck. They knew for certain that she wasn't Verity's mother, as she had claimed to be. Verity's mother not only had short blond hair, but tipped the scale at around two-hundred fifty pounds.

Reading about the crime scene, Kira remembered sneaking into one of Oliveros' zombie movies when she was only ten years old. It was so gory it had an R rating. Her father had a fit when he learned she had seen it, saying that sort of thing would rot her mind. His anger only made her want to see even more horror films. No matter how many such films she saw, Oliveros did them best. He understood the legends and psychological fears that underlay human reactions to evil, and particular the demonic. As a result, his films went beyond shots of blood and gruesome ways to die. They toyed with one's deepest, unspoken fears.

She remembered that the philosopher Nietzsche once wrote, *What if a demon were to creep after you one night, in your loneliest loneliness...?* It was that innate, Jungian collective unconscious fear of demons and evil that made Oliveros' films powerful, and made him rich.

"You aren't supposed to be here," Scoggs said. Kira jumped, so startled was she by his voice. "Take some bereavement time off. You need it."

It took a moment for her to breathe again. "Please, have a seat." She pointed at the guest chair by her desk. "I have something to show you."

She placed the photo of the seven Navy men flat on her desk. It was in a clear evidence bag. "I took this from my father's house last night. Here's my father"—she pointed to one sailor—"and this"—her finger moved to another—"is Gene Oliveros. Do any of your investigators know that Oliveros was in the same squad as my father? Has anybody else discovered this connection? It's too much for a coincidence."

"Whoa! Hold on a minute!" Scoggs picked up the photo. His expression went from skeptical to astonished. "What is this? It sure as hell does look like Oliveros."

"It *is* Oliveros. This photo matches one we put into evidence from Oliveros' home two days ago," she said. "Has anyone paid any attention to that photo? Looked to see who the other sailors were with him?"

"Not yet," he replied.

She gritted her teeth. "This is exactly why I need to be in this investigation, not home licking my wounds!"

"We'll look into everything, but it takes time."

"I know it takes time! That's why I want to help. I want to do more than sit on my ass waiting for the murderer to waltz in here and confess."

"Kira, calm down."

"What about the burner phone and the text to my father's housekeeper? That proves it was a premeditated murder."

"How many people knew your father's housekeeper's name or her cell phone number? We haven't found a single person. Do you?"

"No, but—"

"It could have been him, Kira. Those phones are a dime a dozen."

"No way! There's a reason those two men were killed within a day of each other." She rubbed her forehead, trying to make sense out of all this. "This picture proves there's some connection between them."

He grimaced. "This is Los Angeles, lots of people die here every day. We hadn't found any connection between Oliveros and the judge until right this second. Cut me some slack, okay?"

She couldn't believe what she was hearing. "Two deaths in two days is just a big, fat coincidence? Shit happens, is that it? What I want you to do is investigate the connection between the two men."

"We will, Kira—now that we know there is a connection. Tell me, did your dad ever talk about Oliveros?" Scoggs asked, trying to remain unruffled at her harangue.

"My dad didn't talk to me about anybody." She tried to make it sound as if it didn't matter. "Anyway, the proof is right in front of your eyes. Are you going to check into this or not?"

"Sure thing, Killer," he said, with a shake of the head. "Do you take me for an idiot? I like my balls where they are. Look, I know sitting this out is hard on you, but you've got to think of the whole picture.

And the public. They have it in for the Feds, say we protect our own. If word got out among the newsies, those who don't know you and only heard rumors that you and your old man ... well, you know."

"Didn't get along? Barely spoke to each other?"

"That sounds harsh," Scoggs said, trying not to meet her hard glare.

"Don't give me that bull crap." She tried to calm down. "None of that means a thing when it comes to investigating his murder."

"Kira, you can't get involved any more than you have. You're too close to it, and if you take part it could even cause some trouble-makers to get suspicious. We don't know it's a murder," Scoggs whispered. "I'm sorry."

She froze, then stared at him. Her shoulders sagged at the implication behind his words. She had no business taking her anguish out on the closest thing she had to a partner in the FBI. "Suicide? You can't be serious. That's such shit!" She bit her bottom lip, trying to measure her words. "He was too proud, too arrogant. He would never harm himself. I'm supposed to be the profiler around here, except no one I work with believes me when I talk about my own father."

"Kira, that's not it."

Her hands curled into fists of despair. "I always hoped my father would eventually see that I had become a halfway decent clinical and forensic psychologist, and in time would get over being pissed off that I didn't follow in his footsteps to become Judge Holt *numero dos*. Maybe he was right. Maybe I've just been fooling myself."

"He wasn't right," Scoggs said. "You're good at what you do. Just like him."

"I'm like him?" She grimaced. "Is that a joke?"

"Would I dare to joke with you, Killer?"

"Screw you, Scoggs," she muttered, hurt and distraught.

He stood, giving her a look filled with pity. "I'll see what I can find out." He placed a hand on her shoulder. "For now, go home and take care of yourself. We're on this."

She nodded and looked away. Her eyes got misty at his words and tears were the last thing she would let him see. She hated it when people were nice to her, and she despised their pity.

She took a deep breath then placed her hands on her computer keyboard. She needed to do more investigating on her own.

CHAPTER 17

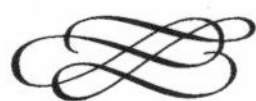

Idaho

"I could not find it, my friend." Lorenzo Fermi spoke softly, then stopped, and waited for the explosion from the other end of the phone line.

"You're saying it's gone?" Bennett roared.

"All I can tell you is that the man asking questions about the old priest is an archeologist named Michael Rempart."

"An archeologist?" For some reason, the name sounded familiar to Bennett. "Are you watching him?"

"More than that, we searched him and tossed his apartment. As well as checking out Chaldean monasteries. We found Rempart at one of them. I think he doesn't have the pearl. He told us he didn't, and if he did, why would he have gone to the Chaldean monastery?"

There was a long silence, and Fermi became hopeful, but then Bennett's harsh, ugly voice said, "Of course, he would never lie to you!"

"Well ..." Lorenzo Fermi hesitated. He wasn't sure what to say, all he knew was that this whole business had spiraled way over his head.

"One. Hundred. Thousand. U.S. dollars." Bennett's words were crisp, distinct. And then he lost all control. "That's what you'll get when you hand me the fucking pearl. I should think that would be enough incentive for you *to search a little bit more!*"

"I'll try, *signore*."

Bennett slammed down the phone without as much as a goodbye, then didn't move for a long while as he tamped down his anger. He wasn't a patient man. He had already waited long enough for this day. Waited for it. Expected it. Feared it.

Two sailors down—Oliveros and Holt. Five to go. Including him.

His living room was filled with computer equipment, and he had set up a powerful network, knowing that someday this might happen. Eventually, he would use it to search for Michael Rempart, but that would have to wait. Why the hell was that name so god-damned familiar?

He shoved it aside. His first task, as always when he sat before the network, was to run a search on the known quantities.

The satellite reception for his computers was working as it should, and he quickly saw that no new evidence had turned up in the murders of Oliveros and Holt. He hadn't expected any. At least no one else had died ... yet.

CHAPTER 18

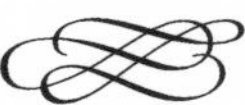

*A**nyang**, China 1150 B.C.*

The young King Zhou Xin could barely eat or sleep after looking upon the face and figure of the Goddess Nüwa. None of his wives or concubines could hold a candle to the beautiful goddess. Finally, in despair, his advisors suggested he search for the most attractive human female in the kingdom, and use her to help him forget about the one he could never possess.

Eventually, word came to him that the woman he sought was the exquisite daughter of the powerful Duke Su Hu of Ji.

The king asked Duke Su to allow his daughter, Daji, to become his concubine—a request that the king considered to be a high honor.

To his amazement, the duke refused. At that, the king sent an army to persuade him, but the duke met them with an army of his own. Their clash resulted in the deaths of many good men.

The fighting continued until the duke's son was captured and threatened with death, and the duke realized he must give in, or he and his people would be annihilated. His heart broke, but he agreed that in exchange for the return of his son, he would give Daji to the king.

The duke arranged to travel to the palace with his daughter, knowing that once she became a concubine, he very likely would never see her again. He included a retinue of fifty warriors to protect them both.

Now, the Thousand Year Vixen had watched all of this with great interest.

*When the retinue stopped at an inn for the night, the duke chose a large room for himself, his daughter, and ten of his most trusted retainers. He and his daughter were given soft feathered mattresses, while the guards slept on the floor. At one point a great chill came over them, and all the candles went out, leaving the room in darkness. The guards murmured "*yaojing,*" meaning a demon must be near.*

Frightened, Daji cried out and sat up from her bed.

"Are you all right, Daughter?" the duke asked.

"Yes, Honorable Father," she said meekly. "Thank you." With that, she quietly lay back down. She was a gentle, modest girl of fifteen years, who had lived a soft and pleasant life. She and her mother had shed many tears at her departure, but she knew she must obey her father's decision to save her brother's life. Thoughts of the king and what was to come filled her with dread.

Now, she felt something near her. She would have cried out, but did not want to again disturb her father. Whatever crept near—something she could feel, but not touch; sense but not see; smell but not hear—covered her and pressed her down hard against the mattress. At first it seemed like an animal, a fox perhaps, but then it changed, and grew much, much larger. It covered her mouth and slowly sucked out her breath, her very essence, her life ...

The guards continued to whisper their fears.

"Quiet!" the duke roared as he ordered his servants to relight the candles. "It was only a gust of wind, you fools!"

He saw that his daughter's eyes were on him, and she stretched out her hand. He went to her and sat. "Daughter, don't be frightened. All is fine."

She turned onto her side facing him, letting the blanket that had modestly covered her slide down to her narrow waist. From there, it rose over full, lush hips. As she leaned closer to the old duke, her nightdress gaped open, allowing him a glimpse of her breasts. Then she looked coyly up at him and smiled. Something about her eyes gripped his attention, something almost alien ...

In a voice lower, huskier than she had ever used before, she murmured, "I'm fine ... Daddy ... now that you're here to protect me."

The duke's chest swelled with pride at her use of "Daddy"—she had never been so bold as to call him that before, even as he was taken aback at noticing the lushness of his daughter's body. She placed her hand on his knee and squeezed, then slid her hand up onto his thigh as she met and held his gaze. As their eyes met, in hers he saw something knowing, inviting. No, he told himself, impossible. And yet, he felt a quickening in his loins. Suddenly, he not only could understand the king's demand for her, but he felt a surprising and deep stab of jealousy ... and desire. He gasped and turned away, horrified and disgusted with himself, ashamed and sickened by such evil thoughts.

The party continued on to the king's palace without further incident.

When King Zhou Xin learned of the arrival, he considered killing the duke for having defied his initial order, but his ministers convinced him that the duke should live since he sought peace and had brought his daughter to the palace. The king decided the duke's life or death would depend on what he thought when he finally looked upon the woman that had cost so many lives.

When the time came for the daughter of Duke Su Hu to be escorted to stand before the king, Zhou Xin entered in his palace hall early and took his seat at the end of a long corridor. He was excited, but anxious at the prospect, sure he would once again be met with disappointment.

Daji dressed in white and pink silk robes that skimmed, but did not completely hide, her lithe figure. She entered the hall on the arm of her father, but then walked in tiny steps, her head bowed, until she was about five feet from the king. Liking what he saw thus far, the king's heart pounded in anticipation.

Then she lifted her head. Boldly she met his gaze and held it a long moment before she said, "I am Daji. May my king, my lord, live ten thousand years."

Although King Zhou Xin was sitting, he felt weak all over at the sight of her. She was more than he had imagined, more than he had dared to dream. All he could think of was a desire to possess such perfection. He immediately jumped to his feet and walked around her several times, then he took her arms and held them out wide as he inspected her up close. She swayed towards him, as if desiring him as much as he did her. He smiled, nodded, and ordered his servants to take her to his rooms to await his visit.

His ministers were dismayed. They wanted him to get over his fascination with the Goddess Nüwa, but they never expected him to lose his head the way he seemed to at the very sight of the duke's daughter. To them, she was lovely, but not enough to cause King Zhou Xin's strange reaction.

The king sent the duke home with vast quantities of food for his people, and then rushed off to be alone with his newest concubine.

CHAPTER 19

Florence, Italy

Michael had set up his cell phone to give him a special alert whenever an email, text, or call came in from Jianjun. When it sounded in the middle of the night, he opened up the email. The news about the seven men in Berosus' photo was mind-blowing.

Each of the seven had become important in his own right. But it wasn't as if they were top graduates of the U.S. Naval Academy or some other university. They had all enlisted out of high school.

Jianjun had listed the men's names and titles:

Gene Oliveros—Highest paid movie director in Hollywood.

Daniel Holt—Federal Appeals Court Judge, 9th Circuit; top prospect for U.S. Supreme Court

Kevin Wilson—U.S. Senator from California, said to be a top candidate for a Presidential run.

Jonathan Vogel—Director of JV Global Energy, world's largest energy-based hedge fund.

Scott Jones—Owner and publisher of the *Los Angeles Post,* second only to the *L.A. Times* in influence on the West Coast.

Stuart Eliot—Founder of Powermore Industries, top mining company in the U.S., now retired.

Hank Bennett—Founder of VaultGuard, the top internet security company in the world, now retired.

Jianjun also included a lot of accompanying information. He noted that movie director Gene Oliveros had died two days earlier. The evidence indicated that he blew up the deck of his house while he, his wife and daughter stood on it, killing all of them instantly. No one could understand why he would have done it. The next day, Judge Daniel Holt had died under mysterious circumstances. The news report's description of his death hinted at murder or suicide, but gave no details as to why the FBI was confused. The piece also stated that Holt's daughter often worked as a criminal profiler with the FBI. A photo of her leaving her father's home ran in the news article, and Jianjun had included it with the e-mail.

Michael's nerves went on alert at the odd expression on the woman's face. Sadness, disbelief, and even lack of emotion due to shock were common expressions at such times, but one that evinced horror was not.

Recent news photographs of Daniel Holt showed him to be surprisingly youthful for a man sixty-two years of age. Even judges liked face lifts, Michael guessed. Gene Oliveros looked equally young, but that was par for the course with Hollywood types.

Vogel, the hedge fund manager, Eliot from Powermore Industries, and even Jones, owner of the *L.A. Post,* had nothing but public relations blurbs and puff pieces about them on the internet. Senator Kevin Wilson had more information than anyone would ever want to read, and Hank Bennett had apparently scrubbed the Internet clean of all information about him, as would be only fitting of the man whose security systems were used by the Pentagon.

Michael saw that Oliveros' death happened after Father Berosus died.

Three men, dying one after the other, all somehow connected by a photo taken years earlier. Why? How?

Michael studied the documents Jianjun sent. As usual, his assistant was incredibly thorough. His phone rang. It was Jianjun.

"Hey," he said when Michael answered. "I got into the FBI database, and what I found deserved a phone call."

"Fantastic!"

"You better believe it. You know, Michael, I wouldn't mind a trip to Los Angeles. I'm a little bored up here in Vancouver. I mean, not that I haven't got anything to do, and I'm here with my wife and all, not that she's boring—well, maybe—but if you'd like me to head south to L.A., Hollywood, Disneyland, I'm just saying, I wouldn't refuse."

Michael rubbed his forehead. Jianjun didn't fool him. His assistant was ready for action. He wished he felt the same. "Tell me what you've got," he said.

Jianjun's information was straightforward. The men varied in age from eighteen to twenty-four when they enlisted in the Navy. They all joined in 1975 or 1976 and came from all over the country. "The seven were on the U.S.S. *Saratoga* in nineteen seventy-seven, part of the Atlantic fleet. They were given leave at the same time and apparently all ended up in Cairo. For over a week, they dropped off the grid. When they reappeared, they were late returning from leave and all ended up in the brig. The strange part was that none of them remembered what made them late. Reports from their superiors, who had sent out search teams, was that they arrived back at the ship on their own volition, confused and terrified. The military blamed it on them having been drugged—either on purpose or because someone spiked their food or drink. In any case, after their tours of duty, every one of them went back to school. That was baffling because, before being drafted, these guys weren't the top of the heap, if you know what I mean, most of these guys were a banana peel away from a life behind bars."

"And then they all went to college," Michael observed.

"They gravitated to the Los Angeles area, started out in junior colleges, did well, and from there went to universities where they all graduated at the top of their class Afterward, each one went onto a mega successful career in various and unrelated fields. I know your country has this mystique about the American Dream and all, but as they say in my country, if it smells like bull shit, it probably is."

"So," Michael puzzled. "What happened to them during the week they can't remember? And why are they being targeted now?"

CHAPTER 20

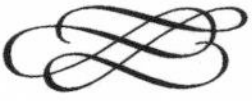

—The new keeper of the pearl has identified our old friends.

—We can make sure they don't meet.

—Or, make it even more interesting if they do.

—Then, we can kill them all at once.

Idaho

Hank Bennett rode his all-terrain vehicle five miles over rugged, roadless mountains to the home of Stuart Eliot. They helped build each other's log cabins, but despite being the other's closest neighbor, neither cared all that much for the other and rarely visited. They communicated every week or so via e-mail, more to make sure the other was still alive than anything.

Since the ATV could be heard several miles away, Stuart stood in his doorway as Hank arrived. Stuart was a big man, pushing two-hundred eighty pounds in a six-foot two frame. He had wavy brown hair, thinning at the crown.

Hank followed him into the cabin. The small main room had a TV, sofa, and a recliner on one end, and a table and chairs on the other covered with papers, three computer monitors, and a printer/scanner/copier/fax. The kitchen area looked more like a chemical laboratory than a place to prepare food, with a multitude of beakers, flasks, heating equipment, glass and metal tubing, plus a large number of containers of chemicals, rare earth elements, and ores.

Stuart, like Hank, traveled every month or two northwest to Elk City to pick up mail and products ordered online. Both had set up false identities for all public interactions. Elk City claimed a population of two hundred, but Hank was sure that included tourists and bears. When they needed more anonymity, they would head southeast to Salmon City. That, however, rarely happened.

On a corner table sat an automatic espresso machine that Stuart used to make Hank a strong Americano. He also gave him a shot of whiskey, neat. Hank knocked back the whiskey in one swallow, then said, "It's time to leave."

"Leave? Why? We're safe here."

Hank grimaced. "Don't you believe in any of the work we've done? All we've studied and learned? We've figured out how to keep ourselves safe anywhere, but if one of the others gets the pearl, we can't be sure they won't cause a huge problem. Right now, with proper precautions, we'll be fine."

Stuart's heart pounded with fear at the thought of leaving the area he had called home for nearly ten years. "I don't know," he whispered.

"I can't do it alone," Hank said. "And you know I'm right."

Stuart took a shuddering breath, then nodded. "Okay, where do we start?"

"Do you remember hearing of an archeologist named Michael Rempart?"

CHAPTER 21

Los Angeles, California

Seventeen hours after he received the news from Jianjun about the strange deaths of two of the men in Berosus' photo, Michael walked through LAX to the car rental area. At first, he told himself to ignore the deaths. They had nothing to do with him. But they ate at him. Father Berosus had called the pearl evil and said it would harm people. Plus, it was a philosopher's stone, something he took personally. Ever since he looked at it, he sensed its presence, felt as if it were near and watching.

The only personal object the priest had carried was a photo of seven men, and now two of those men were dead. Even if nothing mystical was involved, the deaths had to be more than a weird coincidence.

Michael found himself particularly haunted by the frightened look on Judge Daniel Holt's daughter's face in the newspaper article Jianjun sent him. Finally, he gave up arguing with himself, and headed for Los Angeles.

The bright, cloudless sky, warm sunshine, and rows of palm trees filled him with the beauty of southern California as he drove away from the airport. Whenever he came here and saw weather like this, he wondered why he didn't simply move back to his beach house a couple of hours north.

The feeling usually lasted until he got stuck in traffic on the 405. Then, sanity prevailed. He had bought the house some years back after hearing his father was going to sell it. He lived in it for a while, but now used it solely as a mail drop and "permanent" address when needed.

Jianjun had given him information on how to reach Kira Holt. He wanted to speak to her and hopefully get some answers about Father Berosus and the men in the photo. Maybe even about the pearl. He first went to the offices where she conducted her private practice and was told she was on "sabbatical." Next, at the FBI office, he learned she would be out of the office a while, taking some personal days.

He doubted he would find her at the crime scene, but he wanted to see it, and drove by Judge Holt's address. He found a small home on a million dollar location in Laurel Heights. From there, he went to Kira Holt's townhouse in Santa Monica.

A woman opened the door. She wore no make-up, and her blue eyes had a look of deep sorrow. She was tall and stood ramrod straight. Bright red hair pulled into a pony tail revealed a high forehead and lightly freckled pale white skin. "Miss Holt?" he asked.

Her face and demeanor stiffened. "If you're a reporter, you should be showing your credentials. But don't bother because I have nothing to say." She began to close the door.

He put his hand out to stop it. "Wait. I'm not a reporter. I have information for you."

She regarded him with caution, her brow wrinkled. "You seem familiar. Have we met before?"

"No. My name is Michael Rempart," he said, and then felt relief when his name meant nothing to her. During the short time he lived in the area, he had become a bit of a television "darling" because of his archeological exploits, hosting a couple of National Geographic channel specials, dating Hollywood stars, and appearing regularly in *People* and other magazines. That prior fame—or infamy—had caused the press to take notice when he became involved in the Idaho disappearances last year. He was glad to have nothing more to do with that phase of his life and felt vaguely disgusted that he had ever embraced it. "I was living in Florence, Italy, when I received some startling information. The newspapers describe the deaths as possible suicides. I don't believe it."

The way she scrutinized him was so fierce it felt like an assault. "What do you know about them?"

He lifted his hand. "Only what was reported. I'm here to ask you what happened."

She folded her arms. "Who are you that I should tell you anything? I suggest you leave before I call the cops." She again reached for the door.

"Look at this." He held, at eye level, the photo of the seven sailors. "We need to talk about it."

She scrutinized his face as if trying to remember where she had seen him, or if she dared to trust him. "Come inside."

She led him past a living room done in tans and browns and devoid of personality—sofa, two chairs, end tables, coffee table, and a big screen TV. The eating nook had a little color—yellow cushions on the two chairs at a small round table. The kitchen wasn't much bigger than his alcove in Italy.

She walked over to an electric coffee maker that held a half-empty pot of coffee. "Would you like some?"

"Yes, thanks," he said. "I just got off a flight from Rome. It's"—he looked at his watch—"already night there."

"Which means you probably haven't slept for, what, a day?"

"Well over twenty-four hours." He took a sip of the coffee. It was no espresso, but it helped. He placed the photo on the table. "I understand this is your father," he said, pointing to Daniel Holt.

She took a deep breath and nodded.

"Also, here are"—his finger hovered over each figure as he spoke —"Gene Oliveros, Senator Kevin Wilson, Jonathan Vogel, Scott Jones, Stuart Eliot, and Hank Bennett."

"How do you know their names?"

"They're all wealthy, important men." A thought struck Michael. "Didn't your father talk about them?

She shifted uncomfortably. "No, he didn't. I recognize the senator."

Michael was surprised her father hadn't talked about knowing such influential people. Michael told her the job title of each man in the photo.

A stunned expression filled her face. She placed her fingers on the photo. "Where did you get this?"

"A priest."

She looked skeptical. "A priest? Who is he? Where?"

"He's dead."

Her brow furrowed. "Was he related to one of these men?"

"Not that I could find."

"How did he die?" Her face paled. "Was it like—"

"No. Let me try to explain." He worked to keep his voice calm and soothing. He wondered how much he dared to reveal, and quickly decided: not much. "First, let me say none of it makes much sense—not yet, at least. Three nights ago in Florence, a stranger, a Chaldean priest, came to my apartment and gave me a certain artifact, a bronze receptacle containing a kind of amalgam. Shortly after that, he died. I was going through his few possessions to find a relative to give the bronze to, and came across this photo. When I looked into who the men were, I learned that Gene Oliveros died after the priest, and your father a day later." He took out the newspaper photo of the priest. "Have you ever seen this man before? Or heard of him? His name was Father Yosip Berosus."

She studied the photo and shook her head. Her blue eyes twinkled with intelligence and he knew the question that was coming: "Why did he go to you?"

He hated lying, but couldn't tell her the truth. "I have no idea."

She squeezed her hands together. "Your explanation of finding out the names of the men in the photo was too facile. You had to have some idea of the date of the photo, the name of the ship they were on—something. But there's nothing of that sort in the photo as far as I can see."

He shrugged and didn't meet her gaze. "I have clever friends."

"No one's that clever. If the priest didn't tell you, you must have access to government records."

He slid the photo from her and put it in the breast pocket of his sports jacket. "Enough of that. What's important is what happened to the men who died, who killed them and why—and if the men still alive are in danger."

"I've asked the FBI to look into the photo," she said coolly.

He lifted his brows.

"And perhaps they will. Eventually."

He actually felt good about her answer. It showed she was as skeptical of the FBI satisfactorily handling these weird deaths as he was. But then he shook his head. "I'm sorry. I came here because I thought you would have answers for me about the men in the photo, and possibly the old priest. But it seems you're as much in the dark as I am. Maybe more."

"My father never showed me the photo or talked about the men with him" she admitted.

He tried a different tack. "Did your father ever talk about any problems he had when he was in the Navy? Or his shore leave in Egypt? Perhaps he mentioned something about a priest, or a religion, or anything at all that can help me with the task the priest gave me. It would make it easier if I knew why the priest carried this photo when he died."

"What task?"

"It's complicated."

"Isn't everything?" She rubbed her arms as if chilled. "I'm afraid you've wasted your time coming here. My father told me he joined the Navy because jobs were difficult to come by in the 1970s. Back then, he had no ambition beyond drinking and hanging out with the guys, but he returned a new man, and ended up with a full fellowship to UCLA's School of Law."

"Remarkable," Michael said flatly.

"Not really. I suspect his time in the service taught him to focus, to realize he'd just been wasting his life."

"Right. And it's just a coincidence that the same thing happened to the other six men in the photo with him. They all enlisted, joined the Navy with no more than a high school diploma, and a few years later were top men in their fields. What's strange about that?"

She blanched, and in a small voice, said, "What are you suggesting?"

He stared back. "I'm not sure."

"It's time for you to be honest with me," she said, her blue eyes boring into him. "I'm supposed to believe that a priest you don't know gave you a valuable artifact, then died, and you traveled all the way to Los Angeles to try to find out about a photo he carried?"

"I've seen much in this world that's inexplicable," Michael said. "And something about the old priest caused me to take him seriously. Something's going on, a great evil. And when I put that together with the two deaths—"

"Evil?" Her mouth wrinkled with disdain. "What men call evil is simply someone choosing to do something bad."

He wished it were that simple. He leaned back in the chair. "Would it be more believable to you if I said I have a professional as well as an innate interest in anything that is old, rare, and culturally significant?"

She frowned, but then her eyes grew wide. "Now I remember who you are. I've seen articles about you. The Indiana Jones guy. You were going out with some starlet"—an eyebrow quirked up—"more than one, now that I think about it. And there was talk about using some of your adventures in a new mov ..." Her expression dropped from awe to dismay to pure scorn, and she stood. "My God, are you wheedling your way into the investigation of a judge's death for some entertainment show?"

"Of course not. Don't be silly. Sit down."

"Just get out of here and leave me alone." Angry tears filled her eyes.

He remained at the table and spoke more calmly. "Miss Holt, Kira, there was no truth to those stories. Well, maybe a bit, but none of it was serious, and has nothing to do with me being here." He paused a moment. "Think about it. A publicity stunt wouldn't have given me the Egyptian photo of your father, and it sure as hell wouldn't have had me traveling overnight from Italy."

Hands on hips, she blinked away her tears. "I'm a trained clinical psychologist and I can tell when someone is lying or holding back necessary information."

He admired her strength. She was hurting, confused and overwhelmed by her father's horrific death, yet she continued to question, to investigate. He owed her the truth. "All right. I'll tell you what I know, but it'll be difficult to believe."

She folded her arms. "Try me."

"It began with Marco Polo—"

"Marco Polo!" She nearly spat the name out. "Marco Polo, evil pearls, and bull shit! You almost got me. Now get out!"

Michael raked his fingers through his hair, pushing it back off his forehead. He was too tired for this. "All right. Here's my card. Call me when you're ready to talk."

With that, he left.

Scott Jones tilted back in the executive leather chair behind his desk in his walnut-paneled corner office at the *Los Angeles Post.* He read, and then reread, his staff's news articles about his two former Navy buddies' deaths. It had to be a coincidence, he told himself. He wasn't in any danger.

Why should he be? He'd done everything right, and everything had happened just as predicted.

His life was fine, great in fact. No, it was better than great. All he had ever wanted was to be a reporter, and now, not only had that happened, but he owned the goddamn newspaper. Still, he had to admit that covering stories was a lot more fun than running a newspaper. But it didn't pay near as well.

He sighed as he thought back on his reporter days. Reagan's "Western White House" gave him lots of exposure back in the day. Of course, he couldn't talk about it anymore, because when he did, people looked at him strangely as they calculated how old he must be, and then tried to understand how he could look so young. He chuckled. Just dumb luck, he guessed.

Hank Bennett had phoned him yesterday. He refused to take his call, refused to listen to what that paranoid bastard had to say. Last he heard, Bennett had pulled a Unabomber and was living in some outhouse in the hills of Montana or some such place.

Jones wished the lunatic would simply leave him alone. Bennett was the reason he'd love to find the pearl himself. He'd use it to wipe Bennett off the face of this earth, just so he'd never have to hear the testy bastard again. That the guy was certifiable was evident by his walking away from his multi-billion dollar computer security firm. He sold it for big bucks, but it wasn't as if he wanted to spend more time with his family. He had no family.

Jones, too, had no family, but in his case the reason had been the law—until recently, it hadn't allowed the kind of marriage he would have wanted. The end result was fine, however, since Raymond—the man he would have married—turned old, gray, and flabby, while Jones remained youthful and trim. He eventually walked out on Raymond—the guy just didn't excite him anymore. Raymond looked old at fifty-two, and Jones—ten years his senior—didn't.

Things were looking up, however, with Leland, his latest fling. He was so busy thinking about Leland and the excitement the coming evening would bring, that he paid little attention to the window washer's platform outside window directly behind him. Little attention, that is, until the platform began to sway.

At the squeal of the equipment, Jones swiveled his chair to face the windows with their view of exciting, albeit smoggy, downtown Los Angeles. He watched as the platform swung back and forth, farther each time, and finally bumped against the window.

"What the hell?" Jones said, standing now. The window washer, if one had ever been there, was gone.

But as he stared, he noticed something lying on the washer platform. At first, it looked like an animal, but then it pulled itself up and turned into a man—a naked man who would make Adonis weep with jealousy. His hair was blond, long and straight, reaching past his shoulders. He was tanned and shiny, as if he had oiled his body to better show off the beautifully sculpted contours of the muscles on his arms, thighs, and chest. Jones swooned. This must be a gift from one of his cronies—a sex toy sent to him in this most outlandish way.

Only once before had he seen such beauty in the male body—in Egypt. God, how had he forgotten? Before that, he had been too naïve to even realize that there was more to life and love than the few women he had dated.

On the other side of the window, the man stared, and then cocked his head slightly. Jones heard the sound of a nearby helicopter, and he stepped closer to the window to see where it was.

The sounds of war filled the room, turning his blood to ice.

"No," he whispered.

Gunfire, shouted orders, cries from the wounded. Memories of servicemen fighting, running, and dying, flooded his brain until it felt ready to burst. He put his hands over his ears.

"No!" he shouted. "I won't have it!"

The window washer platform swung away from the window, then slammed back against it, striking with a hard, glassy pang. The Adonis pressed his hands to the window, his face on the other side of the glass. And that was when Jones noticed his green eyes. Jones quaked, but couldn't turn away as the platform swung back again. His Adonis vanished, and in his place stood a black fox.

With tears rolling down his cheeks, Jones cried out. "Please. You can't do this. Talk to me, damn it! Talk to me!"

He tried to run, but terror and memories filled his heart. The platform swayed back, much farther than before.

Then, as if in slow motion, the platform began a relentless, steady arc towards the window. This time, when it struck, the safety glass crumbled like sand.

Jones' terrified screams stopped abruptly as the platform struck his neck and severed his head.

CHAPTER 22

MICHAEL HEADED TOWARDS DOWNTOWN. It was more crowded than ever, and the traffic crawled. The first time he saw L.A., he was a child. His parents owned a beach house near Santa Barbara—the one that was now his. They would spend a month there every July when he was a boy, and they'd often head south to Los Angeles and Disneyland. Adventureland was Michael's favorite.

Now, William Claude Rempart rarely left Wintersgate, his estate overlooking Cape Cod. Even before his wife died, he was a strange man. After her death, he became even more reclusive.

Michael's mother had died at age forty-four, only three years older than he was now. She was only eighteen when she married William Claude. He was thirty, and already a wealthy recluse. Their first child, a girl, was born a little over a year after the marriage, but soon died. The birth was difficult and losing the child even harder. Five years passed before she conceived again, giving birth to Michael's older brother. Another ten years passed before Michael entered the world.

By then, all his mother's dreams had vanished into the netherworld in which she seemed to live. She would often sit on a rocking chair in the study on the third floor of the mansion they called home. Michael would crawl up on her lap, and she would hold him and rock.

Sometimes, she would speak to him about her life, but she always couched such thoughts around books, as if they were the only thing real to her.

He remembered her love of classical mythology. Her favorite bedtime reading to him was *Bullfinch's Mythology* in which Greek and Roman gods wandered the earth. She read him *The Iliad* and *The Odyssey* when he was only six and read them again several times thereafter. No wonder he became an archeologist.

A few years after her death, he came across her book of Longfellow's poem, *Evangeline.* He remembered that she often reread it, or sat with the book open on her lap, staring out at the sea. He sometimes read it simply to feel her presence around him once more, romanticizing her as the Evangeline of the poem and telling himself she hadn't died, but had gone away to search for her lost love. He practically memorized the poem, half believing Longfellow wrote it to explain his mother's grief:

Fair was she and young, when in hope began the long journey;
Faded was she and old, when in disappointment it ended.
Each succeeding year stole something away from her beauty,
Leaving behind it, broader and deeper, the gloom and the shadow...

As a child, Michael hadn't understood half of what she'd said, but he remembered her words, and eventually they began to make sense. He even remembered her saying she used to see herself as a poor waif like Jane Eyre, and her husband as the wild, exciting Mr. Rochester. The way she sighed, he knew such romantic dreams had come to nothing.

And then she died.

William Claude, who never paid much attention to his sons, was even less of a father after her death. Michael was ten years old at the time, and his older brother was a student at Yale. Michael was pretty much raised by Magda—the woman he thought of as a gypsy. When she came to live in Wintersgate as its housekeeper, Michael was nine. She brought with her a daughter, Irina, who was four at the time.

They were more of a family to Michael than his father ever was. And Irina …

No, he wouldn't go there. He shook away a memory that still held too much power over him.

Up ahead, Michael saw the Ritz Carlton, where he'd booked a room before leaving Italy. He checked in, but felt too antsy to stay in the hotel room, and decided to walk around for a while.

After a couple of busy blocks, he turned into a Starbucks.

Standing off to the side, waiting for the barista to make her latte, was a woman he couldn't help but appreciate. Her hair was long and lush, a shiny rich brown color. Her white and mauve dress showed off a trim waist and nicely rounded hips, while shapely legs stretched way, way down to sky-high strappy heels. When the barista handed over her coffee, she took it, turned around, and then looked up.

Their eyes met, and Michael's world stopped. Even after all these years …

She almost dropped her coffee.

He jumped out of the line and reached for the cup to help her hold it. Their fingers touched.

"Michael," she whispered.

Nothing about her had changed—not her face, her voice, or those eyes, a blue so light they sometimes sparkled white—eyes that seemed to see into his soul. And always had. "Irina."

She smiled at that.

"Let's sit," he said. "There's a table in the corner."

"Sir?" the barista asked.

He ordered an Americano and then led Irina to a table where he pulled out the chair for her.

"Is it really you?" she murmured.

He also sat and scooted his chair a little closer.

Neither spoke, but searched the other's face, and then both began.

"What are you doing …?"

"Why are you …?"

They stopped and stared into each other's eyes.

"You first," Michael said.

She admitted that she kept up with his exploits and exciting life. That was why she was momentarily taken aback when she saw him. It was as if a magazine article or TV special had suddenly come to life right there in Westwood.

In a matter of minutes, the years melted away. The way she spoke, the way she cocked her head, the way with each move her hair swung freely, sensually, against her shoulders, enchanted him. He never remembered it being as straight as it was now, but it certainly suited her. The hint of green in her eyes was another surprise. How had he forgotten that about her eye color? He didn't think he had ever forgotten anything about her—especially not the way they parted some fifteen years ago.

A strange foreboding filled him. How could it be that she was suddenly here? He tried to shake off the feeling. He had become too jaded about life, too suspicious. Meeting Irina again—why couldn't it truly be what it seemed: a wonderful and fortunate accident.

"Michael?" She had a smile in her voice and on her face. "You look a million miles away. Am I so boring?"

A powerful attraction surged through him, just as when they were young. God, but he had loved her. He once thought he could never forgive her, that he never wanted to see her again, but seeing her now, he realized how wrong he had been. Over an hour flew by as they talked about their lives.

She had married about eight years ago, and last year she and her husband had divorced. He asked if she had children. She didn't. And then he asked if she was seeing anyone at the moment. She shook her head and looked away.

"But your marriage was happy until recently?" he asked.

She hesitated, then said, "Not particularly." Maybe he shouldn't have been elated to hear her admit that to him, but he was. "Let's talk about something else," she said. "About you. Tell me about the galleon you found, pieces of eight, and all that."

When it was time to leave, she gave him her phone number, but told him she didn't expect him to call. So he leaned across the table and kissed her. She looked pleased and taken aback all at once.

"I'll call." He promised. "And if I can get away, I'll call tonight."

"Please do," she said as they stood. "But what's on your busy agenda?"

He stared at her, confused. "Come to think of it, I'm not sure."

She took his arm, tilted her head, and gave him a shy smile. "Well, what if we went *nowhere* and did *nothing* together?"

A shiver rippled down his back, but he chose to ignore it as he pulled his arm free and wrapped it snugly around her waist. Holding her at his side, although not nearly close enough, he wondered how he could ever leave her. "I never imagined I would find you again," he said, his voice husky. "It's a miracle."

"Yes," she whispered. "It is."

CHAPTER 23

THE NEWS OF SCOTT JONES' shocking and horrible death hit the FBI office almost immediately.

Kira read the police reports from the window-washing company which stated that the company had no idea how their equipment, which was permanently installed on the roof, could have been lowered. They found no signs of tampering. Even more shocking to all was that the equipment could have struck the window with such force as to not only shatter it, but continue into the office and kill Mr. Jones.

The police were inclined to chalk it up to a freak accident.

Kira understood how they reached such a conclusion, but they were wrong.

Her thoughts turned to Michael Rempart. Was he nothing but a publicity-seeking charlatan, or had he been telling her the truth? Something about the way he had looked at her, openly yet with dark and troubled eyes, made her want to believe him even though everything rational told her not to.

Using FBI systems, she checked his flight information. He was listed as traveling from Rome to Los Angeles, arriving before noon that day. Perhaps that part of his story was true, but the rest was outlandish.

She keyed in the names Rempart had given her of the men in the photo, and found information including their tours of duty, university experiences, and current lofty positions. Again, each man was as Rempart had claimed. She smirked—who was she kidding? She knew they would be.

Finally, she investigated Michael Rempart. She read a surprisingly glowing write-up in the FBI database that gave a brief biography, his education, his archeological discoveries, and his publications. Nothing else gave her cause for alarm, not even his brief foray into television.

Her first impression of Rempart had been of a troubled but honest man. He was also very good-looking, but surprisingly thin and pale, as if he had been sick or dealing with pain for a long time. She read that he had nearly died after an accident, but no details about that "accident" had been given.

He had regarded her with no wavering, no shiftiness, and yet with an intensity that she could almost touch, like a cloud of despair that hovered around him. What, she wondered, could do that to a man?

She rubbed her temples, trying to clear her head, and get a clear picture of what all this meant. Michael Rempart made her nervous, but although he was probably wrong about some of what he said, it didn't mean he was lying.

All of which meant that the other men in the photo—now only four remained alive—had to be contacted and warned. The FBI needed to do that and to use the information she had to track down the killer or, more likely, killers. These deaths were incredibly clever and sophisticated to carry out. Almost unbelievably so, she had to admit. She gathered the photo and printouts about each sailor and then added a big red check mark beside each man who had died in the past three days. She gave everything to Scoggins.

He let out a whistle as he looked over the material. "An impressive bunch," he said.

"Yes, it is."

"How did you find all this out?" he asked.

She told him about meeting Rempart, stating that he seemed to have a bit too much information about the murders. He might, she said, be involved in the deaths.

"I'll check him and everything else out," Scoggins said, then bowed his head and went back to his paperwork.

"Good." She waited a moment hoping he would ask her to help, but he didn't.

Back at her desk, she put in a call to Jonathan Vogel, chairman of the hedge fund, JV Global Energy, but could do no more than leave an urgent message with his secretary. Not even with FBI resources could she locate Hank Bennett or Stuart Eliot. Not yet, anyway. She was sure they would be found eventually, but for the moment, she felt frustrated at being unable to reach them.

The only good news was that Senator Kevin Wilson was in town. Kira drove to his office, planning a sit-in if necessary. To her surprise, he was not only in the office, but within minutes, a staff assistant led her to him.

Wilson stood as she entered. He looked handsome enough on TV and in the news, but in person, he was jaw-dropping. He reminded her of a middle-aged Robert Redford with rugged good looks, a trim, well-toned physique, and reddish blond hair with a hint of gray at the temples. "Kira Holt." He flashed a politician-perfect smile as he held out his hand. "Are you related to Judge Holt?"

"Yes, he was my father." They shook hands. "You knew him?"

"Slightly. Have a seat." He gestured towards a chair as he sat behind his desk. "Your father and I were in the Navy together. You have my deepest condolences. I understand he was a good man, and a great judge."

"Thank you, Senator," she murmured.

"I'm told you're with the FBI," he said. "What can I help you with?"

She said she was looking into the death of Gene Oliveros. "He was also on the *Saratoga* in the late seventies."

His eyebrows lifted. "He was?"

"Do you remember the day this was taken?" She showed him a copy of the photo of the seven men.

As he looked at the photo, his face turned ashen. "I don't

remember the day, precisely, but I was obviously on shore leave. Is there a problem?"

"Three of the men in that photo have died within days of each other. Gene Oliveros, Scott Jones, and Judge Daniel Holt—my father. All three were killed in horrible ways."

He looked stricken. "I heard about two deaths, but ... Scott Jones is dead? You're sure?"

"Yes. Mr. Jones' death happened today. Some will say it was a horrible accident, but I don't think so. You're in that photo; it's why I'm here to see you, to warn you."

He frowned. "You think these deaths weren't accidents or suicides?"

She nodded. "Do you know any reason why those men, or any of you, would be targeted?"

He pressed his lips together. "No. I wasn't friends with any of them. I learned your father and I were in the service together, but I don't remember him from the ship, or having that photo taken. I suspect I just happened along, stepped into the picture at the last minute."

"I see," she said, taking back the photo.

"That part of the world is known for honor killings. If someone was insulted, maybe they're just now taking revenge."

She shook her head. "Something more is going on here."

"Whatever." He sounded displeased and twisted his signet ring several times. "I would appreciate it, Ms. Holt, if you would keep that photo away from the press. This is the sort of ugliness that can lead to false smears. If my name becomes linked to these deaths in any way, I will hold the FBI responsible."

"Anything you can remember about this photo or these men might help," she said. "I want to know why my father died, Senator Wilson, and who killed him."

"I told you, that photo means nothing to me."

She hesitated a moment, but then decided to go ahead and ask. "What about Yosip Berosus?"

His eyes widened with surprise. “Never heard of him.” He checked his watched. “I’m afraid I have a meeting now.” They both stood.

“If anything comes to mind, please contact me directly.” She handed him her card.

He put it in his pocket. “Goodbye, Agent Holt.”

She left the office. As much as she wished it were otherwise, she realized the person who seemed to know the most about all this was Michael Rempart. She called his cell phone. It rang several times, but he didn’t answer. She left a message.

When he didn’t get back to her after an hour, she tried again, and then several more times throughout the day and evening, always with the same result.

CHAPTER 24

VANCOUVER, B.C.

"So, now your women come to my house!"

Linda Li's sharp voice woke Jianjun. It was only ten-thirty in the morning. He wondered what in the world was going on. Linda proceeded to yell at him in Mandarin.

Jianjun burrowed deeper into his bed, but his wife's piercing voice was like a corkscrew in his ears. Finally, he sat up and blinked, trying to adjust to reality after a pleasant dream.

He'd been awake until five A.M. learning about the men in the photo Michael had sent. One story led to another, all quite interesting, and definitely more interesting than his home life. "What did you say?" he mumbled.

"Wake up!" Linda shrieked. "Some American woman is in my living room. She wants to see you. I tell her you're sleeping, and she says, 'Wake him up. It's important.' But she won't tell me why. I can imagine! You and your so-called boss, running all over the world, gone for weeks and months at a time! And now! So help me, Jianjun, if she's pregnant, you can pack up and never come back." Jianjun's desire not to have children was a constant sore point in their marriage. But he couldn't see bringing a child into such an angry household.

"Stop!" Jianjun rubbed his eyes and stood, hiking up his pajama bottoms which tended to dip a bit low on his thin hips. His thick black hair stuck straight up. "Your imagination gets crazier every day. I have no idea who or what you're talking about."

Linda folded her arms and fumed at him. She was petite and wore her hair in a short pixie cut. To Jianjun's eye, she was a "kinda" woman —kinda attractive, kinda smart, kinda okay. He was also sure she hated him, but was either too proud or too stubborn to admit it. And he knew he disappointed her.

That he didn't care spoke volumes.

He put his feet in his slippers. "She's in the living room?"

"Didn't you hear me? Now you don't listen to me at all, do you?" It was difficult to speak through gritted teeth, but she managed.

"Tell her I'll be right there. I've got to wake up, first." He padded into the bathroom to take a shower before dressing.

"Tell her yourself!" The door to her own bedroom slammed shut.

Ten minutes later, he entered the living room in jeans, a white T-shirt, and flip-flops, then stopped and gawked. The woman before him was attractive, exceptionally attractive. In fact, downright beautiful … except for the scowl on her face.

She was tall, practically eye to eye with him. But his mouth went dry as his eyes skimmed over a toned and curvaceous body. Very nicely curvaceous, in fact. Her hair was red, and pulled back tight, but the bone structure of her face was gorgeous. He tried to swallow, but it was difficult with his mouth feeling like he had tried to eat cotton. Her cheekbones were pronounced, her nose small, her mouth lush, and her clear blue eyes seemed to look right into his head and know what he was thinking. *Uh oh.*

"Hello." His voice scarcely worked. "You asked to see me?"

"You're AceDragon?" she asked.

His left eye twitched. How did she know the user name for his secure computer network? "Who are you?"

"I'll take that as a yes." Her frown changed into a small, I've-got-you-now smirk as she walked to an easy chair and sat down. "My name is Kira Holt. Doctor Kira Holt. I understand you know quite a bit about my father."

"You're Kira Holt?" In person, she looked completely different from the scared, bedraggled woman in the black-and-white news photos. "Of course! How could I miss it, but you're so much prettier than … I mean, I'm sorry, I don't mean the photo in the newspaper wasn't, uh …." He stopped talking.

She looked momentarily perplexed by his rambling.

He sat on the sofa catty-corner to her, perched on the edge of the seat. "I'm sorry about the loss of your father."

"I need to know why you're looking into his life and the circumstances of his death."

He opened and shut his mouth a moment. "It was by chance. Only by chance. I was doing a study of the U.S. Supreme Court—who the current judges are and those who might replace some of the very old justices. Your father was one of them. His name turned up time and again. Yes, I kept seeing it." Michael had often complained about Jianjun's propensity to chatter and repeat himself when he was nervous … or lying … but he couldn't stop. "That's why I was studying about him, but then I saw that he had died. I was surprised. Very surprised. And sorry, too … as I said."

She gave him a skeptical stare. "I'm a consultant with the FBI." Her tone carried more than a hint of warning. "You also looked into the death of Gene Oliveros. Why are you snooping?"

Jianjun scooted back against the sofa, wishing he could crawl under it. "FBI. That's right, you do work for them. I knew that, I think. And you know about AceDragon, too, and that's saying something because no one else knows. I should have put two and two together. And I would have except"—he almost confessed that when he looked at her, his brain seemed to shrivel to the size of a walnut—"except, I just woke up. I must still be a bit groggy. Yeah, that explains it perfectly. I mean, the FBI figuring out my hacker handle is one thing, but if you were just anybody and hacked *me* … Oh, well, there is the NSA too, I mean, they could have done it. Yeah, I guess such governmental computer spying isn't illegal in the USA."

She looked pained. "I'm not here to discuss hacking, Mr. Li."

"Oh! That's good." He jumped up. "I think I need some tea. Would you like some? Or coffee? I know how much you Americans like coffee."

"Tea is fine."

He dashed out to the kitchen, filled a couple of cups with water, and put them in the microwave to heat. While they did, he took several deep breaths. Why was he acting like such a jerk? Was it because his wife had called her "your woman"?

He should be so lucky.

He found a couple bags of some kind of black tea, and stuck one in each cup, then carried them to the living room and put them on the coffee table.

Milk and sugar, he thought. He ran back into the kitchen … and was halfway back in the living room when he went back again for a teaspoon. He put everything in front of Kira, then sat.

"Now," she said, lifting out the tea bag by its string. She held it a moment, then placed it on the teaspoon. "Please tell me what's going on. You didn't only investigate Gene Oliveros. You also looked at the records of a U.S. Senator and several other powerful men."

"I did nothing but look around at names I'd heard of," he said. Her skin looked nearly translucent in the way of some people with red hair, and she had light freckles across her nose. They looked, he thought, kind of cute. "I was curious. That's all."

She looked directly into his eyes. It still bothered him, the way Western women did that, as opposed to Chinese women who tended to look up through their lashes. Or, maybe what bothered him was this particular Western woman with big, blue eyes that he could get lost in. He picked up his tea and then noticed his tea bag. He took an empty candy dish from an end table, put the bag in it, and took a big sip of tea. It was hot. Very hot.

He swallowed.

"You investigated seven men," she said. "And they were the only seven you looked into the past three or four days. I know, because I searched for tracks that you might have been elsewhere. You weren't

—except to try to find a good price on some new computer parts. That aside, what I want to know is, why those particular men?"

Jianjun dropped his gaze. "No reason."

"I don't believe you."

He didn't like it that she thought of him as a liar. "Miss Holt. We're in Canada." His voice, even to his own ear, sounded much deeper and harsher than usual. And his heart beat so loudly, he was sure she could hear it. "You don't have any jurisdiction here, so it doesn't matter what you believe. I mean, with all due respect, of course."

She raised her eyebrows, looking at him with astonishment. "True," she admitted, then asked, "Do you know Michael Rempart?"

"Should I?"

"Why should I believe any of your answers?" Her tone was harsh.

He looked her in the eye, his jaw clenched. "It doesn't matter if you do or not."

To his complete horror, her face twisted with emotion. She turned away.

"Um ..." he said stupidly.

"They're saying my father killed himself, but I know he didn't. I've got to find out what was going on, but I'm starting from ground zero. All I've got is that a fellow sailor died the day before, and another the day after, and a forty-year-old photo that shows the three of them together. Their deaths are more than tragic, but they are not a coincidence. That's why I'm here. You know something, and I'm asking you to please tell me what it is."

Her plea somehow ended his resolve to keep Michael's secret. He had to help her. Now.

"I was sent a copy of a photo and asked to find out who the men in it were," he said softly.

She shut her eyes a moment and nodded. "May I see it?"

"Of course." He went into his bedroom to make a print out, but when he turned around, she was right behind him. He nearly jumped out of his skin and then gave a quick glance at his underwear and dirty clothes on the floor and his unmade bed.

"Quite a set up," she said, looking at three computer monitors and a mid-size network server in the corner. "You could run a small country with this much power."

"I do." He was glad she faced his computer and not his messy bedroom. "I call it Freedonia."

She lifted an eyebrow. "A Marx Brothers fan, huh? Are you Rufus T. Firefly?"

She knows Freedonia! "When I'm not Captain Spaulding," he said with a grin. Her mouth curved into a smile as well. He was half in love. "How do you know the Marx Brothers?"

Her smile vanished. "My father liked them. Sometimes, when I was young, I'd sit down and watch, too."

Jianjun noticed the odd construction of her words—that she'd "sit and watch," but not that they watched the shows together. "Since you're here," he sat before the computer and typed in a command, "you may as well see the enhanced version of the photo."

She stood behind him, then leaned forward as she peered at his monitor. "It's similar to the photo that I have, but with some differences." She strained closer to see. "That name … you can read the name on the duffle bag."

He couldn't take her so near to him. Her clean, rose-scented perfume, her full breasts lightly brushing his shoulder—he was no saint. He stood up and, feigning the gentleman, gave her his chair, then pulled up another beside her.

"Something may have happened out there in the desert." Jianjun spoke softly, worried that his words would upset her again. "Something that, perhaps, someone now needs to keep quiet."

"You think one of these men is behind the deaths?" she asked. Her gaze was penetrating, as if she were trying to decide if he might be lying, or might know a lot more than he was saying.

"Yes, I do. Or, perhaps, the photographer. We don't know who took the photo." He thought a moment, then frowned. "On the other hand, what could have happened forty years ago that's worth killing over?"

"I've given this a lot of thought, and considering the horrendous ways the murders were committed," she said, "whoever was involved had to be rich enough to hire some very clever killers, and rich enough to keep them quiet. I suspect some kind of scandal happened that, if it became known, would hurt the career of one of these men. They've all become huge in their respective fields."

"The one who would worry the most about that, I imagine, is the senator," Jianjun added.

"Practically speaking, yes, but where ego and self-worth are involved, everyone can be equally dangerous," Kira said. "High school kids who can't even spell the word will kill each other because they feel they've been 'disrespected.' But I can't help but wonder how a priest came to have this photo."

Jianjun nodded, then caught himself. "Priest?"

"I've spoken to Michael Rempart." Kira again eyed him closely. "He told me a lot."

Jianjun quietly absorbed this, although his mind was shouting, *damn, damn, damn*. He hadn't heard from Michael since he arrived in the U.S., and now he learned Michael and Doctor Holt had met. Was she playing him for a fool, trying to get him to say things she already knew or suspected? As if he didn't already feel foolish enough because of the way he was acting around her.

His jaw tightened.

"Please, Mr. Li," she said, "if Michael Rempart is your source, tell me. If not, who is it? If someone else is looking into these men, I've got to know."

He drew in his breath, then said simply, "Call me Jianjun."

She looked surprised, then carefully pronounced, "*Jee-ahn-june.*"

He smiled. Her pronunciation was all wrong, but for a Westerner, pretty good. "Michael Rempart is my friend and my employer. He didn't tell me he spoke with you or I would have said something sooner. I'm sorry."

She nodded. "I tried to reach him last night, until late, but I couldn't. I went into the office to look through the FBI's data bank for the men in the photo and discovered that I wasn't the only person out there searching for all seven of them. I tracked AceDragon, then took the first plane to Vancouver this morning. And here I am."

"Michael didn't return your calls last night?" Jianjun reached for his cell phone and punched in a number on speed dial. "He didn't get back to me either. I started trying to reach him as soon as the news broke of Scott Jones' death."

"He seems able to take care of himself," Kira observed.

Jianjun scoffed. "You don't know him like I do."

No answer on Michael's phone. Jianjun called again, with the same result. He then phoned the Ritz-Carlton to direct the call to his room, but again, Michael didn't answer. No one could tell if he had come in last night or not.

"He's probably out on the town," Kira mused. "Living up to those gossip column stories about the dashing archeologist suddenly showing up at all the Hollywood parties and—"

"That was before," Jianjun said gravely.

"Before what?"

"Other things started to happen. Well, they always happened, but he used to ignore them, tell himself he wasn't really seeing or feeling things that were kind of, well, supernatural."

She eyed him suspiciously, but he went on.

"The world we see is just one of the worlds Michael sees," Jianjun explained. "He won't talk much about it and I can't explain it. But when he told me about getting a red pearl and a photo from a strange old priest, I got worried."

Jianjun called housekeeping, gave them Michael's room number and asked if the room had been made up. The supervisor said it had a "Do Not Disturb" sign on the door, so they had not gone inside. He thanked her and hung up.

"I think I need to go to Los Angeles," he said.

"To find Michael Rempart?"

"That's right."

Her eyes were steely. "I'm coming with you."

From his closet, he pulled out the carry-on suitcase he kept packed at all times since working for Michael, put on a jacket, and then stuck his head into his wife's room to tell her he was leaving for California with the beautiful American. He strutted out the door under a diatribe of Mandarin fury.

CHAPTER 25

ANYANG, China 1142 B.C.

The more of the "essence" of a human male that the Thousand Year Vixen, who now called herself Daji absorbed, the stronger she became. Her sexual talents quickly enslaved King Zhou Xin, who could focus on nothing but his newest wife and the pleasure she gave him. As she had been ordered to do by Goddess Nüwa, she soon drained the king of all strength and common sense.

Daji's fellow demons, the Nine-Headed Pheasant and the Jade Pipa, also took over the bodies of beautiful women or men, depending on the proclivities of their prey, and soon joined in the debauchery with the most powerful and influential of the king's men.

But Daji was not satisfied with carnal pleasures, and, with the king basically out of the way, she soon began running the government. Like all specters, she was an amoral being. Not immoral, but simply without any sense of right or wrong. She would do whatever brought her fun and excitement, and due to her demonic nature, found that watching death and suffering was great fun indeed. The more suffering she caused, the more excitement she felt.

Soon she, the pheasant, and the jade pipa completely forgot the Goddess Nüwa's orders not to hurt anyone but the king, and became so filled with their own power that they imposed a horrific reign of terror, torturing people in ways previously unheard of before putting them to death.

Any nobleman or woman who garnered her attention in a bad way or a way that caused her a twinge of jealousy soon found themselves arrested, declared guilty, and then impaled, dropped into pits of snakes, boiled, hacked to pieces, and on and on, as Daji dreamed up numerous new, vicious, repulsive ways to inflict pain before death. Her most horrible invention was called a "paolou" in which a metal pillar, about six feet tall and one foot wide, was heated red hot. The victim's naked body would be tied to it, suffering indescribable pain as he or she slowly cooked to death.

"It is time for the people to call me Queen," Daji announced one morning to the king's counselors.

They glanced at each other, horrified.

"What's wrong with you?" she asked. "Command them!"

None of the ministers wished to speak, but finally, one brave soul did. "But Lady, only the first wife is given the title Queen. She is the mother of the people, as the king is their father. The people love Queen Jiang, and her family is powerful."

Daji's glare caused them all to quake in terror. "I have it on good authority," she announced, "that the Queen plans treason. She is working to have her followers kill Zhou Xin and give the throne to her father, the Duke of the East. She must be imprisoned, and if she does not confess this treason, you will tear out her eyes."

When the counselors presented King Zhou Xin with Daji's horrible lies against the Queen who had remained loyal to him despite his bizarre affliction with his latest concubine, he chose to support Daji, and ordered Queen Jiang's imprisonment.

Queen Jiang, being innocent, refused to confess to any involvement in planning the king's overthrow. She was cruelly tortured, including having both her eyes removed, and was then locked away in a dungeon.

Daji assumed the title of queen. As queen, she imposed ever more harsh and terrible tortures on the people, devising particularly horrible punishments for those counselors who had supported Queen Jiang. She built grandstands for herself and her supporters to watch the torments and death of all who dared oppose her. And when she could find no opposition, she would make something up for the pleasure of watching an innocent person die.

The action against Queen Jiang caused the Duke of the East to go to the stronger, more powerful Grand Duke of the West and ask for help in ridding the land of the pestilence known as the king and queen of the Shang dynasty.

The Grand Duke of the West agreed, and drew up secret plans to lead an army not only to rescue Queen Jiang from prison, but also to overthrow King Zhou Xin.

Daji learned of his plans, however, and before he could amass an army, she sent thousands of warriors to the West to capture both the Grand Duke and his eldest son. When the son was brought to her, she gave an order. "Kill him and mince his body into tiny pieces."

Later, she ordered the Grand Duke to stand before her. "You have committed treason," she said. "For that, the punishment is death. But the death of one so powerful will tear apart this realm. My soldiers have remained at your castle, and await my word to kill everyone within—including your wives, young sons and daughters. But if you agree to reject your past treasonous thoughts, we will let you go. As a sign of our kindness, we offer you a meat pie." She gave him a smile that chilled him to the bone and then clapped her hands. Her servants brought out a pie made with the Grand Duke's son's flesh.

The duke went ashen, and would have fallen to his knees except that Daji's soldiers held him up.

"Eat it!" she ordered, "and the rest of your family will be spared."

The Grand Duke understood what she had done. He could not bear the thought of losing more of his family. He ate as she had ordered.

CHAPTER 26

Los Angeles, California

From Starbucks, Irina led Michael to a bistro located near his hotel. "Our meeting deserves to be toasted with something better than coffee," she said with a smile. After a couple of drinks, they walked back to Michael's hotel.

Michael was stunned at how quiet and empty the streets had become. That he lost track of the hour had to be the effect of Scotch on the rocks after little sleep and even less food since he'd left Italy.

When the elevator doors open, he took Irina's hand and got on. They were alone. "Since you're tired," Irina said archly, jokingly, "I'll ride up to your room with you. I wouldn't want you to fall asleep, and then ride up and down, over and over, until someone decides you're casing the place and has you arrested."

He chuckled. "We couldn't have that, could we?" He drew her closer and kissed her. The scent of her perfume was intoxicating, the feel of her body against his, irresistible.

When the elevator doors opened on his floor, he stumbled slightly. "Whoa, I don't know why I feel so woozy," he said sheepishly. "I can usually hold my liquor."

"It's jet lag. It won't last." She took his key card and opened his hotel door, then gave him a quick kiss on the lips.

He pulled her into his room and let the door swing shut. The next kiss wasn't so quick.

He opened his eyes.

He recognized his hotel room, but noticed sunlight peeked along the edges of the drapery. Something was wrong. He lay naked on the bed, on the sheets.

"You're awake," Irina said. She sat up then turned so she was facing him, her hip nestled against his. She wore nothing and looked beautiful. Her hands rubbed over his chest. He wanted to touch her, hold her, but he lay as if drugged, helpless, unable to move. He felt spent, while she looked more desirable, more vibrant than ever, and her eyes more green. Green … her eyes had never been green.

An overwhelming sense of something terribly, horribly wrong swept over him. She wasn't speaking, but he heard her voice in his head, demanding an answer. Why did she ask about the red pearl? He hadn't told her about it, had he?

They had made love but …

They had grown up together, from the best of friends as children, to lovers as adults. The closeness they had shared was so strong he sometimes felt they were one person. But now, he felt none of that. It was as if he had made love to a stranger.

Why should he expect anything different? Fifteen years had passed, so of course she would seem different now. She was young then, twenty-one. Inexperienced. And now she was a divorcee in her thirties. Naturally she wouldn't seem the same.

"Michael?"

He was about to speak when she placed her finger against his lips.

"No. Don't say it. Don't think about anything but the pearl," she whispered. "Think of the pearl and where you hid it."

Don't do it! And yet, she was so compelling the thought of revealing all his secrets, of completely unburdening himself, was all but irresistible.

She smiled. Snake-like, she coiled herself around him, her head to his chest, her hands everywhere. "Tell me Michael." Her voice purred. "I know you have the pearl. Where is it? Picture it in your mind, picture hiding it. You want to tell me where you've hidden it, don't you? It will be so much pleasanter for you if you just tell me."

She's right, he thought, as her slow seduction continued. *Tell her.*

But even as he thought that, another, more rational side of him, knew it would be wrong.

And knew that she was not Irina.

"Of course I'm Irina." She propped herself up, her hands on the mattress by his shoulders, then leaned forward to kiss him again. "I want to see Florence with you. Once we're there, you would give me the pearl, wouldn't you? Promise. I'm told it's a beautiful pearl. You would give it to me to show how much you love me."

He felt as if he was being torn in two—his body crying out to tell her, to take and enjoy all she offered, while his mind shouted that something was wrong, that *she* was wrong.

He tried to shove her away, to sit up, but he had no strength.

"You can't ignore me." Irina sat up and placed her palm flat against his chest. "Not after the way you treated me. You owe me!"

"What—"

"You thought I left you for no reason. I had plenty of reasons."

Was she bringing up the way they had parted years ago? He shook his head, not wanting to remember the way she had walked out.

"When we were young, when we were lovers"—her mouth wrinkled into a sneer—"I thought the sun rose and set on you, but then I found out the truth."

"What are you saying?" he asked. *No, don't ask her!* He remembered Magda's warning, "Demons lie."

"I found out that you're no good—that you just used me."

He said nothing.

"You're cruel. Thoughtless. What woman would want to stay with you?" Her features twisted into a rictus of disgust. "Who could love someone as pathetic and worthless as you? No one. You're scum. A fucking prick."

He felt unable to breathe. "You're not her."

"You'll do what I want because you're nothing." Her voice became low, guttural, and echoed deep inside him. "Of course I left you. What woman wouldn't? Who could ever love or care about you? Your own mother killed herself because she was sickened by the thought of you."

"Stop it!"

"Your own father hates you. He knows how filthy—"

"Damn you to hell!" He tried even harder to push her aside, but her hand on his chest held him down with unbelievable strength. It seemed to press hard against his heart, his lungs, stopping them from expanding, from breathing. His head felt light.

"Give me the pearl and I'll forgive you. I'll take you back. We'll be together again, the way it used to be between us."

He remembered the warning of Father Berosus: not to listen, not to *think* because they could read your thoughts. He needed to concentrate on something else. A solution came to him, a wonderfully ironic solution. He shut his eyes, sure this was the best way to fight her—it.

Pater noster, qui es in caelis ...

"I'm Irina," she said gently, her voice again sounding exactly like the woman he loved. "You love me. You always have."

... santificetur Nomen Tuum ...

"Bastard!" she cried, pulling herself up, away from his body.

And instead of Irina looming over him, he saw a black fox.

CHAPTER 27

Washington D. C.

Senator Kevin Wilson walked to the parking garage with his cell phone firmly planted against his ear. He had taken a flight that morning back to Washington D. C., but because of losing three hours traveling there from California, he was late to his own meeting, meaning he had rushed to the meeting straight from the airport, not bothering with drivers or special parking privileges. Sometimes a person just had to handle things like the common people.

Then, because of the late start, his meeting ran long.

He was exhausted. The hour was late, and the garage was all but empty. His cell phone dropped the call as he rode in the elevator.

Wilson stepped off the elevator on the seventh floor and tried his phone again. Still no service. Well, he'd reach the would-be donor eventually, and everything would be set up, fairly and honestly—for Washington. Wilson chuckled at that. He hadn't been around such a gang of thieves since his last visit to San Quentin.

At least in Washington, everyone knew how to skirt just enough on the right side of the law to claim privilege, and they never—well, rarely ever—skirted over it. And he was one of the best. Not only had he survived every administration since Bill Clinton's first term, but he could work with both sides of the aisle, and he did—which meant he never let politics or party get in the way of a lucrative deal, and neither did the politicians he dealt with. Any deal could be spun in any direction if one was clever enough, and Kevin Wilson was nothing if not clever. The youthful boyishness he'd somehow been blessed with was an asset to his work. Newcomers to Washington didn't exactly take him for a kid, but few realized he'd been there long enough to know where *all* the bodies were buried—not only ten years ago, but thirty.

Clinton used to ask him his secret to staying young. He was forty when Clinton first took office, but the President swore he looked like a kid of about twenty-five. He didn't think much about it, but as years went by, he noticed that he seemed to age about one year for every two of his life.

This being Washington, foes were beginning to whisper about the "picture in his closet" *à la* Dorian Gray. He chuckled. If the fools wanted to chalk up his success to something demonic, that only gave him that much more power over them. And in government and politics, power was money.

He needed to get back on the phone and continue his conversation. He tried calling again. At times, pockets of service exist in the strangest places.

He had just hit the "call" button on his phone when he noticed a pair of red high-heeled shoes on the pavement before him.

His gaze drifted from the shoes, to thin ankles and shapely legs that rose to a pencil thin black dress—a novelty in these days of pants suits. The woman was young and beautiful. Her eyes had a slightly Oriental tilt which was especially intriguing because the color of her eyes was green. Emerald green, in fact, bright and sparkling as the gemstone. Her platinum blonde hair was straight, chin length with bangs, making her eyes even more prominent above a small nose and cherry-red lips.

He neared. She didn't move, but stood staring at him. There was something definitely familiar about her, but how in the world could he have forgotten anyone so stunning? No way. His mind rushed, trying to remember who she was.

Wilson flashed a megawatt smile at the woman, even as his wariness increased. A man in his position always had to be wary for set-ups, such as people wanting to get photos of him in compromising positions with hookers. But if she was a hooker, she was the classiest one he'd ever encountered. In fact, if this was a set-up, bring it on. "Hello," he said.

"Don't you remember me?" she asked.

Uh, oh. "Remember you? Should I?"

"Yes, definitely."

Something niggled at the back of his mind. Something dark. Something he'd worked hard to forget. "I'm sorry, I—" He tried to walk around her. His Mercedes was just behind her.

"I'm sorry, too," she replied. With a movement so fast he scarcely saw it happen, she ran her hand near his neck. He felt a sting, a trickle of blood.

"What are you—"

"Get up there," she commanded, pointing at the heavy railing circling the perimeter of the garage's seventh floor.

As he hesitated, she reached out her hand again. It seemed to stretch towards him. He felt too petrified to turn and his legs too heavy to do anything to defend himself. In terror, as if he had no control over his own body, he began to climb the railing.

When he looked down, he saw a construction zone. An extension to the lower floors was being erected and rows of rebar jutted up out of a cement slab. He stood up on the railing by holding tight to the post beside him. "What is this about?" he asked. "Please, tell me. Is it about money? I'll pay you. Anything. Whatever is wrong, you've got to tell me. I can't fix it unless you talk to me."

"You make me laugh."

He glanced down once more, and then behind him. He saw no way out. And then he was surrounded by the desert, saw the Great Pyramid in the distance. In horror, he stared at her. "It can't be."

She laughed at him. "So, you do remember."

Tears sprang to his eyes. "Work with me!" he cried. "We can make a deal—one that works for both of us. I've got a lead on the pearl. I'm sure you want it. I can get it for you—for us!"

"Do you really think I want to share?"

"No, please!" He began to sob, and through his tears, he saw a black fox lunge at him. With a scream, he felt himself knocked from the railing. Six floors down, the rebar impaled him. With his dying breath he looked up at the fox. "Daji," he whispered.

CHAPTER 28

Los Angeles, California

A fox, but not a fox, with black fur, claws, and a long snout stood over Michael. It curled back its lips and snarled, baring its teeth, its green eyes fixated on him. A distant pounding filled his ears. He ignored it and wrapped his hands around the fox's neck, trying, but failing, to find the strength to shove it away. The pounding continued. He fought the fox, its strength incredible.

"Michael!"

The fox vanished, and he froze. *Where did it go?*

Slowly, consciousness made him realize his eyes were shut. He forced them open, looking wildly all around. The fox was gone. Irina was gone.

Jianjun's form came into focus, pulling a blanket over him, a worried look on his face.

Behind him stood a red-haired woman … a familiar woman …

Kira Holt.

"What happened, Michael?" Jianjun lay a cool hand on his forehead. "Do you feel sick?"

He felt nauseous; his stomach flip-flopped. Abruptly, he sat up. "What are you doing here? What's going on?"

Jianjun lifted the pillows from the floor and placed them against the headboard. "That's what you need to explain to us. You were delirious, tossing and turning as if fighting with some—*thing*. Only because Kira, I mean, Doctor Holt, has FBI credentials were we able to get rid of hotel security who wanted to call the paramedics."

Michael eased himself back onto the pillows, his breathing fast, his mouth dry, as he tried to put together all that Jianjun was saying, and to ignore the fierce scowl Kira Holt threw his way. "How did you get here so quickly?" he asked.

"Quickly? It's nearly six o'clock."

"Morning or night?"

"Night. I haven't spoken with you since you landed in L.A. yesterday morning."

He stared in disbelief.

"You didn't answer Kira's calls or mine," Jianjun explained. "I had to come and find out why."

When Michael made no response, Jianjun added, "Also, there's been another death. Scott Jones, owner of the *Los Angeles Post.* They're calling it an accident, but we know that's not true."

"Another death?" Michael looked from one to the other. "And you really weren't able to reach me for over twenty-four hours?"

Jianjun looked worried. "That's right. What happened? Where were you?"

"I don't know." Memories washed over him of the coffee shop, of his happiness when he thought he had found Irina again. He couldn't remember the last time he had felt such joy. But it was all a lie. A demonic lie.

That sickened him worst of all.

But if she was a demon, why didn't she kill him the way the men in the photo had been killed? But then he thought about her words. She hadn't simply asked where the pearl was located, she wanted him to *give* it to her. That had to be significant.

Kira spoke softly to Jianjun. "I'll order some broth and light food for him from room service. He needs to eat and drink something."

Michael shut his eyes. He couldn't remember what he and Irina had talked about, only that it felt as if all the time between them—the fifteen years that had passed since he last saw her—had vanished. But at the same time, something was slightly out of kilter, and then he began to suspect.

His mind went to the accusations the demon had flung at him ... that he was vile, unlovable ...

Ironically, those words, those accusations, mirrored everything he had said to himself after Irina left him. Accusations he believed to this day were all too true. *Don't look at the pearl or it will look back at you,* Berosus had said, *and it will read your mind.*

He must have blacked out again, because he woke up in the shower, standing under a jet of hot water, soap suds sliding down his chest.

He suspected Jianjun and Kira waited in the bedroom for him, and wanted some sort of explanation of what had happened, of how he had spent the time when he was out of reach. How could he explain? Should he tell them how he and "Irina" had made wild, passionate love, and then she turned into a demonic fox? Yeah, he could see that going over real well.

He wished he'd simply been drugged, that meeting Irina had been a drug-induced illusion. But more than truth serum had happened. Something had read his deepest thoughts, had looked into his soul and found one woman branded there.

A knock sounded. "You okay, boss?" Jianjun's worry was evident.

"Yes. Be right there." He shut off the shower, dried off, and put on clean clothes. Back in the bedroom, he saw that room service had already made its delivery. He guessed it paid to have the FBI call in an order. He went over to the table where the food tray had been placed. A straight-back chair was in front of it. Kira sat in an easy chair, and Jianjun on a corner of the bed.

Michael's stomach churned at the thought of eating, but he needed to. First, he downed a bottle of water. Kira had been right about him being dehydrated. Then, a cup of coffee helped clear his head. The food was mercifully light—scrambled eggs, toast, chicken broth.

Kira explained how she tracked down Jianjun. She thought Jianjun would lead her to whoever was murdering the men in the photo, but instead, he led her back to Michael. "I tried to warn the four men in the photo who are still alive," she said. "But so far, not even FBI resources can find Hank Bennett or Stu Eliot. I spoke with Senator Wilson in person, and after five tries Jonathan Vogel returned my call. Neither of them believe they're in danger. But what worries me is that both Wilson and Vogel took what I said very calmly. The normal reaction would be to call anyone with such a tale crazy. But they didn't. They should have had a lot of questions for me. But neither did."

"Did they do anything at all?" Michael asked.

Her expression turned rueful. "Other than Senator Kevin Wilson calling my boss at the FBI and warning him that if anyone from the FBI bothered him again, he'd have his job, and as a result, my boss telling me I no longer had a consulting job with them since I had 'impersonated' a federal official, no, nothing at all."

He reached for the carafe and poured himself more coffee. His head still felt fuzzy. "I'm not sure what's going on here," he said. "But one thing I am sure of is that I have no information for you, Doctor Holt. I'm as much in the dark as you are."

She glanced at Jianjun, then back to Michael. "Someone murdered my father. Do you really expect me to walk away from this?"

Kira's unnerving blue eyes caught and held Michael's gaze. "On the long flight here from Vancouver, Jianjun told me a bit about some of the strange adventures the two of you have experienced. I'll admit that at times I didn't want to believe him. I used my education to explain the mass psychosis that must have affected you and others. It frankly bothers me that he seems surprisingly sane."

Michael nearly choked on his coffee.

"What I'm trying to say is, I'm ready to listen."

"You refused last time I tried," he reminded her.

"Well, I'm ready to hear it now. Including"—she pursed her lips—"the stuff about Marco Effing Polo."

With that, she folded her hands on her lap and waited. She looked ready to sit like that forever if need be. Jianjun looked uncomfortably from Kira to Michael.

She was good, Michael thought. She knew exactly what to say to wear away his concerns. The few psychologists he met in the past had seemed crazier than their patients and all he wanted to do was get away from them. She was different. Something told him that no matter how much he objected, in the end, he would give in.

He decided to tell them about everything he knew … everything except Irina.

"It all happened almost a week ago," he said. "Very late at night, a stranger came to my door…"

A couple of hours later, Jianjun lay fast asleep, stretched out on the easy chair and ottoman. Michael pulled a spare blanket from a closet and covered him. Michael wasn't in the least sleepy, and Kira seemed too keyed up to sleep, so they stepped out onto the narrow balcony overlooking Westwood.

Confusion and misery over all that had happened were etched on Kira's face. He remembered the grief and loneliness that blanketed his days after his mother's death, and he saw the similar distress and unwarranted guilt in Kira's eyes.

She stared out over the city, hands against the railing. "I'd like to believe your story about the red pearl, but I find it impossible."

"Nobody says you have to. You can always go back to the FBI and look for a serial killer."

"I can also bang my head against a wall."

"True," he admitted. "I can't help but think … for seven sailors to share an experience and then all become tops in their fields is so bizarre, I wonder if that's what kept your father from mentioning the names of men he served with. I also wonder if all of them didn't have a good idea of exactly what was going on."

"A secret he carried for forty years? I don't know." She thought a moment, then shook her head and dropped her gaze. "Something was always a bit odd."

He took in the lights and traffic of the city, then said, "Some things aren't understandable, no matter how much science and education you bring to them. They just happen."

"That's supposed to be comforting?"

He felt bad; he was speaking in platitudes, and they did no one any good. Especially not a psychologist. But what could he say when he saw sadness and deaths all around them? He had talked to a ghost and then screwed a demon. Great! Which way to the nearest funny farm? The worst part was that he believed it was all real. The red pearl was drawing him more forcefully into its web. He had a strong desire, even now, to hold it, to see what he could do with it. It was a philosopher's stone, and he had studied quite a bit about alchemy since learning of the many alchemists in his family. The desire to hold it, use it, was almost a physical ache.

He was glad he had left it in Florence. He tried to shake the feeling, but knew it would come back, always stronger, the more he thought about the pearl, and the closer the demons who wanted it got to him.

He had to fight them—and fight the pearl's allure.

"I'm going to do what the old priest asked," he said to Kira. "Go to the Old Silk Road and look for the monastery from Marco Polo's time."

"Whoa! Wait a minute." She looked at him as if he had gone over the edge. "The murders are happening here. You can't believe bringing the pearl back to the monastery will stop them or help us find the killers."

"Why not?"

"People aren't dying because a pearl was stolen seven hundred years ago."

"Then explain what happened to your father and those other men? And since we're looking into it, how safe are we?"

She opened her mouth as if to object.

"I believe the old priest's story," he said.

"I can't quite make that leap."

"No one's asking you to. Stay here. Maybe you, or the FBI, will find an explanation you can accept."

She stared hard at him. "Damn! Why does talking to you make me feel that an 'acceptable' explanation won't be the truth?"

He grinned. "Why don't you get some sleep? Use the bed. I'm not tired at all. Maybe tomorrow everything will be much clearer."

—He's stronger than we imagined.

—We'll wear him down.

—We are the stuff from which dreams are made.

—And nightmares.

CHAPTER 29

ALTHOUGH MICHAEL KNEW he had not been with Irina, he couldn't get her out of his head. And he couldn't take off for the other side of the world without trying to find her.

The next morning, he asked Jianjun to search for Irina Petrescu, or possibly some Anglicized version of the Romanian name, such as Irene Peters. She would be in her mid-thirties. Her mother's name was Magda Petrescu. The two formerly lived in the vicinity of Cape Cod, Massachusetts.

Jianjun searched everywhere for Irina, including death records, but came up blank. She seemed to have disappeared off the grid. He did, however, find a Magda Petrescu, age sixty, living in the town of Apex, North Carolina.

"I'm going there. I want to see her before I return to Italy," Michael said. He didn't say why, but knowing Jianjun he didn't need to.

"I'm coming, too," Jianjun announced.

"So am I," Kira said, then folded her arms. "And from there, I'm going with you to Italy and Central Asia."

"Central Asia?" Jianjun asked.

Michael nodded.

"Hell, yes!" Jianjun said, then smiled.

"In that case, I think the two of you should go straight to Florence." Michael felt his side trip was a bit of a fool's errand. No sense "sharing" it. "Stay at my place. I'll meet you there."

"No way, boss," Jianjun insisted. "I don't know what happened to you while you were here alone, but someone—or something—put you in some kind of trance. If that happens again, I'm going to be with you. Anyway, North Carolina sounds dangerous."

"If you ask me," Kira added before Michael had a chance to object. "Someone needs to protect both of you."

"Hold it," Hank Bennett said as his cell phone sounded an alert.

He and Stuart Eliot had just parked in a lot across from the Ritz Carlton in Los Angeles. They had chartered a private plane and used fake identities to travel from Missoula, Montana—the largest airport near them—and then rented a car at the Burbank airport where they landed. They planned to meet Michael Rempart and were prepared to do whatever it took to get the pearl from him.

Hank read the alert. "What the fuck is this? The bastard is at LAX. He just bought airline tickets to North Carolina." Hank glowered at his phone.

"You think that means he didn't come here to sell the pearl?" Stuart asked.

"He couldn't possibly have sold it already. If he did, we'd know. God damn. I wonder if he has any idea of what's in his hands."

"What should we do now?" Stuart's voice was small.

Hank thought a moment, then reached the only possible conclusion. "We follow."

Michael, Jianjun, and Kira traveled to the address Jianjun had found, a small, tidy house on a quiet country lane.

Michael got out of the rental car slowly. He licked his lips and stuffed his hands in the pockets of his slacks.

"You okay?" Jianjun mouthed.

Michael nodded, then began the walk up the driveway as if he were headed to a guillotine. He hadn't seen Magda for fifteen years and had no idea if she'd greet him or slam the door in his face. He would have turned around except that Jianjun would give him no peace until he explained why.

He half hoped no one was home. He rang the bell.

Magda Petrescu opened the door. Michael stiffened. He recognized her immediately. She had been a round-faced, attractive, salt-of-the-earth woman when she first came to live at Wintersgate, and now she was plump, and her short black hair peppered with gray.

His heart was in his throat. "Hello, Magda."

She put her hands over her mouth even as her face curled into a huge smile. Her blue eyes filled with tears. "Michael! Oh, my dear boy!" She threw her arms around him. She didn't even reach his shoulders. He returned her embrace, holding her a long time. He could scarcely breathe for the emotions that washed over him.

She stepped back, then reached up and brushed a lock of hair off his forehead as she had so many times when he was young.

"I never thought I'd see you again," she said, her eyes sparkling with unshed tears. "You're even more handsome than all those magazine pictures I have of you. Come inside, all of you."

Michael took her work-worn hand and held it in both of his as he introduced his friends. Magda led them to the kitchen where she immediately began pulling cheeses and sausages out of the refrigerator. She spread them on the table as one might for a holiday get together. Some things she heated, some were best cold. They made small talk as she put the food out, about Michael's life in Florence, and hers in North Carolina. She had her health and lived among nice people. It was enough to make her content.

When they sat down to eat, Magda kept rubbing Michael's shoulder and patting his arm, as if she could scarcely believe he was real. He reveled in her simple touch, he, who most people considered cold and unfeeling, had turned into a grinning kid around this woman.

"You are too headstrong, Michael," she said at one point, waggling her finger at him as she used to do when he got into trouble. "You must listen to Jianjun. He sounds like someone much more careful!"

Michael was taken aback, but saw the nods that passed between Magda and Jianjun. "No comment," he said with a laugh.

"It's called 'caution,' and you could use some." Magda took on the familiar tone she had used years ago with him. He realized he had been more to her than simply her employer's son. He had been so wrapped up with Irina, he had paid little attention to how Magda felt. But now he did, and was warmed by it. He kissed her cheek, which caused her to beam with joy.

Once finished, and with the table cleared, Magda brewed cups of dark, Romanian *cafea lunga* for everyone. Michael hadn't yet asked her about Irina. He was dying to know what she had done with her life, but was also scared of what he might find out. He didn't know if he'd feel better to hear she was happily married with children or a drifter, much like he was. But, God, that was selfish. It almost made him ashamed. Almost.

"How is Irina?" he asked, when he couldn't take not knowing any longer.

He wrapped long, thin fingers tightly around the warm coffee mug as the words hung in the air. He hoped no one else had detected the quaver in his voice.

"It's strange," Magda said, "but you aren't the first one this week to ask me that. A woman came here two days ago looking for her."

"Why?"

"She never said, just asked where to find her."

His pulse quickened. Two days ago he'd met the demonic Irina. "What was the woman's name?"

Magda shrugged. "She never said it."

"What did she look like?"

Magda wrinkled her mouth. "She was beautiful, but she only *looked* it. She had no warmth, no soul. I felt like I was standing in a pool of ice just talking to her, and when she left, I said many prayers for protection. She had long hair, dark brown, and it was straight like a board, reaching almost to her *cur*—you remember that word, Michael?" she asked with a grin. "But her eyes, they were green like an emerald, and she gave me such a hard, cold look I thought, my God, if she could strike me dead with those eyes, she would do it."

"Did you tell her how to find Irina?" Michael held his breath, awaiting the answer.

"No, never. I told her I had not seen Irina for many years, and that I have no idea where she is now."

"Is it true?" Michael asked. "That you don't know where Irina is?"

Magda took his hand and regarded him with compassion. "I can reach her. If she is in danger—and I think she is because of the way you are looking at me—I'll warn her." She let him go. "But only if you tell me why. What has happened?"

Michael's voice dropped to little more than a whisper as he asked, "How is she?"

Magda's lips tightened, but then she lifted her hands and flopped them back down, as if to say, who knows? "She lives in Paris, so how bad can it be?"

"I always assumed she'd married, had children. Was I right?" he asked.

Magda shook her head. "She never married. Not that she wasn't asked, several times. Over the years, she has lived with two different men that I know of. Nice men, I think. One French, one English. I hoped one of them would work out, that she would marry and find happiness. I haven't talked to her for three or four months, so for all I know, she found somebody new. We do this e-mail stuff, but I don't like it. She even bought me a computer to use. With these fat fingers? But half the questions I ask her, she doesn't answer anyway."

"Is she working?"

"Oh, yes. In an art gallery."

He gave a small smile. "I should have known.

Magda joined him in their private joke. "Yes, you should."

"Does she have children?"

Magda dropped her gaze. “No, no children.” She drew in her breath. “Now, stop stalling. I’m worried. I e-mailed her when that strange woman showed up. She told me to ignore it. Is my daughter in danger?”

“I don’t know.”

“Michael, I know you too well for you to hide things. Why are you worried about her?”

He glanced at Jianjun and Kira. “Some dangerous people have been looking closely at my life, and making threats. If they find Irina, I don’t know what they might do.”

Magda nodded. “I see.”

“Maybe I should go to her, warn her,” he said.

Magda’s expressive face turned sad and troubled. Then, she shook her head.

Michael felt empty. Being here with Magda, hearing about Irina, brought home to him all he had lost in his life. And that there was nothing he could do about it. “You’re right. It’s probably better if you don’t tell me how to find her. But warn her.” He could scarcely get the words out. “Do that for me, please.”

She patted his arm. “Of course. But, tell me, does your father know you are looking for Irina?”

Her question surprised him. “No. Why?”

She shook her head. “It’s nothing; I shouldn’t have asked.”

“Magda, tell me. What’s this about?”

Magda shut her eyes and stayed that way a long time as if she didn’t dare look at him. “I’ll let Irina know you were here, and that you’re worried about her.” Her words were flat, and he knew she would say nothing more to him about her daughter.

Soon, it was time to leave to make the flight to Italy. Michael hugged Magda goodbye, and she kissed his cheek. When he stepped back, the tears in her eyes matched his own.

CHAPTER 30

Florence, Italy

Michael, Jianjun, and Kira reached Florence the next afternoon.

They walked down the narrow cobblestone street to Michael's apartment and had just turned onto the courtyard when out of the darkness appeared a black fox. A demon, Michael thought, like the one that had attacked him in Los Angeles. The same that had been watching him here in Florence ever since the priest had given him the pearl.

"Stay back," he told Jianjun and Kira. The fox stood still and fixed its emerald eyes on Kira. The three backed to one side of the courtyard, inching towards Michael's door.

"Get!" Michael shouted, but the fox stood its ground.

Michael and Jianjun attempted to scare it off with a short sprint towards it, but the fox darted around them and lunged at Kira. She flung her arm out. The fox hit it, snapping at her, the force of its impact nearly toppling her, and then it fled to the street.

Jianjun ran to Kira. "Are you all right?"

"I think so." She pulled back the sleeves of her leather jacket and sweater, then unbuttoned the cuff of her shirt and folded it back. All were relieved to see that the fox's teeth hadn't broken the skin.

"Do you think it's rabid?" Jianjun asked Michael.

No, I think it's a demon. He decided he had better not say that. "I understand rabies is all but eradicated here. Would you like to go to a hospital, Kira?"

"Not necessary," she said. "Although the way it came at me was weird. But a fox, a black fox. It's like a dream I've had …"

"A dream?" Jianjun asked.

Her eyes were wide and scared, but then she tightened her lips. "Nothing. It's nothing."

They walked through the courtyard to Michael's door where he discovered his old apartment key still worked. So much for getting the lock changed quickly.

It had been a long, exhausting day. Michael gave Kira his bedroom so she could sleep well. She had been very quiet since the fox attack and readily hurried off to bed. Jianjun used the sofa, and Michael got a rollaway bed from his landlady.

Michael gave Jianjun a bottle of beer, and took one for himself as they sat in the living room, Michael at one end of the sofa, Jianjun on the other. One soft lamplight lit the room.

"How about you tell me what's going on, Michael," Jianjun said after a while. "This is kind of weird, even for you."

"It's freaky." Michael agreed, popping the cap off his beer. "I'm pretty sure that I encountered a demon in Los Angeles, a demon that looked like someone I was once very close to."

"Irina Petrescu?" Jianjun asked. "I heard the change in your voice when you talked about her. You were in love with her, weren't you?"

"Why do I try to keep anything from you?" Michael drank some beer.

Jianjun knocked back more beer, then shook his head. "Man, I've been around you too long. Just think, I let a comment about demons slide so I could ask you about an old girlfriend. But maybe this old girlfriend is bothering you the point of seeing demons?"

"You think I'm creating all this in my mind?"

Jianjun shrugged. "I don't know, because you won't tell me."

Michael slowly rotated the beer bottle. "Maybe because it sounds too much like a soap opera, even to me. And I lived it."

"Now, I want to hear it even more."

He let himself remember. "She was always tagging after me when we were little. She used to make me promise to wait for her to grow up. I knew what she meant. She was always a romantic, even as a kid."

Jianjun nodded and waited.

"Well, one summer, I went home, and discovered that she had grown up. But I was twenty-one and she was only sixteen—still a little girl, while I was a college man of the world—or so I thought. The summer she turned eighteen, I couldn't dismiss her any longer. But she knew nothing of the world, or of life. I wanted her to be sure what she felt for me was mature, you know. Not hero worship for her rich employer's son. There are too many sappy romances where that's the theme, and it seemed Irina had read every one of them."

"What did you do?"

"I planned to propose on her twenty-first birthday. But it never happened. When I was in my last year of graduate school, it all came to an end."

"Why?"

Michael took a long swallow of beer. "It's not important."

"I think it is."

Michael ran his hands over his face. He had never told anyone what had happened, never spoke of the time his world turned upside down. "My father showed me a check that had been cashed. It was made out to Irina for a small fortune. Two-million dollars. That was chump change to my old man. That's what happens when you grow up in a family of alchemists." He took another gulp of beer. "I recognized her signature, her endorsement, on the back of the check. He had paid her to never see me again, and she took the money and ran—her and Magda both. But I never blamed Magda. Only Irina. I found out the value of love that summer—the cash value of love."

Jianjun frowned. "You believed your father? The man that, all these years, I've never heard you talk about except to let me know he was alive. Why would you believe him that she left for money?"

Michael finished the beer. "Irina knew how to get hold of me. We e-mailed, talked on the phone. She knew I had money of my own—not as much as my father, but more than adequate. She could have contacted me, told me what was going on, done anything. She knew how I felt about her. Instead of doing any of that, she took the money and signed the agreement, and then she and Magda vanished. I tried to find her, but couldn't."

"Something's missing; something you don't know," Jianjun insisted.

If only. He grimaced. "I thought that for a while. I searched, tried to find something that could explain Irina's deception, but there was nothing." He wondered if he should tell Jianjun the rest, and then did. "My father told me the experience with Irina was proof that, like all Rempart men, my life would be different, that *we* were different. He said being with a Rempart would break her, as it had my mother. He thought it best if I learned the lesson early, and in that way I could be spared the pain he faced in his life."

"Is that why you never talk about him, never go to visit him?" Jianjun asked.

"I haven't been back to Wintersgate since that summer."

"He was wrong," Jianjun said. "Doing what he did to you was cruel. You aren't like him; you don't have a cruel bone in your body."

"Sometimes, I know I do. But anyway, that's the story," Michael said dismissively.

He wondered if it even mattered anymore. Until all this had gotten stirred back up again, he had thought he'd put it all aside, both in his life and in his mind. He hadn't thought about Irina in years, making him wonder, why now?

"It's long over," he said. "The only reason it's in my head is that the demon looked like Irina. For a short while, I told myself it was her, but when I stopped lying about it, it turned into a black fox."

"Like the one in the courtyard?" Jianjun asked.

"Exactly."

Jianjun took a deep breath. "Demons are something I grew up

hearing about in old Chinese tales. They love to kill and maim, but they aren't real. They're like 'boogeymen' in the West. Just a myth."

Michael never tried to convince Jianjun of anything. He always hoped Jianjun-the-practical was right, and Michael-the-intuitive wasn't. So far, he was, unfortunately, batting a thousand. "Enough about demons and foxes and me. I noticed the way you look at Kira."

Jianjun's head snapped towards him. "Am I that obvious?"

Michael grinned.

Jianjun's mouth wrinkled. "She's smart and beautiful," he said. "But I know that even if I were single, someone like her would never be interested in someone like me."

"Why not? There's nothing wrong with you."

"Nothing a few more pounds of muscles, several inches of height, hair that behaves, and a handsome face wouldn't cure."

Michael shook his head. "You're too hard on yourself. You look fine. Do you want to talk about it?"

"What can I say? I'm married. End of story."

"Right. You don't want that kind of complexity in your life."

Jianjun caught his eye, then smiled. "Like hell, I don't."

The next morning, Jianjun and Kira left the apartment to buy supplies and warm clothes for their trip to Central Asia. The first stop Jianjun made, however, was at a store that sold switchblades. He wanted to be prepared in case any more aggressive foxes showed up to attack Kira.

At the same time, Michael went to visit a woman named Renata Corbi at her home just outside of Florence along the Arno River. She was a small woman, in her mid-forties, with short, curly brown hair, and narrow black-frame glasses over dark brown eyes.

Michael had met her a few months earlier, and she gave the clear impression she would welcome more contact. She was an ethnographer, a cultural anthropologist who relied on up-close, personal experiences. Her primary area of study was the population from the eastern edge of the Pamir Mountains in what is now Uzbekistan, to the Taklamakan Desert in the western Chinese province of Xinjiang—a region that caused her to learn quite a bit about Marco Polo's travels. After preliminary pleasantries and discussions, Michael asked if she knew any Nestorian monasteries along the Old Silk Road. He explained that a priest, now dead, claimed to have a pearl that Marco Polo stole from such a place.

"Marco, his father and uncle brought many jewels with them when they returned home from China," Renata said. "In fact, one of the stories Marco told was that they sewed the most valuable jewels into the lining of their coats."

"This gem is red, and most likely not a pearl at all. I suspect it's a philosopher's stone—assuming there are such things as philosopher's stones, that is," Michael quickly added.

"Well, we know there are no such things," Renata said, her dark eyes curious as she studied him. "I've never heard of a red pearl stolen by Marco Polo, but there is a famous Chinese tale about one."

"Oh? What story is that?"

"The Chinese call it *Fengshen Yanyi,* usually translated as *Investiture of the Gods,* or *Creation of the Gods* which isn't as accurate but used since many people don't know what 'investiture' means. Have you ever heard of it?"

"I've heard the name," Michael said. "But I don't know the story."

"It was written down during the Ming dynasty, in the 1500s, but it is much, much older than that, perhaps from the Shang dynasty, and tells stories about gods, demons, and kings, with a lot of sex thrown in. It's very famous in China, but not in the West, and is a horrible story filled with the most awful torture and mutilations."

"As would be typical of a story about demons," Michael said with a grimace, remembering his eerie encounter.

"Well, anyway, it's not important," Renata said, opening a map of Uzbekistan, Tajikistan, and Kyrgyzstan. "Let me tell you about the Nestorian monasteries along the Old Silk Road. We have records of where some once were, but not a single one remains."

When Michael left Renata's home, he once again felt he was being watched. He steeled himself for another demonic attack. The only thing keeping him alive, he suspected, was not revealing the pearl's location. He also remembered that the demon kept asking him to give it the pearl.

To get the pearl to the Nestorian monastery, he needed to disguise it to keep it safe from demons and also from thieves who swarmed out-of-the-way parts of Central Asia. He expected any surviving Nestorian monastery would be far from civilization. As he rode back to his apartment, a way to do it struck. Father Berosus had warned him, and he learned for himself, that demons were quite good at getting into his head. He needed to be sure not to think about the hiding place he would use to carry the pearl to Central Asia.

But trying not to think about something was the surest way to think about it. He concentrated on his purchases, not thinking of why he was buying them, and then headed for his safe deposit box.

Since the demon posing as Irina had become infuriated over his simple "Our Father" in Latin, he decided to use a longer prayer he had once memorized, one that would require even more concentration on his part. *Gloria in excelsius Deo* should cause any demon to flee in terror.

As with *Pater noster,* he had learned the prayer years ago, not because he was Catholic—he wasn't—but because Latin, classical Greek, and Syriac were important in his archeological work. As a student he would go to a Tridentine Latin mass or to older liturgies in a Greek Orthodox or Eastern Rite church to hear a spoken version of a language he was studying.

He had been raised without God and had turned his back on religion except for his language interests. But then, other-worldly things happened in his life, things that caused him to question all that was around him. Now, since coming to Florence, he found himself spending a fair amount of time in churches. He wasn't sure what that was all about, but he particularly enjoyed attending the Tridentine mass with its candles, incense, and bells. Many of the Latin prayers and songs he had learned as a student came back to him.

Now, alone in a bank cubicle, he opened the bronze and lifted out the pearl, softly murmuring the *Gloria*. He worked to concentrate hard on the Latin words, but the allure of the pearl, the power it would give him, rushed through him. He could practically feel a long line of ancestors whispering to him to keep the pearl for himself. To use it himself. He fought their call, concentrating ever harder on the prayer ...

If only I used the pearl as it was meant to be used ...

"Laudámus te,"

I might find Irina, I might get her back ...

"Benedícimus te,"

I would have more power than imaginable in the modern world ...

"Adorámus te,"

The power of the alchemist.

"Glorificámus te ..."

He concentrated hard on the rest of the prayer as he wrapped the pearl into a soft cloth, returned the bronze to the safe deposit box, and went home. Fortunately, Jianjun and Kira were still out, giving him time to hide the pearl so it could safely travel with him to Central Asia.

But simply knowing it was near gave him a strange, overpowering joy.

CHAPTER 31

"SINCE I'M HERE," Kira said later that evening in Michael's apartment, "I'd like to see the red pearl. I'm sure Jianjun would as well."

"Actually," Jianjun said. "You're wrong. I don't want to have anything to do with it."

Kira's words not only surprised Michael, but ratcheted up his suspicions about her. Why, he wondered, had the fox singled her out for the attack? Did it have something to do with her father, since a demon—he suspected—was the cause of his death? Were they now after Kira as well, or was she somehow connected to them because she carried her father's genes? Was the attraction she held over Jianjun natural or demonic? "Until we find out more about the pearl and what it does, that's not a good idea."

"Is it in the apartment?" she asked.

"Let's just say it's safely hidden."

"Where? Shouldn't Jianjun and I also know? Don't we need a back-up plan, just in case?"

His eyes narrowed. "I don't think that's wise."

"But I—"

"How about I make some coffee?" Jianjun jumped to his feet. "Who'd like some? Michael? Kira?"

Both nodded.

Kira glared at Jianjun and Michael both. "So much for the pearl. All right, if you don't trust me. Can we discuss our trip or is that also on a need-to-know?"

Jianjun looked ready to crawl into the coffee press.

"We'll talk about whatever you'd like," Michael said.

She looked from one to the other. "Let's start with the Old Silk Road? What do we expect there?"

"Frankly," he began, "I was disappointed in it after the way I'd romanticized it. In Central Asia, it was more of a network than a single road, and most of it has vanished. In China, government agents make it difficult to correctly follow Marco Polo's footsteps, although they do have routes they've set up to make money from Western tourists. Then, Shang-du, poetically known as Xanadu, has all but vanished in what's now Inner Mongolia. It's been leveled to almost nothing."

"That's terrible," Kira said. *"In Xanadu did Kubla Khan a stately pleasure dome decree...* And that's as much as I know."

"Where Alph, the sacred river, ran through caverns measureless to man down to a sunless sea." Michael concluded Coleridge's opening lines.

Kira nodded. "Very nice. What a pity Xanadu is no more."

"I agree," Michael said, remembering one of the disappointments of his early archeological studies. "We have very little remaining from that period. Even the burial sites of Genghis and Kublai Khan are lost. After the thousands, if not millions of people Genghis Khan killed, his family feared his grave would be desecrated, so they kept it a secret. The slaves who helped build his tomb were all killed to assure its location remained secret. Kublai Khan supposedly was buried near his grandfather. Over time, people no longer know where the graves are."

"Amazing."

"It's one of the biggest archeological mysteries," Michael added "In 2003, some Japanese archeologists announced they had found the sites, and were promptly chased off the land, fearful for their lives. The Mongolian people consider digging up a grave a desecration, and they revere Genghis Khan, no matter what the West thinks of him."

"But he was a butcher."

"Genghis Khan conquered the known world from the Pacific to the edge of Europe. When his grandson, Kublai, took the throne, he didn't allow his subjects to wage war against each other. When skirmishes broke out, they were quickly and mercilessly put down. They called it the *Pax Mongolica,* the Mongolian Peace. A common saying at the time was that a maiden bearing a nugget of gold on her head could wander safely throughout the realm. Trade flourished between the East and West using the Silk Road as the heart of the commerce. Genghis Khan may have created the largest contiguous empire ever known—second only in scope to the far flung British empire."

"It's interesting," Jianjun said, bring them coffee, "that although many people traveled back and forth between China and Europe, including Chinese people, Marco Polo is the one everyone knows."

"The way it happened is actually kind of funny," Michael said. "After Polo returned to Venice, he got caught up in a war between Venice and Genoa, and was imprisoned. His cellmate was Luigi Rustichello, an author of 'romances.' As Polo relayed tales of his travels, Luigi wrote them down in French, the most widely used language at the time. They became *The Travels of Marco Polo.* But since Rustichello was known as a fiction writer, Polo's travels were looked upon as fiction. To make matters worse, since there were no printing presses yet, as scribes copied the words, some added their own embellishments, some left parts of the original out, and others made up their own stories and threw them in.

"As a result, Polo was tarnished with the name, *il milioni,* because the Venetians believed that he had told a million lies. On his deathbed, when pressed to admit that his travels were a lie, he said, 'I have not told the half of what I saw and did.'"

"Poor Marco," Kira said. "To have done all that, and not be believed."

"We now have Chinese records from the time," Michael said, "that tell of Europeans who meet the description of Marco, his father, and uncle in the court of Kublai Khan."

Kira nodded. "I'm glad to hear that. It would be a shame if all the stories children are told of Marco Polo are false."

"That's what I enjoy most about archeology," Michael admitted. "It gives the true picture of life at the time, not what some historian tells you about it."

"Is there anything in Polo's *Travels* about such a pearl?"

"Not that I recall."

"What if everything that the old priest told you is a lie?" Kira asked.

"Then we have nothing," Michael said. "But consider … what if it's true?"

Kira looked from Michael to Jianjun. "What do you have to say?"

"Nothing! I can't take all this history when I'm starving," Jianjun announced. "It gives me a headache! I told Kira about my favorite soup in Florence, ribollita—twice-cooked. Let's go eat some, and then decide what we do next."

The other two concurred.

CHAPTER 32

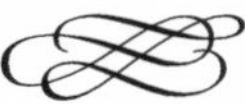

Anyang, China 1122 B.C.

The Grand Duke of the West returned to his palace and once there bided his time. Outwardly, he showed allegiance to the king and queen because Zhou Xin and Daji not only controlled a vast army, but they also had spies throughout the land, many of whom had been willing recruits because of their own avarice and sexual proclivities.

Slowly, the desire for rebellion swept over the land. For years, noblemen felt a duty to remain true to the king, but as the cruelty of Daji continued, the feeling dissipated. Peasants who had been taught obedience above everything else, also turned against the royal couple. Quietly, the Grand Duke of the West amassed enough supporters and power to declare war.

The warring states continued for many years and caused vast amounts of blood to be shed before the uprising succeeded. With the overthrow of Zhou Xin and Daji, the Shang dynasty came to an end. The people so hated King Zhou Xin that, to ensure no one with his blood remained alive, they slaughtered all his relatives up to seven times removed from him.

The victorious leaders of the war established the Chou dynasty which ruled China for eight-hundred years.

After the king and queen were put to death, the Goddess Nüwa called the

Thousand-Year Vixen, the Nine-Headed Pheasant, and the Jade Pipa to stand before her. "You have disobeyed my orders."

"I believe we obeyed them with great zeal," protested the Vixen who had been Daji. "We destroyed not only Zhou Xin, but his dynasty, and all his relatives. His name will be forever reviled"—she bowed low—"as you commanded."

"I told you to harm no one else, and you did nothing but harm others!" Nüwa shrieked. "I am also disgusted with the men around you who allowed such vile terror for the sake of their own filthy lust and power."

"Yes!" the Vixen shouted. "It was their fault. And they have been punished for it."

"Quiet, demon!" Nüwa stormed back and forth before the three demons who quaked with fear at the goddess's wrath. "The people have destroyed your earthly bodies, and now your demonic spirits will be placed in this stone." She held up a small red pearl-shaped pebble. "Whoever owns it will have power over you. And when the stone is in a special rare earth, you will feel as if the soil is smothering you, and you will gasp for breath only to have dirt fill your demonic mouths causing the terror of believing each moment may be your last.

"If, by chance, you break free of this prison, then mankind is yours, for I will do nothing more to help them, or to stop you."

With that, Nüwa commanded the demons into the pearl, and placed the pearl in a small bronze vessel. She then returned to earth and gave the vessel to the new king of the Chou dynasty, commanding him to cast it far from his people in a land not yet named, a land north of the Gobi desert, where only nomads roamed, and where a rare and wondrous soil would entrap the demons.

Many of the brave victims who had been killed by King Zhou Xin and Daji, as well as the heroic warriors who had died during the years of battle, were invested as gods in Heaven. And they were remembered and honored from that time forward by everyone from the highest nobleman to the lowliest peasant.

CHAPTER 33

News of the death, called a "possible murder-suicide" of Jonathan Vogel, hedge fund CEO, his wife, and a son who was being groomed to take over the business, flashed across the news wires the next morning. Michael, Jianjun, and Kira scoured the Internet for details.

"It isn't stopping, is it?" Dejection filled Kira as she sat at the table with her morning cappuccino and a croissant.

"Let's just hope, whatever it is," Jianjun said, "doesn't follow us to the Silk Road."

Michael's phone rang. His friend, Charlotte Reed, was calling from Salmon, Idaho.

"Your story about the strange pearl of Marco Polo made me curious," Charlotte said, not bothering with pleasantries. "I've done some research and even contacted a few old friends from my university days. It's fascinating! There actually are legends about a red pearl. Most people, of course, don't believe any of them, but I'll leave it up to you to decide."

Michael put his phone on speaker so the others could hear what she had to report and quickly introduced her to Kira.

"More history," Jianjun grumbled to Kira, standing close. She jabbed him in the ribs with her elbow.

"The red pearl was used to explain some of the vicious things that certain men did in Europe after the time of Marco Polo," Charlotte began. "Historians agree that it wasn't a pearl at all, but a philosopher's stone conjured by Chinese alchemists thousands of years ago. It had nothing to do the usual tenets of alchemy, creating gold, the perfect and incorruptible metal, or even with creating a perfect and incorruptible man, one who was immortal. Instead, whoever owned it could control demons. Unfortunately, the demons influenced its owner as well, making men who might have been only a little shady, turn into monsters.

"Apparently, if the pearl is buried in some special earth found in the north China-Inner Mongolia area, the demons lose their power. Somehow, Genghis Khan learned about the pearl, and used it to cruelly take over most of the known world. Then, when Kublai Khan became Emperor, Kublai's mother understood how evil the pearl was, and gave it to Nestorian monks to hide. Did you know she was a Nestorian Christian?" Charlotte asked.

"I didn't," Michael admitted.

"I find that fascinating!" Charlotte was bursting with enthusiasm. "In fact, she was the reason Kublai Khan was so open to other ways of thinking, and invited Westerners to his court. But I digress. Kublai's mother asked the monks to put the pearl into that special earth so her son wouldn't be influenced by demons the way Genghis Khan had been. She wanted him to be a kind and compassionate ruler.

"For the most part, her wishes worked. But the empire was so vast and diffuse that as Kublai Khan grew old, it began to break down. One theory is that the breakdown happened after Marco stole the pearl.

"In any case, Marco Polo had three daughters. After he died, his daughters split up his fortune, but the red pearl wasn't mentioned. No one knows if it was still part of his fortune, or if Marco gave it away or threw it away earlier. Rumor had it, he thought the pearl had brought him bad luck.

"But the pearl does pop up throughout European history, always connected with unnaturally evil men. This is where it gets really fascinating."

Michael and Jianjun grinned at each other. They both could imagine Charlotte pouring over history books, gleefully rubbing her hands together over discoveries, and loving every minute of her research.

"Vlad the Impaler was said to have been one of its owners—the sadist who was so cruel in Romania he was fictionalized as Dracula. It's theorized that Henry the Eighth became increasingly heartless not only because of his alleged syphilis and festering sore that never healed, but because he gained possession of the pearl.

"Mad King Ludwig of Bavaria is believed to have owned the pearl. He was a patron of the composer Richard Wagner, whose *Ring of the Nibelung* is said to be a parable about the pearl. Wagner was a onetime friend and father figure to Nietzsche before their falling out.

"Nietzsche went mad after writing books that ultimately influenced Hitler, a man fascinated by all things connected with the occult and alchemy. The red pearl supposedly reached Der Führer, and shortly after, he began to build concentration camps.

"After Hitler's downfall, the pearl somehow ended up in Egypt. But exactly where it's been since it was last seen, around 1946, is unknown. And that's as much as I've been able to find."

Michael and the others thanked Charlotte for her research.

"Might I ask what you plan to do next?" Charlotte asked.

Michael noticed a figure dart past his window out in the courtyard. Sheer curtains covered the window so people couldn't see into his apartment, but the morning sunlight allowed him to see a little outside. "It's believed that the Nestorian monastery that housed the pearl when Marco Polo stole it is still on the Old Silk Road, and if the pearl were returned, it would cease to be powerful. I guess that special earth you spoke of is also in that area." He moved to the edge of the window and pushed a sliver of curtain out of the way to see outside. "We're going to go look for it."

Two men crept towards his door.

"I can't begin to tell you how tempted I am to join with you," Charlotte said ruefully. "But I'll—"

"Got to go," he whispered. He hung up, motioned for Jianjun and

Kira to go into the kitchen while he hurried to the far side of the front door.

They waited, staying quiet. Before long, they heard a key in the lock, and the apartment door slowly opened.

As an intruder crept into the room, a revolver was the first thing Michael saw from his hiding place behind the door. He reached out, grabbed the hand holding it, and jerked it forward. As the gunman stumbled, Michael kneed him in the sternum, lifting him off his feet, then gave him a chop to the back of the neck that dropped him to the floor.

Michael reached for the gun as a second gunman stepped into the room.

"Don't touch it! Get back!" he ordered, his pistol pointed at Michael.

Michael froze, his shoulder once again throbbing. He had seen both these men before—the same two at the monastery in Rome. Jianjun crept up behind the gunman, a cast iron frying pan in hand.

"I said let the gun go, or I shoot!" the gunman ordered.

Jianjun slammed the frying pan down on the gunman's head. He dropped, out cold.

The larger man awoke to find Michael pointing a gun at his head. Michael grabbed his jacket and dragged him to his feet.

"I'm sick of you two following me," he said. "What the hell is going on? Talk!"

"We weren't going to hurt you. In fact, we thought no one was home," the big man said.

"What do you want here?"

"A red pearl. That's all I know. We were promised a lot of money if we got it away from you. We were told that, for sure, the red pearl was here now, and we just needed to get it." He shook his head, then winced and put his hand against the back of his neck.

"Who told you all that?"

"An American. I've got his phone number. Nothing else."

"Give it to me.

He carefully reached inside his jacket pocket and held out a scrap of paper. Michael took it. It was a U.S. phone number. The 208 area code was familiar because he had just used it to call Idaho.

"No name?"

"Never."

"Why do you trust he'd pay you?"

"He's in the U.S., I'm here. If I didn't get the money, I wouldn't send him what he wanted."

"He trusted you to send it?"

"Why not? I prefer money over a red pearl."

"How forgiving will he be that you failed him?" Michael asked.

The man glanced nervously at his cohort, still unconscious. "Not very," he mumbled.

Michael called the police and his landlady, saying he had caught two men who broke into his apartment. Mrs. Silvestri was more fearsome than the police. She was infuriated that anyone would try to bother her nice tenant, *il professore,* and immediately noticed that his shoulder was hurting him again. She found pain medicine and a heating pad for him. She liked trying to make Michael happy and well cared for in his adopted home, and apologized for the slowness of the locksmiths, swearing she would change the lock herself if she couldn't get one to come the very next day.

To go from someone wanting to shoot or at least pummel him, to someone who pampered him in a matter of minutes made his head spin.

The robbers had little to say when the police arrived. They took the robbers to jail, while an inspector took statements from Michael, Kira, Jianjun, and Mrs. Silvestri.

Inspector Lucca, a thin man of medium height, intense brown eyes, and a small mustache, told Michael he would need to come down to the police station to press charges.

"No," Michael said.

"No?"

"They didn't take anything. This was more than a robbery, and they're just pawns. Let them worry about what might happen, and then let them go. They won't be back."

"That's not a good idea, *signore,*" the inspector said.

"It's what I want."

Inspector Lucca tightened his lips. "I hope you don't regret it." He gave a brusk nod, then left the apartment.

"Do you think it's wise to let them go?" Jianjun asked.

"The less the police look into any of this, the better off we are."

"Could be," Jianjun admitted. "Now, what?"

"I'm going to call Charlotte Reed, apologize for hanging up on her, and ask if she can get the sheriff to find out about this Idaho phone number," Michael said. "Then we're going to leave Florence tonight. The sooner we're away from whoever is sending goons after me, the better I'll like it."

Ethnographer Renata Corbi phoned Michael with names of guides to hire when he reached Tashkent, but then added, "If you don't mind, I'd love to come with you. The search for a Nestorian monastery would make a great topic for a paper."

"If you'd like to come, that's fine," Michael said. "I know you'll be helpful—but, will you be ready to leave tomorrow? We're already in Rome. We're taking a seven P.M. flight tomorrow night."

She didn't hesitate. "See you in Rome."

Michael hung up his cell phone and gave Kira and Jianjun the news. They sat in Kira's hotel room, having ordered focaccia and beer. The TV was on. Breaking news from Florence caught their attention. Two men were gunned down as they left a police station. The shooter was in a car that immediately sped away.

When the photos of the deceased were shown, they were the two men who had broken into Michael's apartment earlier that day.

PART II

The Journey

CENTRAL ASIA

CHAPTER 34

TASHKENT, Uzbekistan

Michael never cared to spend a lot of time in Tashkent because it reminded him of all that had been lost in Central Asia. Home to over three million people, the heart of Tashkent was now a modern capital —big and sprawling, with high-rises, traffic jams, and numerous government institutions. Some cement-block reminders of the failed USSR's onetime power and hold over the land could still be found, and there remained an ever-shrinking traditional Uzbek town of narrow streets lined with mud-walled houses interspersed with ornate blue-domed mosques.

The old Tashkent that Michael enjoyed had been one of the major stops along the caravan route between Europe and China. Not only was most of that gone, but even moderately aging areas were being destroyed by the new Uzbek government. In a few more years, he probably wouldn't recognize the city at all.

He and his companions flew into Tashkent, or "Toshkent" in the local language, as the best spot to start searching for Father Berosus' monastery. From there, they would follow the Old Silk Road eastward.

"Remember, we're tourists," Renata said as they headed to a Hyatt

Hotel with lots of other tourists to blend in with. "Two couples traveling together. It's what people here are used to, and they won't take much notice of us. So, you two are a couple," she pointed at Jianjun and Kira, "and I'm Michael's Italian girlfriend." She took Michael's arm. "Got it?"

Jianjun looked uncomfortably at Kira. "Is it okay with you?"

She shrugged. "Whatever it takes."

"After we check in, Renata and I will go in search of guides who know the route best aligned with that of the Old Silk Road," Michael said. "You two need to be on the lookout around the hotel. There shouldn't be anyone or anything to worry about, but we need to be vigilant. So far, things are progressing almost too smoothly."

After registering for their room, Jianjun took Kira's arm and led her toward the elevator. She gave him a harsh look, but didn't pull away. A guy could dream, couldn't he?

Up ahead, he saw Michael and Renata waiting for the elevator. They all got off on the same floor.

Jianjun watched Michael open the door to his room and disappear inside with Renata.

He faced his door, holding the key card. He felt as if he were all thumbs, but steadied himself. The card easily fit into the slot and the lock clicked. He pushed the door open and held it to allow Kira to enter first.

He followed her into the room and froze. The queen-size bed practically filled the entire space. He gawked, not sure what to do.

"This is awkward." Kira put her hands on her hips as she looked around, as if expecting a second bed to miraculously appear.

He darted across the room to the closet. "Ah! Here's an extra blanket. And a pillow. Which is okay. I mean, not that it's okay that there's nowhere else to sleep. But there's the floor. It's comfortable enough, I'm sure. I mean, not comfortable as such, but better than standing. Or, there's a chair—"

"Jianjun, it's all right. We'll manage," she said.

"Uh … Maybe I can request a rollaway bed."

"And blow our cover?" She put her knapsack on a chair, upzipped it, and started digging through her things. "Don't worry. I know you're married. You can trust me to leave you alone."

"No." *Where had that come from?* "I mean, of course."

She suddenly stopped what she was doing, faced him, and then grinned.

He wished the floor would open and swallow him. But instead something—maybe one of Michael's demons—caused him to say, "It was an arranged marriage in the Chinese tradition."

Her eyebrows rose high.

The silence stretched out before she said, "Maybe we should freshen up and then go for a walk before dinner." She headed towards the bathroom. "I'd like to see a bit of Tashkent while we're here."

"Yes! Good idea!" He sat down on the bed to wait and then jumped to his feet. "I'm sorry! I forgot to ask … which side do you want?"

Michael and Renata wandered through old, bazaar sections of Tashkent in search of the guide she had used in the past. Stalls around them sold everything from pots and pans to used shoes and old spoons. The crowded markets supported a number of outdoor cafes, called chaikhanas or tea rooms, that sold kebabs, shawarma, samosa, and pilaf. The two were tempted to stop and eat, but they decided to locate the guide first.

Michael's cell phone rang. It was Charlotte, telling him the phone number he gave her was from a burner *satellite* phone. She hadn't known burner satellite phones existed. "Apparently they cost beaucoup bucks," she added. "We're trying, but so far, no clue as to who it belongs to."

"Okay—thanks. That gives us some idea, at least," Michael said. He soon hung up because Renata found her contact.

The guide, however, refused to help, saying it had become too dangerous beyond Tashkent with marauding bands of thieves, and government soldiers looking for spies, terrorists, and opposing government militants. If they insisted on going anyway, he knew two men willing, for enough money, to lead them across the steppes and through Kyrgyzstan to the Chinese border. After that, they were on their own.

A sinking feeling hit Michael. They weren't even out of Tashkent, and already they had a problem.

Marco Polo had followed the Silk Road through Tashkent to the Chinese cities of Kashgar and Khotan (or Hotan as it was now known since the conquering Chinese didn't have the guttural "kh" sound of the Turkic languages), and then across the desert to Kublai Khan's capital city of Cambaluc, now present day Beijing, or some two hundred plus miles north to the ruins of Khan's summer palace, Xanadu, in Inner Mongolia. Somewhere between those cities lay the Nestorian monastery for which they searched. It was a ridiculously long distance—about 1800 miles—but Father Berosus had sounded convinced the monastery they sought was in the Central Asian part of the journey, or at worst, not far into land now owned by China. Michael hoped he was right.

Eventually, they found the guides and agreed on a price, place and time to meet. Michael rented a Japanese four-wheel-drive van fitted with enormous tires for the dire snow conditions, and then, with satellite phones on his mind, he bought one for their trip into the back roads of Central Asia. Most of the time, it would be their only means of communication with the outside world.

He and Renata returned to the hotel after that and joined Jianjun and Kira for dinner. They agreed to meet in the lobby at six o'clock the next morning.

Renata and Michael entered their room. He took out his computer and checked on US and British news sources while Renata showered. She came out with her skin warm and glowing, and wearing a short, thin nightgown. He did a double-take. She might be a scholar, but she was full-bodied and womanly. His gaze followed her as she got into bed.

"Come join me," she said, patting the mattress beside her.

He was tempted until Irina and the demon, never far from his thoughts, swept over him. Who or what was Renata Corbi? He had met the real woman months earlier, but could he be sure this was her? Her nightgown dipped provocatively low, making her almost too tempting—just as the demon had been.

"We'll be working together many days," he said. "It's not a good idea."

She cocked her head. "You Americans, too many of you are still Puritans. I find you attractive, Michael. What's the problem?"

"And I find you incredibly sexy. If I were someone else, you wouldn't get any sleep tonight. But I'm me, and now, I'm going to read."

She shrugged her shoulder. "As you wish." She shut the lamp on the nightstand, leaving only the light in his side of the room, then turned onto her side. "Good night, Michael."

Michael gazed at the hills and valleys of the blanket that covered her and wondered if he was being ten-times a fool.

Down the hall, Jianjun went into the bathroom to change into sweat pants and a sweat shirt. Ever since he nearly froze to death on a trip with Michael to fjords in Norway, he made sure he always had something warm to sleep in. He padded into the bedroom. Kira sat on the one comfortable chair in the room, reading something on her computer tablet. The lamp beside her was the only one in the room still lit. He stood in the middle of the floor, then decided the least awkward thing to do was to get into bed. He lay on his back and shut his eyes.

Sleep refused to come.

An hour passed before Kira went into the bathroom. He listened to the water running for a while, then heard her come back out. He opened his eyes just a little. Her hair was down. She went over to her knapsack, pulled out heavy flannel PJs, and then shut the lamp. Moonlight against the thin drapery sent enough light in the room that he could make out her long, lithe silhouette as she pulled off her top, unhooked her bra and removed it, stepped out of her slacks, socks and panties, and then put on the pajamas.

He squeezed his eyes tight as she walked to the bed and got into her side. He could smell the flowery soap she had used, could hear her breathing, could sense her nearness.

The space between them felt simultaneously as narrow as tissue paper, and as wide and empty as the Gobi desert.

He wondered if he would be able to sleep at all that night.

CHAPTER 35

Early the next morning, the four met with the two guides. They had brought food and supplies, including thick parkas and extra blankets in case they got stuck somewhere out in the snow, and soon everything was loaded into the van Michael had rented.

Once past Tashkent, law and order broke down even though the Uzbek government, plus Russian, Chinese, and most likely American operatives, closely watched the region and any travelers. Both Russians and Chinese governments worried about the country being used to stage terrorist attacks on them, and all three foreign governments used the area to spy on each other.

As they headed eastward, against the sky, they could see a faint silhouette in the distance. As they neared, it became a snow-white wall with blue shadows—the T'ian Shan, or "heaven's mountains." More than 10,000 feet high, an eternal blanket of snow covered the tops of the peaks.

The guides took them along Old Silk Road caravan routes used by Marco Polo rather than the busier main highway until they neared the border between Uzbekistan and the small, politically unstable country of Kyrgyzstan. Once there, the guides returned to the highway and crossed only in areas known to be safe, since a number of landmines had been planted along the border by the Uzbek government during a time they feared Islamic militants coming through Kyrgyzstan and Tajikistan. Some had been removed, but many were still buried.

Once in Kyrgyzstan, they traveled even more slowly, searching the area, talking to local people, doing whatever they could to find any hint of a Christian monastery having once existed in the area. The road took them along streams from the snow-covered peaks. Winter weather hadn't yet hit or the area would have been impassable. The autumn landscape had patches of snow alternating with boggy soil and thick, coarse grass, but beyond the small roadway, glaciers and lakes dotted the mountains. Once, they even spied a pair of large, spiral-horned Marco Polo sheep along a riverbank. But they found nothing that could have been a monastery. Even the Silk Road itself was hard to locate most of the time, and a great deal of guesswork was involved by the guides and Renata.

They spent two nights camping, and when they reached the small strip town of Naryn, wedged in a foreboding canyon and called the gateway to the mountain passes into China, they were glad to spend a night in an inn, much as a caravansary welcomed travelers during the time of Marco Polo.

"Don't shoot! It's just me," Kira said as she crossed the inn's barren courtyard to Michael's side. He sat alone on a rickety wooden bench.

The women had been given one room, and the men, including the guides, shared another that was set up dormitory style. Here, in the courtyard, a blanket of stars created a brilliant canopy in the night sky.

"Are you all right?" Michael asked.

"Yes." She joined him on the bench. "Actually, that's not true. Something is bothering me. You don't let anyone but Jianjun get close. Why is that?"

"That sounds like a profiler's question."

"I'm a psychologist, what can I say? And believe me, that question was way too straightforward for profiling."

He could understand her uneasiness. If he were in her position, he doubted he'd trust himself either. "I'm sorry, Kira. I'm not an 'open up' kind of person."

She gazed up at the stars awhile before saying, "Come to think of it, neither am I. I shouldn't have pried. I'll just continue to drive poor Jianjun crazy with my questions."

"I'm quite sure Jianjun doesn't mind," he said.

"He's a good man." Her words were soft. "I just don't know what's going on. My father and I weren't even close, yet since his death, I feel lost."

"I understand," he said.

"I doubt it." Her tone was bitter.

They sat in silence a moment, then he said, "My mother died suddenly when I was only ten. That kind of death of a parent gets deep into one's bones and leaves a person uncertain."

"What happened to her?"

He still saw that day clearly. He was at Wintersgate. His mother stood at a third-floor balcony outside what they called 'the study,' a library filled with his parents' books. He had been playing in the garden, and knew if she saw how filthy he'd gotten, she'd be unhappy. So he hid behind a tree, waiting for her to go back inside, planning to sneak up to his room to change. Next thing he knew, she fell … or jumped … or was pushed, from that balcony.

He would never forget the blood on the patio soon after she hit. So much blood. And his screams.

He shut his eyes, trying to forget.

But he always wondered if he had made some simple gesture, if he'd waved in her direction, called up to her, done anything instead of running past so she wouldn't see him, if that might have changed everything.

Friends, even psychologists, told him he had to stop blaming himself for what had happened, that he couldn't have known what she was going to do, couldn't stop her from taking her own life. But he had been there, and no one else was.

He believed his father never forgave him. And he never forgave himself.

Instead of telling Kira any of this, he simply said, "An accident."

"How awful," Kira said.

"Yes." His tone clearly said it was not a topic for discussion.

"What about your father?" Kira asked. "Is he alive?"

She *was* profiling him. "He's alive. After my mother's death, he became even more of a recluse than he had been previously. People say he has the gift—or curse—to see more than the physical in this world. Apparently, I have the same affliction."

"Do you and your father get along?"

He found this tedious. "We've never been close," he snapped. "And that, Doctor Holt, should give you plenty to think about as you work up a psychological profile for me. Isn't it better than thinking about demons?"

"No, Michael, it's sad," she said, her gaze filled with sympathy. The last thing he wanted was anyone's sympathy. "But it helps me to understand."

"Oh, great." The words were dry, sarcastic.

"It's fine. And I'm sure that someday, you'll find Irina again."

His head jerked towards her.

She stood to leave. "I saw the expression on your face as you talked to Magda about her. A person doesn't need to be a psychologist to understand what's going on. Thank you for talking to me."

CHAPTER 36

Once past Naryn, the road became increasingly rugged and difficult as they climbed ever higher into the T'ian Shan range. They headed toward the Torugart Pass border crossing into China. It was 12,300 feet, well over two miles, above sea level. The guides told them the pass was currently open, but would shut if a storm came in. They hoped to reach it before that happened. But more than that, they hoped to find the Nestorian monastery without needing to enter China.

Along the narrow, mountain road wending through Kyrgystan, they saw mostly bare land with occasional rocky outcrops and banks of snow. The last time Michael had been here, it was summer, and he remembered seeing migrating tribesmen in the valleys far below. Some yurts had been erected, and near them horses stood, lambs cavorted, and yaks slowly meandered, followed by their calves. Now, the valleys were bleak and empty, the air so icy and thin the boiling point of water had dropped to 188 degrees Fahrenheit, and tufts of grass cast long shadows on the stony ground.

"Shouldn't we have found some sign of at least one Nestorian monastery by now?" Kira asked as they bounced over a particularly bumpy patch of narrow roadway that wended between rocky inclines on both sides.

Renata answered. "Since Marco Polo traveled here over seven hundred years ago, it would be amazing to find any structure in this area from his time."

Michael said nothing. He was tired of this argument with Renata. He wasn't giving up, no matter how impossible she found his quest.

The sun set quickly, dropping behind the mountains, as they searched for a place where the road widened enough to make camp for the night. But then the driver abruptly stopped the van.

He and the other guide spoke to Renata in Uzbek as they loaded their rifles. "They're worried about the headlights," Renata said as she pointed to what appeared to be lights on a truck or other large vehicle heading their way. "It could be nothing, or they could be bandits. This area is filled with them. They especially go after people after dark, and target tourists they think might not be able to defend themselves."

Michael grabbed rifles from the back of the van and handed one each to Jianjun, Renata, and Kira, plus extra ammunition. He kept one for himself. The headlights sped closer. "Jianjun, be ready to drive Kira and Renata out of here if things go south."

"I'll head to the turnout area a few miles back, and wait there," Jianjun said.

Michael nodded as he and the guides got out. Usually, bandits would turn around if they saw rifles pointing at them. But as the gray truck drew near, the men inside it fired at them.

Michael and the guides returned fire.

"Damn it all!" Jianjun muttered and furiously backed the van to a spot where the road was wide enough for him to make a three-point U-turn.

Michael blasted a tire on the approaching truck, flattening it and sending the truck into a spin.

The bandits jumped out of the truck, still firing. Michael scrambled up the rocky mountainside and ducked behind some boulders.

From there, he shot back, hitting one in the shoulder, then ran farther uphill as did the guards. At the crest, they split up. Michael kept going as the gunfire continued. When he reached a rocky outcrop, he stopped, and squatted behind some rocks.

He stayed hidden as he heard an occasional volley of shots.

Darkness fell, and mist settled over the land, the kind of mist that caused the tops of the T'ian Shan to seem to vanish within the clouds when seen from below.

Eventually, he heard the sound of a truck's engine. The bandits must have managed to change the tire, and were leaving. He listened for more shots, the sounds of the bandits coming up the hill.

All he heard was the truck driving away, and then the sound disappearing altogether.

The fog and haze blotted out the little moon and starlight. Even Marco Polo had written of the heavy ground fog that sometimes blanketed the area and caused men and caravans to lose their way. Michael headed back towards the area where he had last seen the guards. He couldn't see more than a few feet ahead. Despite his heavy jacket, thick socks and hiking boots, the cold seeped into his bones. If the temperature dropped much more, he wondered if he could survive the night.

He headed down mountain, believing he should reach the road at any time, but for some reason, he didn't. He must have gotten turned around somehow, and the hillside he descended wasn't the same as the one he had climbed.

He headed farther down, but then stopped when he reached an area relatively level. He walked along it far enough to know it was as best a pathway, not the main road. Now, he was sure he was in the wrong spot.

He feared if he continued to wander in this murky darkness, he would end up hopelessly lost.

Michael jerked himself awake. Falling asleep in this temperature could be fatal. It was still hours before dawn, and the inversion continued. He kept watching, hoping for a sliver of moonlight, anything to help him find the roadway. But then, a solitary figure stepped out of the fog. He was no more than a shadow. As he neared, he seemed to be wearing a long wool tunic with a cowl. Michael held his rifle ready to fire.

"I am not here to hurt you." The man's accent was thick. "You can lower your rifle."

Michael and his rifle didn't move. "Who are you? What are you doing out here?"

"I'm a monk. I live some distance, but I heard the rifle fire echoing through the mountains. When I thought it safe, I came out here to see if anyone was hurt. Are you?" He lowered his cowl and Michael saw he was an elderly man. His hair was long and white, and he had a wispy white beard. "If you're hiding from bandits, I have not seen any since nightfall."

A monk, out in this nothingness ... and he speaks English?

"How did you find me?" Michael demanded.

"I know places to hide from the cold as well as from bullets. But you are too suspicious. If you do not wish my help, so be it." With that, he started to walk away.

"Wait." Michael stood, still gripping his rifle in case this was a trap. "If you can point me to the road, I'll make my way back to my friends."

"You do not know this area, and its dangers are many, both natural and man-made. Come to the monastery with me. I can give you some food and a bed for the night."

"Are you Buddhist?" Michael asked, not recognizing the clothes the monk wore, and realizing they contained many layers for warmth —a sort of primitive insulation system.

The monk took hold of the silver necklace he wore and lifted it from under his robes. On the end was a cross. It appeared to be Christian, but instead of a crucifix, it had three little circles at each tip of the cross—right and left, top and bottom. "I am a Nestorian Christian. My name is Sirom."

After so many days of searching, this is too easy.

Michael stiffened. "Lucky me, just when I was looking for a Nestorian monastery, you're here to guide my steps."

The monk smiled secretively. "I know. Follow me."

Michael studied the man. "I thought there were no more followers of Nestorius."

The monk's brows lifted, but the rest of his face remained impassive. "Well, you can see I am here, so your world is—as usual—wrong."

Michael wondered if he was having one of those dreams so realistic it left you unsure when you woke which was the dream, and which was reality.

The monk didn't answer, but walked away. Michael hesitated, then followed. They continued along the pathway. It seemed they went in the opposite direction from the one Michael thought he needed to go in, but he couldn't be sure of that.

After a while, Sirom spoke again. He explained that the Nestorian church had gone underground in the area, but it had not disappeared.

"We expected someone would be looking for us," Brother Sirom said. "Someone from the West, trying to right the wrong done by Marco Polo."

"Why would you expect such a thing?"

"Our history has been passed down from one abbot to the next. As you are aware, what you have is not a pearl, but a philosopher's stone."

Michael nodded.

"You are not surprised or troubled by this?" Sirom asked.

"No."

Sirom's eyebrows rose. "What do you plan to do with it?"

The monk spoke as if he assumed Michael had the pearl with him. "A Chaldean priest warned me not to destroy it, but to return it to the monastery from which Marco Polo stole it."

"Good. You must head east. This is not the land you seek."

"What do you know about the pearl?"

"We know its history, and that demons are active because the pearl has been freed."

"Freed? What do you mean?"

"Something happened that freed them. Perhaps the priest who possessed it knew how to fight the demons, to control them. When he died, they were freed—until you or some other new owner learns how to keep them contained. Now, the demons roam the earth. We feel them. I suspect they are following the pearl, which means they are following you."

Michael didn't like the implication he had failed. "Do you know about some special soil that's supposed to control the demons?"

"The soil doesn't control them, it removes their power. Only the keeper of the pearl can control them ... if he knows how. But they're demons and know how to tempt the owner. Far too often, the demons won the power struggle with their owner. Through that owner they inflicted much harm and suffering."

"How can the owner learn to control them?" Michael asked.

Brother Sirom looked coldly at him, not answering his question. Michael didn't trust this man, or this situation. He wondered if this was another trap set up by demons in the way they'd fooled him with Irina. Finally Sirom spoke, "There is a reason Father Berosus chose to give you the pearl. He saw something in you. But remember that you never know who or what the demons might attack. Be ready."

Michael stared at the monk. He hadn't mentioned Berosus' name. How did this man know him? "The pearl is a tool of alchemy, which I've studied."

"If you think you can control a demon," Brother Sirom said, "you are mistaken."

"As keeper of the pearl, I should know how. Perhaps the same way Father Berosus did."

"But he was a holy man. Do you plan to draw them to you?"

"That's preferable to having them roam the world, isn't it?"

"Not for you, or for your friends," Sirom warned.

"When I find my friends, I'll pass on your warning."

"Those friends will be better off if you confront the demons alone, especially if you attempt to thwart their will and not succumb to the temptations they throw your way," Sirom said. "Demons are known to attack not only their prime target, but also anyone close to that target. They torture and kill in the most horrifying ways."

They soon reached an area with a few piles of stones that looked like nothing more than crumbled fireplaces and stone foundations. Any wood used to form the walls and roof was gone.

"This was once our monastery. Out here, it's nothing, but it backs into the mountain. Inside we have carved out a decent shelter. You will spend the night here," Sirom said. "You will be safe. I will return in the morning."

Sirom entered an opening that looked like an abandoned mine, one that should be covered with warnings not to enter. Michael followed and found himself in a long tunnel. At the far end, Sirom opened a heavy door. Beyond was a lit corridor with walls painted white, and several doors on both sides of it. Sirom stopped at the first door on the right, and turned the knob. The door was unlocked, and he pushed it open. "This is for you," Sirom said. "Use it or not, as you wish." He then walked back into the tunnel.

Michael hesitated, but then went to the door Sirom had opened. Past it was a small, windowless room, empty except for one candle and a thin mattress. Over it hung a cross similar to the one Sirom wore, but larger and fancier. Michael remembered reading that Nestorians venerated the cross, but not the crucifix.

The room was hardly inviting, but was warm and sheltered. Just looking at it made Michael realize how cold and exhausted he was.

Almost immediately a slight, elderly man dressed like Brother Sirom appeared in the doorway. He carried a tray with a cup and bowl, placed it by the door, then bowed and left the room, quietly pulling the door shut behind him.

Michael went to the tray to find green tea, rice and pickled vegetables. Dare he eat? The monk had plenty of chances to kill him, if that was what he wanted to do.

He ate; the warm tea felt especially good. Soon after finishing, he lay down to sleep. He looked around the strange monk's cell, and as his eyes shut in sleep, the thought flitted past at how odd it was that now, over seven hundred years after Marco Polo's journey, he was the reason Michael found himself in this strange and unnerving land that time seemed to have forgotten.

The bed, food, warmth might all be a set-up, just as supposedly meeting Irina had been a set-up by demons—perhaps a way to convince him to turn over the pearl to them. But at least for tonight, he'd take advantage of it.

CHAPTER 37

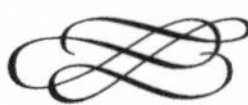

In the morning, Brother Sirom met Michael with a yak-drawn wagon. "I will take you close to the Torugart Pass," Sirom said. "From there, you can cross into China, and you'll be on your own. You must travel to a small town called Baigou on the Old Silk Road." He handed Michael a paper on which he had written out the name of the town in Chinese characters as well as Uyghur script. "It is about fifteen kilometers before Khotan. Go to the monastery there. It is the place you seek."

"Thank you for this." Michael folded the paper and put it in his pocket. "But first I need to go back and find my friends."

"Your journey will bring them too much danger. You must go alone."

"But they'll worry, and come after me," Michael said. Although the satellite phone was in the van with Jianjun, Michael needed cell service to reach it. He wished he'd thought about getting them each a satellite phone. "Is there cell phone service at the border?"

"I have no idea. Also, you must leave your rifle with me. You cannot get into China with it, and it will only create trouble for you."

"No."

Brother Sirom said nothing more, but got onto the wagon.

Michael did as well. They rode for a few miles when Sirom stopped at the side of the main roadway and waited. Michael asked why they had stopped, but he received no answer.

Before long, a bus with Buddhist monks came by. Brother Sirom stopped them and spoke to them, then returned to Michael. "For two hundred euros they will drive you to Kashgar. From there, you will need to make your own way."

"Two hundred euros to go eighty miles?" Michael asked. "Is there a Buddhist term for highway robbery?"

"They use the money for the desperately poor," Brother Sirom said with a scowl. "They will not allow your rifle, however."

This argument was unwinnable, and Michael turned over the money and his gun. Sirom kept the rifle and gave the money to the Buddhists. He returned with a maroon robe for Michael. "Put it on and join them. Many foreigners come here to spend time with them to try to achieve 'satori'—enlightenment. The border guards are used to it, especially if you look both vacant and wide-eyed as they question you."

Brother Sirom gave Michael a backpack with food and some travel necessities like a knife and flashlight, and Michael gave him a donation for the monastery.

A Buddhist monk who spoke a little English saw Michael checking for cell service as they neared the border. He warned Michael not to speak to the guards, and especially not to ask to use a phone. Anything unusual could cause them to detain and question him. Kashgar, he said, was not far.

At the border station, after one look at the scowling guards, Michael took the advice.

As predicted, although the border agent smirked at Michael's passport, visa, and his clothes, he stamped it and let him enter the Xinjiang Uyghur Autonomous Region. Here, the western borders of China rubbed up against the nomads of the 'stans,' Kazakhstan, Uzbekistan, Tajikistan, and others, an ever-changing land that refused to recognize boundaries in both ancient times and modern, populated by peoples for whom extended family was everything, and the concept of a national identity was new and foreign.

Once past the border, the land quickly began a descent to the flat, desert lands of Western China. After time spent in high, snow-covered mountains and narrow gorges, Michael enjoyed the sense of relief and freedom as the little Buddhist bus zipped down the slopes. The land went from bare rock to tufts of greenery and trees, an area with occasional livestock and homes.

Beyond the foothills of the T'ian Shan, however, the landscape again dramatically changed, now to flat and barren plain covered with rocks and a haze of red dust.

The onetime oasis of Kashgar, now a large city, was gray under a sky made yellow from the strong wind and sand of the desert. But the edges of the city still had the noise, jumble, and bazaars of the old city.

The Buddhists stopped the bus at the first market square they reached. It was raucous and crowded with both people and animals. "We must leave you here," said the English speaker. They took back their robe and then drove away.

Stalls with ragged awnings, separated by cloth walls, lined up against old buildings. Vendors displayed their wares and foodstuffs on tables, on racks, and blankets spread over the ground. People and bicycles were everywhere, and in any direction, in the distance, Michael could see a minaret or the dome of a mosque.

The stench was from the many horses tethered to carts in the area, plus separate groups of sheep, donkeys and mules, then camels, and even cattle.

The odor fought with the pleasant aroma of foods being cooked in the stalls for hungry shoppers.

Beyond the aging square loomed tall buildings of a surprisingly large city, but the area immediately around him probably hadn't changed much in centuries. Michael had been to many Central Asian markets, and enjoyed the foods, spices, goods, and humanity.

He checked his cell phone—one bar of service. He tried calling the satellite phone to reach Jianjun, but the call kept dropping. The same thing happened when he phoned Charlotte Reed. He remembered hearing that text messages had a better chance of getting through than voice, so he wrote a text to Jianjun saying he was in Kashgar, China, and that he would meet them in Naryn as soon as possible. He also texted Charlotte and asked her to convey the message to Jianjun's satellite phone.

When he hit "send" the texts appeared to transmit. He hoped they did.

He soon found a money changer and converted his Euros into Chinese yuan. He asked about a way to reach Khotan, the city back on the Old Silk Road. The money changer directed him to a bus station.

Michael headed towards it when a young teen, a nicely dressed, pleasant looking kid, walked by and spat at his feet. Michael was shocked. This wasn't the time or place to react, however, and he pretended not to notice. He never expected that sort of blatant antagonism in China. But this wasn't China, not really, although he was within the country's borders. The Uyghurs were a Muslim people of Central Asian Turkic origin who wanted independence from China.

While everyone who was within the country called China was officially "Chinese," the Han Chinese were those from the heart of the country—the original land ruled by the Han dynasty when China was unified around 200 B.C. The name China, or *Zhong-guo,* means "Middle Kingdom," and the people of the Han believed it to be the center of the world, and that those beyond its borders were barbarians. Today, many of those people and their lands have been conquered by China—areas such as Tibet, Manchuria, Inner Mongolia, and the Uyghur homeland.

Now, the Han Chinese were relocating to Xinjiang in huge, purposeful numbers. They had come to outnumber the Uyghurs in the provincial capital of Ürümqi, held most of the good jobs in the area, and forced Uyghurs to study Mandarin Chinese in schools. As a result, the call for Uyghur independence was increasing daily, with ever-mounting violence.

As Michael continued through the dusty market place, he saw that the crowd was a mixture of Uyghur and Han Chinese, without another European among them. The Uyghur women, especially the older ones, wore colorful headscarves, while most of the men wore brimless caps. Other than that, their clothes were mostly Western, with pants and even jeans being surprisingly common. The burkas and chadors of the Muslim women of the Middle East were not seen.

A Chinese woman, dressed in a traditional full-length black dress, scowled fiercely at him from across the market. He drew back as if struck. Her face would have been lovely were it not for her expression. Her shiny black hair was parted in the middle and pulled into a tight bun. She stared at Michael as if she knew him. He started across the square, but he had only taken a few steps when she disappeared into the crowd.

Something about her unnerved him, but it probably meant nothing. More important was for him to find a bus station, and then to get on a bus that traveled the route between the Taklamakan desert and the Tibetan plateau.

How ironic, he thought, that last year he was near Idaho's Salmon River, called the "river of no return," and now, he headed for the Taklamakan desert—a place the Uyghurs called "the land you can get into, but never get out of." He hoped his luck held.

Up ahead, a bright yellow and green CITS sign hung over a doorway—the Chinese International Tourist Service. CITS was the government-run travel agency. He darted away from the office and hoped no one reported seeing him, although at 6'2", he tended to stand out.

The bus station was next to it. He bought a ticket to Khotan and then looked for a public phone. He would feel better if he could talk to Jianjun or Charlotte, and his cell phone still had only one bar. He eventually found a phone, but the instructions were in Chinese. He put in some money and dialed the number of the satellite phone, and got a recording of a high-pitched female voice shrieking at him in Chinese to do something, but he had no idea what. He tried Charlotte's number and got the same angry-sounding message.

He saw a cell phone vendor and asked how to make a call. The vendor shook his head and handed Michael a photocopy of an article in the English language Shanghai Daily. It reported that anyone buying a mobile phone or a computer in Xinjiang had to register their personal details with police. The measure was to "prevent people spreading harmful information and carrying out illegal activities."

Michael tried to explain that he only wanted to make a call, not buy a phone, but the vendor kept shaking his head and pointing to the article.

Michael gave up, sent two more text messages to Jianjun and Charlotte as insurance, and then got into a line of people and animals waiting for the bus he needed to take. The agent had said it would depart "soon."

Michael stood, ticket in hand, when a lanky man in a blue suit marched towards him, shouting in Chinese. As he neared, Michael saw "CITS" in Roman letters, plus some Chinese and Uyghur script stitched onto the pocket of his jacket. The fellow's hair was clipped short, and a scar from his upper lip across one nostril appeared to be a botched operation to correct a harelip. He held out his palm and barked an order.

Michael didn't have a clue what he said and handed over his passport. He must have guessed right. Officious and irritated, the agent read it over, and then, in Chinese, made it clear he didn't want Michael on the bus.

Michael steeled himself and replied, "*Mei-you.*" He was told it meant "No," but considering the gasps around him when he said it, it must have been a bit stronger. The agent's shoulders stiffened, and he nearly levitated with indignation. Michael fought back a smirk. Police, soldiers, and bureaucrats weren't used to having their requests denied.

When the man returned to earth he asked, in English, with a sneer, "You like girls?" and suggested Shanghai.

Michael's reply was the same. He then used his minimalist Mandarin Chinese to say, "I go to Khotan."

The agent shook his head, then his eyes narrowed and he slapped the passport back into Michael's hand. He told Michael that when he arrived in Khotan, he must immediately report to the Public Security

Bureau, aka the police, to let them know he was there. They would escort him to a hotel for foreigners.

Sure they would. Michael nodded gratefully, not telling his tormentor that he wasn't planning on going all the way to Khotan. Not immediately, in any case.

The official, clearly playing to the crowd, ranted a bit more, raised his chin and all but goose-stepped back to his office.

Michael let out a big sigh of relief.

He faced forward in the bus line when the smell of meat being cooked with ginger, chili and coriander wafted towards him. He noticed many passengers carried food from the market stalls. Much as he tried to ignore them, his mouth began to water, and he doubted he would find another opportunity to eat for several hours.

He left the line for a food stand for hot tea and a pamirdin, a Uyghur meat pie consisting of lamb, carrot and onion. Not until he rejoined the back of the line and boarded the bus did he realize his mistake. The only seats left were those next to sweaty, heavily bundled up men, women with live animals, or squalling kids sprawled several to a seat. He squeezed onto a hard plastic seat next to three chickens with little bags over their heads so that they wouldn't run off. He tried to ignore the fact that he shared the space with someone's dinner.

—He's getting closer.

—He's alone.

—But not for long.

—And then he's ours.

CHAPTER 38

ABOUT FOUR MILES from the encounter with the bandits, the ground surrounding the roadway was wide and flat enough for Jianjun to hide the van among the brush and shrubs. That was where he told Michael he'd wait. He, Kira, and Renata took turns keeping watch along the road for Michael and the guides. It was dark when the two guides reached them. The guides insisted Michael had safely evaded the bandits because they saw the bandits change the tire he had shot out, and leave the way they'd come. They had no idea, however, where Michael had gone. They also refused to do any more "guiding." Renata drove them back to a tiny village some five miles away and paid them more money for their trouble.

Jianjun didn't like any of this. There was something about those bandits that was too violent, too targeted.

Jianjun saw Renata's disappointment when she returned to the camp and Michael still hadn't joined them. She was attracted to his boss, and he hoped she had enough experience to know such infatuation would never go anywhere. Michael was haunted by demons—demons that had been part of his life long before he encountered the red pearl. Jianjun didn't completely understand the cause of them, although meeting Magda and talking with Michael about Irina had gone a long way towards putting together pieces in the mystery that was his friend and employer.

He was worried, but it was too dark, cold, and foggy to search. The three of them slept in the van for warmth, rifles nearby, and prayed Michael would show up the next morning.

He didn't.

At first light, they returned to the road. Jianjun called Michael's phone using the satellite phone, but the calls wouldn't connect. If he'd been thinking straight, he would have insisted they buy two satellite phones in case they got separated. His eye caught a flash of red hair nearby and he knew why he was scarcely thinking at all.

"He's been captured," Renata said. "That's the only explanation."

"No," Jianjun insisted. "It's one explanation, but there are many others. Perhaps he found the monastery and is there now, giving them the pearl."

"Or," Renata all but groaned the words, "something worse has happened to him."

He felt an urge to wrap his fingers around her throat. He had no interest in hearing her conjectures.

"We're going back to the area we last saw Michael," Jianjun said. "We're going to do a thorough search. He might be hurt and needs us to find him."

Both women agreed.

Jianjun drove back and parked on the roadside. He would have liked to park off-road and hide the vehicle in brush, but the gorge was too narrow, and the land too bare. With rifles strapped over their shoulders, they spent the rest of the day searching the mountains for any sign of Michael. They found nothing.

By evening, dejected, they were climbing down the rocky hill above the road to the van when they heard a loud engine. "Go back," Jianjun said, leading them quickly back up the hill to some boulders. They lay down and watched.

An open jeep with six well-armed men stopped at the van. They looked like a group of wandering marauders in search of something to steal—and quite similar to yesterday's bandits.

Jianjun saw Kira shift her weight. He tried to stop her, but before he could, her foot lightly tapped a small rock. It slid from their hiding place and bounded down the hill, cascading into an ever-growing rock slide. One of the marauders saw the rock and angled his gaze upward. With a shout he fired at them, just missing Renata.

Jianjun fired back at the attackers.

He saw that Kira knew next to nothing about using a rifle, and Renata wasn't much better. Kira kept her head down, not daring to move after what she had done, while Renata fired infrequently. Jianjun used up the shells in his rifle, and then Kira's. He wounded two men, but the four remaining were not giving up. When Renata handed over her rifle, their eyes met. They were nearly out of bullets.

He wracked his brain for a way out. There was no cover for them to run. Would these people take them captive, or simply kill them? Given what was sometimes done to captives in this area, he had no choice but to fight on.

He picked off a third attacker when steady rounds of gunfire, as if from semi-automatic rifles, sounded.

Jianjun watched the attackers grab their wounded and flee back to their jeep, spin it around, and drive off.

Jianjun, Kira and Renata looked at each other.

On the road below, all was quiet.

"Michael?" Jianjun called.

"No, it's not Michael, but we know who he is," came the reply.

"Americans," Jianjun whispered, recognizing the accent. "Who are you?" he shouted.

"Hank Bennett and Stuart Eliot. You should know us."

The last two Navy men in the old photo, Jianjun thought, the only two still alive.

"We also know what you look like," Kira called. "Show yourselves."

The two men walked along the road with their arms raised, holding semi-automatic rifles over their heads. "We're here to help you," Hank said. "Can't you see that?"

"Do you trust them?" Renata whispered.

"We may have to," Kira said as three other men, muscular, puffed-up, and also armed with semi-automatic rifles, joined Hank and Stuart.

"Stay down," Jianjun said. "I'll talk to them."

"No." Kira grabbed his jacket, stopping him. She called out, "I'm Daniel Holt's daughter." She slowly got to her feet. Jianjun rose with her, holding his gun on the newcomers, ready to shoot anyone of them who even thought about firing at Kira.

"We know." Hank stepped closer. "We've been tracking you ever since we realized you folks have the pearl. When we figured out what you were up to, we thought we'd better show up in case you got yourselves into a shitload of trouble. Looks like we were right." He and the men around him put their rifles on the ground and waited.

Renata also stood. No one moved a long moment, then Jianjun, Kira, and Renata glanced at each other, nodded, and headed down the hill.

They introduced themselves to each other. The three strangers were former US Army rangers, now working as bodyguards, Carter, Polk and Taft. Hank called them his "three presidents," then gave a boisterous laugh.

Such a wit, Jianjun thought. Hank struck him as the kind of guy who expected to be the center of attention. It took a lot of chutzpah to call three ex-military tough guys as "his" anything. Stuart Eliot, on the other hand, looked like a pudgy wuss.

"Where is Michael Rempart?" Stuart asked.

"We don't know," Jianjun said. "Last night, someone attacked us, and we became separated."

"With all this noise," Hank said, "if he was still around, and alive, he'd have found you. I suspect he's already far from here. He was trying to get into China, right?"

"Most likely."

"Sounds like we need to head towards China ourselves." Squinty-eyed, hands on hips, Hank looked over Jianjun and the two women. "You're welcome to follow our SUV if you want to come along."

"Hold it!" Jianjun shouted as the two started to walk away. "Why aren't you two dead like the others in the photo?"

Hank glanced at Stuart, eyebrows high. Stuart nodded, and then Hank spoke. "Years ago, once we realized what was going on, we sold our businesses. We were both rich beyond our wildest dreams and that bought us a lot of knowledge. We went into hiding in the mountains of Idaho. There, we kept track of what was happening with the five men who were in Egypt with us. When we saw that they were being killed, we knew the time had come to use all we had learned. We have to get the pearl to make sure no one else dies."

"Hank's a computer expert," Stuart said, "so he was able to track you. We want to find Michael Rempart and the red pearl, and make sure no one else is harmed by it again."

"How all this came about is a long story," Hank said. "But right now, our priority is to get out of here in case those guys come back. There's a place not too far, kind of like an old caravan stop where we can refresh ourselves. See you there if you want to join us. But we will find Michael Rempart—and the pearl." Hank and Stuart headed towards their SUV.

"I don't trust these men," Renata confided to Jianjun and Kira.

"Arriving in the nick of time was pretty convenient," Jianjun said. "Almost unbelievably so."

"True. But the sound of gunfire would have echoed far in these mountains, and they were trying to find us," Renata said. "I don't know what else to do. We might have a better chance of finding Michael with them. They seem to know what they're doing, and they're well armed."

"That's true enough," Jianjun said. "But still …"

"May we have a minute?" Kira asked Renata and then moved to Jianjun's side.

Renata looked from Kira to Jianjun, nodded, and went to the van.

Jianjun was surprised at Kira's request. He saw that her worried frown reflected his own. "What are you thinking?" he asked.

"I want to know what you're thinking, just you, not Renata," she said.

Her white skin seemed paler than ever. "Renata was right when she said it'd be easier to find Michael with them than without them," he admitted. "And also, if Michael thought we would be safer if he left us behind, I could see him doing exactly that. He might be in China right now."

She studied his face. "So you think we're better off with them. But do you trust those men?"

"No," he admitted. "Still, they managed to find us. I'm sure they know a lot more about all this than they're saying. I'll drive you and Renata back to Naryn. You'll be safe there. Then, I'll do my best to catch up to them and find Michael."

Kira moved closer and placed her hand on his arm. Her large blue eyes captured his. He saw her sadness, but also her determination. "I'm not going to be shut away like some shrinking violet, and I'm not letting you go off alone with them. For me, this is personal. I'm going with you."

"Kira, it'll be too dangerous—"

"I'm going."

Her lips were firm, and her chin stubbornly tilted. After a moment, he nodded. "We'll get this worked out. I promise you."

He started back to the van, but her hand closed on his arm, stopping him. "Thank you for being here, for helping me," she said. "I don't know how I could handle any of this if you weren't."

He was stunned by her words. To his complete surprise, she kissed him. A light, friendly peck.

He didn't move a long moment, and neither did she. He placed his hands on her waist. Her eyes widened, but she didn't pull away from him, not even when he wrapped his arms around her, not even when he gave her a real kiss, the kind a man gives a woman he cares about. Instead, to his relief and amazement, she clutched him tight and kissed him back.

He broke off the kiss. His heart pounding, he placed his hand against the back of her head, his cheek against her hair, and continued to hold her, as she did him. *Remember this moment,* he ordered himself. *Remember so you never forget how it feels to hold a woman you care about, how it feels to kiss her, and to be kissed in return.*

He took her hand, and they walked together back to the van where they joined Renata.

When Hank, Stuart, and "the three presidents" passed them in a black SUV, Jianjun followed, hoping against hope he was doing the right thing.

CHAPTER 39

Michael got on the bus in Kashgar and tried to ignore the many eyes staring at him. In a great belch of black smoke, the bus left the market and zipped along at a good fifteen miles per hour until it reached a wide road where it rocketed up to twenty-five. He counted six sheep, several cages of birds, and a baby yak on the bus. Within an hour, the smell of dung was so bad he pulled his tee-shirt up over his nose. After another hour, the bus stopped. Michael wasn't sure why, but everyone got off, including the animals. He did, too. Maybe, he prayed, someone would hose the damn bus out. Over a half-hour went by before they all climbed onto the bus again, animals included. No one had cleaned out anything.

Not until a forty-five minute stop at a government checkpoint did someone clean the bus, but that was only so that the government agents wouldn't dirty their shoes as they checked the bus itself for contraband or whatever they were looking for. All Michael knew was that they scowled and yelled at him as they looked over his papers, finally giving them back in disgust and walking away from him. He suspected they wanted to know why he was on a local bus. He played dumb.

People and animals continuously got on and off as the bus drove along the completely flat highway with nothing but rolling sagebrush and a petrol station now and then.

Michael had loaded an e-book of *The Travels of Marco Polo* onto his phone and now looked at the section on the Taklamakan:

There is a marvelous thing related of this desert, which is that when travellers are on the move by night, and one of them chances to lag behind or to fall asleep or the like, when he tries to gain his company again he will hear spirits talking, and will suppose them to be his comrades. Sometimes the spirits will call him by name; and oftimes shall a traveller be led astray so that he never finds his party. And in this way many have perished. Even in the day-time one hears those spirits talking. And sometimes you shall hear the sound of a variety of musical instruments, and still more commonly the sound of drums.

Although the windows were smeared and dirty, there was something serene about the empty beauty before him. The archeologist in Michael knew that the sand dunes of the desert were moving relentlessly southward, and in the centuries since Marco Polo had traveled here, many desert towns and oases had vanished beneath them, such as the town Polo discussed at some length called Pem.

As the bus route edged the desert, it made far fewer lengthy stops. They crossed great parts of it by night but even then the bus crawled between rest stops, to change drivers, and to repair the continuous series of minor breakdowns. Once three hours passed waiting for a part to be delivered. Michael knew getting on that this was not some high speed express bus that would whisk people from one city to the next but it was much worse than he ever imagined. The ride was bone-shaking and Michael often grabbed the back of the seat before him as they bounced over potholes and rocks where a road should have been. Most of the passengers were Uyghur farmers, their features stern, broad, and much more intense than their Chinese rulers. He tried to speak to a few of them, but the men sat in brooding silence, with booted feet spread wide and sturdy on the rollicking, antique bus. Compared to them, Michael seemed happy-go-lucky.

In the morning, a Uyghur student got up nerve to sit next to him and practice his English. He had a map of the highway they were taking. Michael had his own map and had attempted to follow the road signs, but having his location confirmed was a relief. The sun was low in the sky before he saw that his destination was the next stop. He stood to get off. The student grabbed his arm and shook his head, "No. That is not Khotan."

"It's okay," Michael said. "I want to stop here first."

The boy's eyes grew wide and fretful. "No!" He clutched Michael's arm tighter. "It is not a good place."

A twinge of nervousness shifted through Michael.

He pulled his arm free, jokingly telling himself the student was a secret CITS agent making sure Michael went to Khotan. But the joke wasn't the least bit funny.

The bus driver muttered something at him, but he had no idea what the man said.

No one else got off the bus at this stop, and no one else got on, which was a rarity for an area where the bus only traveled four times a week. No vendors' stands were around the bus stop—another rarity. The area was completely still. He saw and heard no birds, no bees. Not even a fly or a gnat. But as strange as it was, it felt like heaven compared to the bus.

He zipped his jacket shut against the chill in the air. Only one narrow, empty road led away from the main road. A painted wooden sign with Chinese writing stood beside it. Michael pulled the piece of paper Brother Sirom had given him from his pocket. Chinese and Uyghur script filled the page and confirmed that he had reached Baigou. Michael scanned the other words Sirom wrote out that he might need to use—words like "bathroom," "man," "woman," "danger," "hospital," and "crazy foreigner." Quite appropriate.

He started down the lonely path.

A sharp, cold wind blew, and dark clouds massed against the horizon, casting a shadow across the land. The area was treeless, an arid expanse of yellow, rocky soil and stubble. A feeling of dread permeated everything. Michael wondered if Brother Sirom had been wrong to send him here. Or worse, if he had been right.

An hour passed before Michael spotted the first sign of human habitation—four small buildings against the setting sun. They were unlit and so dreary looking he wondered if they'd been abandoned. An unnatural stillness blanketed the area, and he feared finding himself out here alone in the dark of night. He was definitely nervous now and searched all around.

On a hilltop high above the road stood an impressive structure. A solid wall surrounded it, but the roof was visible, its eaves curved upward in the style of a Buddhist temple. Hoping to find a welcoming face, he turned his steps in its direction. A narrow footpath led up the hill.

It must have been much farther than it appeared since, by the time he reached the wall, the sky was dark and a gentle rain fell. A wooden gate, rough, splintered with dryness, and nearly six feet tall, served as the entry. Through its slats, Michael saw a courtyard and a small glow of light coming from the building beyond it. His spirits lifted.

A rope dangled beside the gate, and he pulled. A bell clanged. He pulled two more times in rapid succession, then waited.

No one answered. The latch on the gate was rusted, but unlocked. As the rain increased, he pushed, and the gate swung open with a piercing shriek of the hinges.

"Hello? *Ni hao!*" Michael called in the best Chinese accent he could muster.

No plants, not even weeds, grew in the sterile courtyard. A porch stretched across the width of the one-story wooden building. The building's roofline extended over the porch to provide shelter. Michael ran to the door and knocked hard, calling hello again and again. After no response, he discovered that, just as the gate had been unlocked, so was the door.

The floorboards creaked as he entered. A single light bulb dangled from the ceiling and cast a faint glow. He left the door open but, perhaps caught by the wind, it slammed shut with a bang that made him jump. Something was wrong here, something made him feel as if he had stepped into an ancient spiritual building in which he was alien and unwanted.

On one side of the sparse room stood a low table with two lit candles. Small rugs and floor pillows around it were the room's only furnishings. Nothing hung on the walls, and the corners of the room were gloomy and shadowed. The inside was much smaller than it had appeared from the road, and Michael was surprised to find it was in the shape of a cruciform—a Christian church with a long center nave, a transept on each side, and the sanctuary at the top, forming the shape of a cross.

This had to be the Nestorian monastery Brother Sirom told him about, but finding it so easily once he reached Baigou filled him with disquiet.

A small door stood on one side of the sanctuary, or what would have been a sanctuary were this a church. Michael went back there, but the door was locked. The rain fell harder now, creating a drumbeat on the roof, and he was glad to be indoors, unwelcoming as it was.

He took off his jacket and shook the rain off it, then ran his fingers through his wet hair. He turned all the way around, not sure why he felt so ill at ease; why the ever present feeling of being watched still clung to him.

Brother Sirom had said demons followed him because of the pearl. Perhaps he was right. Could they be why he had found the spot Father Berosus directed him to so easily?

Or was something very different going on here—something that involved a Nestorian monk who found him in the middle of nowhere on a foggy night, spoke English, and gave him food and shelter?

He sat on one of the carpets, propped a pillow against the wall and leaned back to listen to the rain. One of the candles burned down, flickered, and went out. He looked at it and when he turned back, he became aware of a presence in the room.

From the dark sanctuary a figure strode towards him. He wore a brown monk's tunic with a cowl, similar to Brother Sirom's, and carried a tray in his hands.

"Hello," Michael said, standing. He gave his name. The man never raised his head. He was bald, his face wrinkled with age, and his features were Chinese or possibly Mongolian.

"Do you live here?" Michael asked in English and then in fractured Mandarin, wishing he had paid more attention to Jianjun's lessons. "Are you a monk? Nestorian? Is there someone in charge, or anyone who speaks English?"

On the low, candlelit table, the old monk placed a cup of tea and a bowl of soup, and then put a thick rolled-up blanket on the floor. He walked out of the building, exiting by the main door.

"Thank you!" Michael called after him, unsure what to make of this.

He hadn't thought he was hungry until he tasted the soup made with noodles and mutton. Considering the strong odor of the mutton, he must have been famished. The tea was made with salted yak butter in the Uyghur tradition. Not long after he finished the meal, he stretched out on the rug and pillows, and covered himself with the blanket to ward off the cold, dampness of the building. He listened to the falling rain and slowly, finally, began to relax.

He opened his eyes with a start. He must have fallen asleep because someone had shut the one light, blown out the candles and removed the dishes. A faint glow of starlight came through the barely opened shutters, but it wasn't enough to see the hands of his wristwatch. His eyelids felt heavy, but something had awakened him, and the little part of his mind that remained clear told him to protect himself.

The rain had stopped. All was quiet, and he was about to berate himself for foolish nerves when something banged hard against a shutter. From his backpack, Michael took out the knife Brother Sirom had given him and held it close as he lay propped up on one elbow.

Whatever it was struck again, but it was more of a knocking this time, as if someone—something—out there wanted to be let it in.

He would have liked to believe the banging was only the branch of a tree, but no trees stood in this barren desert. His tormentor was most likely nothing but a crow that had lost its way. Yet, the thought penetrated of how very alone he was out here, and how very unnatural all this felt.

He had no sooner convinced himself that all was fine around him, when a furious shriek shattered the night, rattling the shutters and doors. He wondered if the window would hold, if the door was locked. He lay still, listening. If whatever was outside came in, he had little with which to protect himself.

He was afraid—he'd be a liar not to admit it. And with that fear, he also admitted that something was in the church with him.

CHAPTER 40

JIANJUN, Kira and Renata found themselves crossing the Torugart Pass into China with Hank Bennett, Stuart Eliot and their bodyguards. Jianjun was curious about the strings Hank Bennett must have pulled to have been allowed to bring rifles into the country. That was all but unheard of. He asked, but Bennett refused to say.

Renata spoke to the guards in the Uyghur language about Michael. They remembered the man she described and told her he had entered China the prior morning traveling with a group of Buddhist monks on the way to Kashgar.

Renata bubbled with joy as she told Jianjun and Kira, who met the news with both relief and not a little wonder. Jianjun had called Charlotte Reed on the satellite phone the night before and again that morning to ask if she had heard from Michael. She had not and promised to phone him if she did.

They reached Kashgar in late morning. It was both larger and more modern than any of them expected, but with areas more ancient looking than expected as well. The streets were packed with people, but few were European. To find Michael in this crush of humanity seemed hopeless.

Jianjun found an Internet café and connected with his phone. He tapped into a program on his home computer and was using it to scan for Michael's cell phone's location when Chinese police came up to him and shut him down. It seemed foreigners weren't allowed to use the Internet without signing up at the police station and giving lots of personal information. Jianjun told them he was only looking up information about hotels and hurried away.

"So much for technology," he said, when he rejoined the others.

"It would have been difficult for Michael to rent a car without the government's involvement as well," Renata said. "It was always that way to a degree in China, but here, after Uyghur riots against the government, things have really cracked down. We should ask about Michael at a CITS office. They keep watch over all foreigners. And we need to check in with them as well."

At the second CITS office they tried, they found an officious agent who definitely remembered Michael. He spoke down to the foreigners, all but sneering at them, until Jianjun spoke to him in Chinese, using better Mandarin than he did. Also, since Jianjun had been born in Beijing, he had the same accent as top government officials. Jianjun found the accent was useful in getting people in China to take him seriously—at least, those who weren't the police.

The agent told them Michael had bought a bus ticket to Khotan, but if he was there, he had not checked in as he had been ordered to do. The agent was most unhappy.

The group got into their vehicles and drove to Khotan. They arrived at night, and Renata went straight to the CITS office to see if Michael had arrived. She learned the agency was searching for him, no one knew where he was, and everyone was furious about it.

"How can that be?" Hank asked Renata. "Surely, people on the bus noticed him."

"Of course they did. But they're Uyghurs, and not about to help Chinese bureaucrats. They simply say they weren't on the bus he was on, or that they saw him, but they got off before he ever did, or whatever. We're going to have to find someone who will talk to us."

Khotan was a much smaller desert town than Kashgar, but old and new also existed here, side-by-side. A few dramatically modern buildings stood near the town's Union Square, and in the area were night clubs, restaurants, coffee bars, and even supermarkets. But away from that area, the old reigned, with crowded, bustling markets and bazaars. As they walked by a market place, they passed a group of performers and stopped to listen, with Renata offering explanations of the music. A man played a *surnay*, an oboe-like wind instrument with a haunting sound; a woman strummed a *dutar*, a Uyghur lute with a long neck and two strings; while another woman dancing to their music. All were dressed in colorful traditional outfits. The dancer's dress was purple and white with elaborate embroidery, high necked, and fitted to the hips which were covered with an elaborate girdle crocheted with gold thread. Below it, the skirt flared out, and hung down to the ankles. On her head was a round hat with a flat top. Sparkling jewels dangled from the front crown of the hat, reaching to the eyebrows and along the sides of the face, essentially framing the woman's large, dark eyes. At the back of the hat, a long scarf reached her waist. As the woman danced, she performed a number of spins, causing the scarf as well as her skirt to flare out and swirl around her. She was beautiful and graceful, as was the woman who played the lute. Her dress was similar, but its main color was red rather than purple. The man's jacket was black with intricate silver embroidery along the front of it. His brimless hat was silver with a black pattern woven in.

The music stopped, and the performers began to walk among the small crowd who had watched them, carrying pails into which people dropped coins. The dancer approached Jianjun and the others, and held out her pail as she asked in English, "Are you American?"

"Most of them are," Jianjun said, looking at her in surprise. He put some coins in the pail, as did Renata and Kira. "Why ask that?"

"CITS is in a tizzy because some American didn't report in to them. We don't get many tourists here anymore, but here you are. I guessed it's all connected."

The two musicians joined the dancer. Renata asked, "So, do you know where the American is?"

"Why?" the man asked.

"He's our friend," Renata said.

The Uyghurs huddled together, whispering. Then, the man approached. "My sisters and I can show you for a small fee."

"How small?" she asked.

They negotiated a bit because the first amount the brother suggested was hardly small. But Renata knew that if the troupe was telling the truth, they would be able to catch up to Michael a lot faster than otherwise.

"Before we pay you anything, how do we know you're telling the truth?" Jianjun asked.

The brother, whose name was Az'har, explained that they had traveled from Kashgar to Khotan, and outside of Khotan they heard about a Westerner who got off the bus in a strange area. He was warned not to get off there, but he didn't listen—or didn't understand.

Az'har's sisters, Dilnar and Paziliya, nodded in agreement. "We heard he is very handsome," Dilnar said. "So we are most interested in meeting him as well." She and Paziliya laughed, while Az'har scowled at them.

"It is a chore having sisters such as these," he said, with a shake of his head.

Renata and Kira met each other's gaze and realized they were having similar thoughts about Az'har. He was remarkably handsome.

Hank and Stuart had approached when they saw that some negotiations were going on. Jianjun filled them in, and the group agreed to give the performers a chance.

"One more thing," Az'har added. "We should stop at an inn for the night, and could use help paying for our rooms. My sisters and I have worked all day, and there are no accommodations in the village we are going to. Plus, we do not wish to arrive there in the middle of the night."

"You aren't the only ones who are tired and in need of a warm bed and a shower," Renata assured them.

"How do you know such good English?" Hank demanded.

Az'har smiled. "We learned it because it's the best way to make a lot of money. Just like we're doing now."

The performers threw their instruments and knapsacks in the back of the van that Jianjun drove, and squeezed in with him, Kira and Renata since five large men filled Hank and Stuart's SUV. As Jianjun drove off in search of an inn, the Uyghurs directed them to the "foreigners" section, since that was the only area in which they'd be allowed to stay.

Near Union Square, they found a hotel, several boarding houses, and inns, all within a few streets of each other. Since no one establishment had enough rooms available for all of them, they spread out and agreed to meet at nine o'clock the next morning, giving them time for a good breakfast.

Jianjun glanced at Kira, and the two went together to find a place to spend the night. They found an inn that was quite nice, and expensive, but it offered suites with soft, thick towels, and even bathrobes. After their last few nights, it sounded heavenly. Kira asked for two rooms. Jianjun felt disappointment, but he hadn't really expected otherwise.

At most, it had been a dim hope.

He had showered and gotten into bed wearing his sweats when he heard a light tap on the door.

It was Kira. "Do you mind?"

She had a bottle of wine in her hand. He opened the door wide. "Of course not."

"I need to unwind." Her voice was overly cheery as she entered. "The owner offered this at a ridiculous price, but tonight, I don't care."

"I, um ..."

"Don't you like wine?"

"I do. It tends to make my cheeks red, though."

She chuckled, seeming relieved. "No problem." She carried two glasses with the wine, put them on the dresser and poured.

Her long red hair was still damp from her shower and hung free. She looked shiny and clean in the fluffy robe and wore socks to keep her feet warm. As he neared her to take the wine she offered, he could smell soap and talc and he didn't know what else, but the combination was intoxicating.

He took the glass and sat on the end of his bed. She sat on the lone chair in the room, next to the bureau.

"Tell me about yourself." She sounded a little nervous. "Have you been married long?"

He was surprised that she should ask such a thing, especially as her first question … and especially in his room. His own nerves strummed, and he gulped some wine. "Five years."

"First marriage?"

"Yes. Were you ever married?"

"One year together, one separated, and then we divorced. It was a few years ago. I haven't been serious about anyone since," she said, then blurted, "I want you to know, I don't make a habit of taking wine to men's rooms."

Ah, the cause of her uneasiness. "I can tell. And I'm glad you're here."

She nodded and took a sip of wine.

"What happened between the two of you?" Jianjun asked softly.

She shrugged. "Lots of little things. A death of a thousand blows. I think we both knew something was wrong right from the start. He didn't understand me and seemed to think I was someone I'm not. And he said I thought the same about him. He's now happily married and even has a daughter. But I had found life with him boring and wanted excitement." She shook her head at that. "Guess I didn't know when I was well off."

"You're a criminal profiler for the FBI and you were bored?"

"The job is fine—or *was* fine. Not sure if I'll get it back. It was my home life I had trouble with."

He nodded, then took another big swallow of wine before admitting, "I know the feeling."

"Yes, I could tell. When I was at your house …" She hesitated. "Is it always that way between you and your wife, or had the two of you just had a fight?"

He gave a half-smile. "We never fight. To fight usually means there's something that you care about in the other person, something that rankles and you wish you could change. I mean, she's a good person. If she was a friend, I probably wouldn't mind going to dinner with her—maybe once a year, even. So I feel bad for her, that she's stuck with me. Some days, I even feel guilty."

"You really are much too nice," she said.

Her words surprised him. "I'm not!"

"Well, all I know is, it's not good for you to live that way. And how happy can she be, knowing her husband doesn't love her?"

"She doesn't know," he said.

"Believe me, she knows."

He finished his wine at that, knowing he had drunk it much too fast. He poured himself a bit more, then sat down again. "Sometimes I think the only reason we're still together is my job with Michael. If I couldn't get away from home, often for months at a time, I don't know what I'd be doing right now."

"You and Michael seem to genuinely like each other," she said.

"He doesn't know it, but he's my best friend."

"And you're his."

"Maybe. I worry about him."

"With good reason from what I've seen. He's lucky to have a good man like you on his side."

He had to ask. "You always say I'm a good man. You don't really know that. Or me, for that matter."

"Don't I? It's my job to know things like that, remember? I see too many men and women who aren't. It makes me enjoy being with you." She stared at the floor a moment, but then looked up at him with blue eyes that were like an arrow to his heart. "No pretense; no trying to show anyone I'm as smart or successful or brave as my father or anyone else." She ran her finger over the rim of her wine glass. "I'll never forget you for that reason, if nothing else."

"Forget me? I'm not going anywhere."

"Yes, you are. You will."

He was puzzled by her words, but then noticed that she had finished her wine. He got up, took the glass from her and refilled it.

She stood, but didn't reach for the glass. Instead, she looked at his face, as he did hers.

And he could see her longing.

He placed her glass atop the dresser. "Kira," he murmured.

She swayed towards him, her hands against his chest. He slid a hand into her hair. It felt damp and cool against his warm fingers. Their eyes met as he drew her closer and then couldn't stop himself from clutching her tight as their lips met.

She drew back a moment, and lightly ran a hand over his cheek, his ear, his hair, then murmured, "I don't want to be alone tonight."

"Stay with me," he whispered.

She nodded, and then untied the sash of her robe, letting it fall open. Besides the robe, all she wore were thick, dopey looking socks. As he took her in his arms, he was sure he had never seen a woman look more beautiful.

CHAPTER 41

MICHAEL QUIETLY WATCHED a procession of six Nestorian monks enter the church. Four carried candles, and the last two swung censers that filled the church with incense. At the area where the altar should have stood, they knelt side-by-side and softly chanted. None of them paid any attention to him.

They moved like robots or replicants—too perfect, too stylized. In fact, everything seemed to be a dream, yet he was sure he was awake. Awake, but having a vision, much like earlier with Irina.

Yet, with this vision, the eerie spookiness of the church vanished. It felt warmer now, comfortably so, and the monks' candles cast a pleasant glow. Even the scent of incense comforted him.

The strong sense struck that this was where he needed to be. No matter how cold and eerie the monastery had felt earlier, the monks gave him a clear message: they wanted him here. They accepted him.

And perhaps they—with Brother Sirom's help—had led him here.

He lay his head down and listened with his heart as well as his ears as the chant softly echoed through the church.

The shutters lay open and daylight streamed through the windows when Michael awoke. He sat up quickly.

A cup of salted tea and a steaming bowl of soup were on the low table. He rubbed his face and eyes, and couldn't help but wonder if the sights and sounds the night before had been real or a dream.

The tea cup felt hot. He drank some, and then went outdoors where he found a basin of warm water, a razor, soap, and a towel on the porch. He washed up and shaved. It felt good to get the scruff off his face.

The courtyard held an outhouse in a far corner, but little else. He found a door in the back of the main building, but it and nearby shutters had been nailed shut.

He saw no sign of the monks, or any housing for them.

Back inside, his soup had cooled enough to eat. Mutton soup was hardly his idea of a tasty breakfast, but Uyghurs didn't consider a meal edible unless it had meat or fish as part of it, and sheep and goat were the most prevalent meats in the area.

After eating, he left the monastery. The rain had stopped and now, in daylight, he headed for the town of Baigou. He hiked down the hill to the tiny huts he had seen coming in. Weeds grew up around them and everything had been boarded shut. He was glad he hadn't wasted time going there the night before.

Continuing along the road, he reached the town market. It was small, dusty, and crowded with people and stalls containing a variety of vegetables, fruit, clothes, herbs and medicines. Michael's entry caused a stir. Uyghur women with lush beauty, captivating dark eyes, and wearing long dresses with colorful scarves, smiled at him. He remembered Marco Polo's tale of the women of Kamel who took providing comfort to travelers to a whole new level. If they looked anything like these women, Marco Polo had been a lucky man indeed.

Older men wearing traditional fur Uyghur hats, often with a rolled brim, pulled so low over their ears that the tops of the ears bent downward, scowled in his direction. A lifetime of bending the ear cartilage permanently stretched the tops of their ears so that even after the hat was removed, their ears angled outward. Younger men preferred the brimless, four-cornered *doppa*, a Uyghur version of a Muslim skull cap.

As Michael walked through the bustling area, one of those older men grabbed his arm. The stranger smiled, showing teeth blackened by heavy cigarette smoke. He appeared to be in his seventies, which in this rugged, harsh land, probably meant he was a lot younger. He wore a long, heavy black coat, brown trousers tucked into black boots, and a black fur hat. He spoke to Michael.

Michael pulled his arm free, and said in Mandarin, "I don't understand."

"You American?" the fellow asked, also in Mandarin.

"Yes."

"I speak English." He had a thick accent and gave Michael a jovial whack on the back. For a while, English and Russian had been taught in schools along with Mandarin to help people learn to deal with the outside world. The man's name was Hajji, and he asked what Michael was doing in Baigou.

"I'm traveling the Old Silk Road." It was one of the few reasons foreigners went to that remote part of the world. The local people, as well as the Chinese government, understood and accepted it.

"Ah, you Marco Polo!" Hajji shouted, then said something, rapid fire, to the men who had gathered around them.

Little did Hajji know how close he came to the truth.

Michael asked about the building on the hill, and learned that it had been built by Christians many, many centuries earlier, and then Buddhists took it over. When Muslim Uyghurs drove the Buddhists away, it fell to ruin. Michael asked about the monks who used the church.

Hajji looked at him strangely, and said no one used it for centuries, and no Christian monks were anywhere near. Hajji's English wasn't good, and Michael's Mandarin was even worse, but no matter how many ways he asked the question, he was told the monastery was an abandoned ruin with rotting, crumbling wood. When Michael mentioned an electric light that must have run off a generator, Hajji frowned and shook his head.

"If you saw anyone or any lights on that hill, it must be a ghost or a demon," Hajji warned. "You must not go there. Come to my house. Down that street, last house." He pointed to a street and told Michael he was welcome to sleep there that night.

Michael thanked him for his generous offer and didn't tell Hajji he had already spent one night at the place. Instead, he said he would explore the area, and might show up later at Hajji's home.

"Tell me," he said. "Are there any other monasteries or old churches or temples nearby?"

Hajji thought a moment. "Nothing. That is the only one."

Michael again thanked him, then went off to buy a meat pie, a slab of goat cheese, and pistachios at the market for his supper. He appreciated the old monk bringing him food, but preferred to pass on the greasy mutton soup.

Somewhat reluctantly, he decided to head back to the monastery. Although he believed it was the place Brother Sirom talked about, he wasn't sure he ought to leave the red pearl there. It felt wrong. To be honest, he didn't like the idea of leaving the red pearl anywhere. How could he be sure it wouldn't fall into the wrong hands? At the same time, thoughts of the power of a philosopher's stone filled him. Thoughts of magical, wondrous power that could be his.

A familiar van followed by a black SUV turned off the road and came to a stop near the market. Michael was astonished to see it, and hurried towards it as his friends got out of the van, along with three classically dressed Uyghurs. Even more surprising, he recognized Hank Bennett and Stuart Eliot when they stepped out of the SUV, along with three muscular strangers. But a dark aura circled Hank and Stuart. It startled him, and he stopped and stared.

Jianjun reached him, put his arms around his boss, but as soon as Michael tried to hug him back, he gave Michael a forceful shove. "What the hell were you thinking? You scared us to death. We didn't know what happened to you."

"I texted you and Charlotte. Didn't you look at the sat phone?" Michael said.

"I never got any texts. Neither did Charlotte. And since the government runs the whole damn internet, I couldn't even use it to track your phone or your messages."

"Maybe you need to hack them next time. But I ran into similar problems just trying to make a phone call."

"Hello, Michael," Kira said, smiling broadly. She gave him a quick hug before Renata threw herself into his arms.

"I'm so glad you're safe," Renata cried. "I was so worried."

"I'm shocked all of you are here. So, how did you find me?"

"You're notorious, how else?" Jianjun admitted. He then introduced Michael to Hank Bennett, Stuart Eliot, their bodyguards, and the three Uyghurs.

"Doctor Michael Rempart, Ph.D. Oxford, I understand," Hank said, extending his hand—a not-so-subtle way to let Michael know he had done his homework.

Jianjun had just begun telling Michael how Hank and Stuart had saved him and the women from bandits when shouts stopped him.

"*Yaojing! Yaojing!*" An elderly vendor of meat pies toddled towards them on thin, rickety legs, pointing and shrieking at the top of his lungs.

Michael wondered what was going on. The others in the market place also stopped everything, their gazes jumping from the old man to the white strangers in their midst. As one, they began to move towards the foreigners.

The old man continued to shout. "What are you saying, old fool?" Jianjun asked, running towards him to stop his cries.

The vendor suddenly gripped his chest and then fell to the ground, his eyes open but unseeing.

Jianjun loosened the vendor's collar as he cried out in Mandarin to get a doctor, that the old man may have had a heart attack, but none of them moved.

"You understood?" Michael asked, kneeling by Jianjun's side.

"*Yaojing* is Chinese, not Uyghur." Jianjun tried CPR on the man's heart, but the vendor made no response.

Renata spoke to the crowd in Uyghur, pleading for a doctor. Still, no one did anything to help the vendor, hopeless though such help might have been. Instead they glared at the foreigners, repeating the vendor's cry of "*Yaojing.*"

Jianjun stood and backed away. "Let's get out of here fast," he said to Michael. "This could get ugly."

"What was the old man saying?" Michael asked.

"Demon. He was yelling the word for demon."

Before they could warn the others, they were hit by a hail of rocks. The villagers ran at them, shouting and pelting them with rocks and anything else they could grab hold of.

Polk and Taft pulled out pistols and pointed them at the villagers, but Michael and Jianjun waved their arms to stop them. "You can't shoot them all," Michael said, "and the survivors will tear you—maybe all of us—limb from limb if you kill anyone."

"Come on!" Hank ordered. They climbed into their vehicles.

Kira told Michael to sit in the bucket seat up front with Jianjun, that she'd squeeze in back with Renata and the Uyghurs. Dilnar, however, didn't get in. "Hurry!" her brother shouted.

"No time to crawl back there," she said, then got in front with Michael, sitting on his lap. "Okay?" she asked.

She was petite and beautiful. "Okay," he said, and shut the door.

Jianjun peeled out of the square behind Hank's SUV.

Bullets pinged against the van as Jianjun drove. "Damn," Michael said. "Duck down. They're shooting." He found himself even closer to Dilnar after ducking, their arms intertwined. Given Uyghur customs, he could end up engaged by the time this ride ended.

Jianjun raced towards the main road. "I'll direct you to the monastery I found," Michael said. "I'm pretty sure it's the one we've been looking for. The villagers think it's haunted. We'll be safe there."

"Haunted? I don't like the sound of that, boss," Jianjun said as he waved to Hank, signaling the other driver to let him get ahead and then to follow him. "But right now, it's better than sticking around these people."

"There it is." Michael pointed to the monastery atop the hill. All were sitting upright again, and Dilnar's arm remained casually flung around his shoulders. He gave up trying not to touch her as she slipped and slid over the bumpy road and put his arms around her waist to steady hear. It earned a smile from her that would have curled his toes had he not been suspicious of exactly who she and her siblings were, and why they were here—particularly after her provocative nearness.

"That?" Jianjun asked. "It looks like a crumbled ruin. How can you even tell what it is?"

Michael glanced at him in surprise. "What do you mean? It's not that bad. You'll see."

"We've heard of this place," Az'har said. "But we've never been inside. The wall around seems very high. Was it difficult to get in?"

"The gate was unlocked," Michael said. "So was the door to what had once been a Christian church."

"A Christian church?" Dilnar asked. "I have never been in such a thing. I shall be happy to see it."

From the backseat, Renata cleared her throat. Loudly.

Hank followed as Jianjun drove onto the footpath to the structure, the leftmost wheels on the path while the rightmost rode over rough land. "Damn, it really is a wall," Jianjun said. "It sure didn't look like there was anything here when we were out on the road."

"I thought the same thing," Renata said. "But now, I see it's remarkably well preserved. What an incredible find."

They parked outside the wall since the wooden gate wasn't wide enough for them to drive through. Although the market in Baigou had been sunny, dark rain clouds now filled the sky, and a strong wind caused all of them to pull their coats and jackets closer.

"I wouldn't worry about anyone coming by to steal the cars," Michael said. "People think the monastery is abandoned, but a monk brought me food last night and again this morning."

"A monk?" Jianjun asked, while Dilnar's brother grabbed her arm and pulled her away from the others, speaking in low, gruff tones. Paziliya smiled and shrugged.

"The monk was dressed similarly to the Nestorian who told me about this place."

"Are you saying you found a Nestorian here? That's impossible." Renata looked at him as if he was quite mad.

Hank, Stuart and the body guards joined them.

"What the hell is this place?" Hank asked, hands in his pockets from the cold as he walked closer to eye the building.

Michael replied. "I spent the night at a Nestorian monastery in Kyrgyzstan, and a monk directed me here."

Hank and Stuart glanced at each other and Renata's eyes narrowed.

Michael pulled on a rope to ring the bell by the front gate. "The person who fed me may come to the gate," he explained. But no one did, so he gave it a push. The gate squealed open.

Everyone was quiet as they crossed the courtyard. Michael led them inside the building. The temperature was cold, much colder than it was outside.

Kira rubbed her arms and voiced what the others thought. "This place is creepy."

Michael remembered the church's warmth the night before although it had no heat source and no fireplace. Now, it felt dark and dank. It was dry and not drafty, but the loneliness of the place and its unnatural silence wormed its way into their bones. Their voices sounded unreal and forced, causing them to whisper.

When the rain began, the group lit candles. Michael and Jianjun went outside to bring in extra blankets and coats from the cars. When they alone, Michael questioned him about the Hank, Stuart, and the Uyghurs. His experience with Irina had left him wary of anyone suddenly latching on to their group.

Jianjun explained, but as they reentered the church, Michael remained guarded.

"Have you looked in there?" Dilnar asked Michael, pointing at the door to the sacristy.

"It's locked tight," Michael said. "It'll need to be pried open."

"I've heard that at the time of the Great Cultural Revolution, groups of students were assigned to buildings like this and took everything of value," Renata said. "What they left behind, they planned to destroy as 'objects of mindless idolatry.'"

Michael nodded. "The destruction done during that time was terrible."

"I've read that in this area," her voice echoed, "the Red Guard students were struck down by some mysterious meningitis-like illness and died. Doctors assumed they had stirred up some long dormant strain of virus or bacteria, perhaps from rat and bird droppings."

"It sounds as if we had better be careful moving things around," Kira said.

"Exactly," Renata agreed. "As if we didn't have enough to worry about. This whole adventure is getting more absurd by the minute. Doesn't anyone see that but me?"

"Maybe those kids were struck down by something altogether different," Hank said with a nod at Stuart, who nodded back at him.

"Okay, ignore me," Renata said. "Don't blame me if you all get sick." She moved away from the others, her arms folded.

Michael sensed another presence with them. He turned in a full circle, but saw nothing. Yet something in the church felt alien. More existed here than what he could see. All sense of the peaceful, chanting monks vanished, and he wondered if what he saw last night had been a dream or a vision, perhaps caused by the demons Hajji, the villager, had described.

With that, the realization struck the way he saw this place was not what the people of the village saw. And Jianjun and Renata's initial reactions had matched Hajji's. At first, they seemed to see only a ruin —but no longer. Were the demons causing that as well?

The dark auras he saw around Hank and Stuart were thicker now, and more unnerving.

"We should keep watch," Michael said, then quickly added, "in case a villager comes up here."

"That's why Stuart and I hired bodyguards," Hank said, then faced the three. "Can you guys handle it?"

Carter, Polk, and Taft nodded. Carter went out to take the first shift.

"We can explore outside once the rain stops," Hank said. "In here, there's nothing."

They sat around the low table. Michael faced Hank and Stuart. No one else seemed as troubled by them as he was. He wondered if the black aura he saw meant death—surely, they were under the same threat as the other sailors in the photo, and they were the only two still alive. They were very likely on borrowed time.

"Why don't you two tell us why you've followed us here," Michael said. "And why you're both still alive."

Hank tried to laugh off Michael's harsh tone. It didn't work. "I figured you'd want to know sooner rather than later. It's a long story, one we spent the last ten years piecing together, trying to make sense of it. Yet, it's still confusing and for many of you, ultimately unbelievable."

Michael leaned back against the wall, his arms folded. "Try us."

Hank nodded and then told his story.

CHAPTER 42

Egypt, Mid-twentieth century

Shortly before the Second World War came to an end, a four-star "Generaloberst" in Hitler's Nazi army abandoned his position and escaped to Egypt, carrying with him some Nazi gold and other riches, including a red pearl that had belonged to Der Führer. The general changed his name and lived in a small town. The only person close to him was his Egyptian servant, a scrawny man with no spouse or children.

As the general's death neared, in 1970, he told the servant he could keep all of his remaining possessions except one. The General said he had done terrible things during the war and had lived these last years in an attempt to correct some of that. But his last act was one the servant had to see was carried out. The general had had a special coffin made for himself, and he told the servant to be sure that his small Chinese bronze and the red pearl inside it be buried with him in the desert.

The Egyptian promised to do as asked, but before burying it, he opened the bronze. When he looked at the red pearl, longing and desire came over him. He felt connected to the pearl, and that it connected with him. He had never experienced anything like it before, and to bury it seemed sacrilegious. The Egyptian had spent his life following his boss's wishes, but this time, he could not.

He soon discovered that when he held the pearl near the eyes of a stranger, the pearl would somehow fill the Egyptian with knowledge of the stranger's future. The pearl never lied; whatever it predicted, happened. The servant became so good at foretelling the future, he came to be considered a holy man, a fakir.

The fakir found that he could make especially large sums of money in Cairo by telling the future to tourists.

Some seven years later, during a time of recession in the United States, many men signed up for military service. One of those men, Hank Bennett, grew tired of working for pennies at a gas station, and thought he might be able to do more with his life than add oil or change fan belts. He was a tall, gangly man, with an overly long face and teeth that seemed too big for his mouth. Handsome wasn't in his vocabulary.

Bennett kept his nose clean, his head down, and quickly rose to seaman third class on the U.S.S. Saratoga. The ship saw plenty of action, all unreported back home, but Bennett liked the order and discipline of Navy life and considered making it a career. When he was given a few days of shore leave in Cairo, Bennett was more than ready.

He was perusing wares in a souk one afternoon with some guys from the ship when a little old man in a turban and white flowing robes ran up to them. "My good men," he said, opening his arms wide. "I would like to show you the wonders of this city. The pyramids, the desert, and many fine places. Secret places. My fee is very, very small. I know what sailors like."

"You do? I doubt that, little man," Hank said. He and the others laughed, but something about the fakir intrigued them, particularly when he mentioned secret places.

"Come with me if you aren't afraid," he said with a sly smile. "And, if you are brave enough, I will also tell you about your future, and what you can do to have the best life you can imagine."

"Brave? You don't know the meaning of the word." Hank laughed, ready to walk away, but then seeing the gleam of curiosity in the other men's eyes. Finally, six decided to go with the fakir, while the others headed off to see the sights on their own. Hank looked from one group to the other. He noticed space left on the jitney the little fakir drove, and at the last minute jumped on.

They rode to the Great Pyramid where the fakir took a photo with his Polaroid camera for each of them as a memento of the day. He told them to be sure to keep the photos and that one day they would enjoy looking back and remembering. "Now," he said, "you must think of your talents, and the kind of life you would like to lead using those abilities."

"What if you ain't got any?" Jonny Vogel said, an arm around Kevin Wilson's neck. "Or if you ain't as pretty as Wilson, here?" Then he rubbed his knuckles in Wilson's hair, giving a noogie.

"In that case, you must leave your mind blank, and the pearl will fill it in for you." He opened a Chinese-style container. It had dirt in it, which he moved aside to reveal what he called a red pearl. None of them had ever seen a red pearl before, and doubted that was what it was, but it hardly mattered. They were amused and having fun. "Who will go first?" the Egyptian asked.

Hank Bennett volunteered. Some of the guys were only eighteen, and Hank at twenty-four was the oldest. The fakir held the pearl against his forehead. "Ah! It is very clear. If you believe, and follow the way of the pearl, you will become a very important man in computer security—one of the most important men in your country."

"Computer security?" Hank looked at the others. "Man, I'm not even sure what a computer looks like, except that they're huge mothers that fill big, cold rooms. Guess this means I'll be a security guard. No, thanks!" He chuckled. "I'll stick to the Navy."

"He just doesn't want to give up his uniform," Dan Holt said.

"As a guard, he'll still get to wear one—a rent-a-cop uniform," Wilson added, rubbing his head where it hurt.

"Hey, man, don't you know nothin'? The gals like Navy whites. Why else did we join, right, Stu?" Gene Oliveros slapped Stu Eliot on the back. Gene was nineteen, handsome, and wild. For him, it was join the Navy or see the inside of San Quentin.

Stuart blushed and nodded. He became the brunt of jokes when the others realized he was a twenty-year-old virgin.

One-by-one, each man let the fakir tell them what the future held. Some were surprises, such as Gene becoming a movie director. He loved that idea. Others weren't a surprise at all, such as Kevin Wilson becoming a senator. He was already considered a class-A brown-noser.

The fakir then offered to take them to see something very special. It was still afternoon. Assured they'd be back in Cairo before the night life started up, they went along. The fakir drove them far out into the desert to see an open pharaoh's tomb. Everything in it had been removed or stolen years earlier, so it wasn't interesting. "Time for Cairo!" Scott Jones shouted to cheers. Enough sight-seeing; other amusements beckoned.

"I take you back," the fakir said, "for twenty dollars each."

"Twenty bucks! You're crazy!" Hank yelled. "We had an agreement!"

"Five dollars to take you to see the sights," the fakir said. "I never told you what it would cost to bring you back."

"You piece of shit. You take us back if you want to keep your teeth." Vogel grew up on the streets with no father and a mother who paid no attention to him. The others agreed with Vogel: the fakir either brought them back or paid the consequences.

The fakir held out the pearl, and to everyone's surprise, it began to glow. "You are in its power," he said. "Pay what I ask, and I will turn its attention elsewhere, sparing you. If you insist on being cheap and arrogant, you will turn into foxes."

"Foxes? That's bat-shit crazy." Oliveros laughed.

"Let's leave him and drive ourselves back," Jones said.

Furious, the sailors tried to grab him and take the jitney's keys. They swung their arms, stamped their feet, but as much as they tried, the young, strong Navy men couldn't touch one short, scrawny little running and darting fakir.

"You are young and foolish." The fakir all but danced with glee at the sailors' growing frustration. "You have taken the first test—to see if you are good or evil. Evil will enter your short, sweet lives, and then you are forever damned."

"Damn you!" They shouted, but couldn't stop the fakir from jumping into his jitney and driving off.

In the middle of nowhere, without another vehicle or person in sight, the sailors trudged in the direction they assumed would lead to Cairo, following the jitney's tracks. It was one thing to ride around in the desert, quite another to try to walk in the heat. They had no supplies, not even water.

Eventually, the jitney's tracks vanished. Despite hours of walking, they found no road. Hot, tired, and desperate, the first sign of life they saw was a single black fox. Its color stood out against the pale sand of the desert. It sat and looked at them.

"What the hell?" Hank said. From the gawking stares of the others, he knew they, like him, remembered the fakir telling them they would become a fox.

"If it's able to live out here," Stuart's voice quavered, "it must know where there's water. We should follow it."

"Follow a fox?" Jones said. "You're crazy as that fucking towelhead."

The fox ran, but then stopped and faced them again as if it expected them to follow. They did.

Not much later, Stuart collapsed. The others coaxed him to his feet, but he was delirious. The second time he collapsed, his mouth was so dry and blistered, he could scarcely speak, but he told the others to go on.

"We'll find help and come back for you," Oliveros promised.

Stuart only managed to nod.

A half hour later, the sailors stopped and stared. Instead of one fox, they saw about ten huddled together eating some small desert animals. From time to time, a fox stopped and looked at them, blood dripping from its mouth. Instead of it looking disgusting, it looked wet—drinkable. The sailors moved closer.

As they did, the foxes left their food and trotted towards them. None had ever seen a fox act that way and wondered if this was some mass hallucination. The sailors backed up, and then, as one, they turned and ran back towards Stuart.

Four foxes stood over him, and they wondered if he had become a meal. They stopped but somehow, what they thought were four foxes, were four women, giving Stuart water to drink, and putting cool water on his brow. When they looked over their shoulders, the foxes chasing them had vanished.

The women offered them pitchers of lemon water. After drinking their fill, the women led them to an enormous tent. Inside the air felt cool, music played, men and women milled about, and tables were filled with a veritable banquet of familiar and exotic foodstuffs, plus wine, beer, and whiskey. All the women were beyond beautiful with the biggest, greenest eyes imaginable, and blonde, red, black, or brown hair that reached down to tiny waists. Handsome men were there as well, some with the physique of a body builder and others delicate and almost effeminate. As the sailors filled their stomachs and drank, the women, and even men, began giving comfort in other ways. The more they drank, and ate, and loved, the more abandoned they became. The men and women of the desert were uninhibited and insatiable. The sailors went from sated to exhausted, but kept crawling back for more. They tried everything and everyone, including each other. It was much more than any had ever experienced, or even imagined.

One-by-one, the desert creatures asked if the sailors would want to spend eternity living that way. They offered the sailors a life of everything they ever dreamed of, and then one day, during the second "Year of the Rat" from that moment, the desert creatures would come for them. One-by-one being held and caressed by the person each found the most attractive, the sailors agreed, none of them even understanding the Year of the Rat reference. When the last person, Stuart Eliot, said "yes" to the offer, the creatures vanished.

The sailors suddenly found themselves in Cairo, back in the same market place in which they had met the fakir. They looked at each other, and were filled with memories of the orgy—all except Stuart, who seemed confused and dehydrated. They said nothing, but hurried back to the ship, each acting as if they scarcely knew the others.

On board, they learned they were five days late returning, and that search parties had been sent out after them. When asked where they had been, none could—or would—answer. They pretended not to remember, except for Stuart Eliot, who truly did not remember.

The officers decided the men must have been drugged and put them in the brig. During that time, the ship was attacked. They heard the battle, felt the blasts as bombs struck, heard the cries as their fellow sailors fought and were killed and wounded, while they sat locked up, safe, but unable to do their jobs, unable to help. They later learned that all seven men who were assigned to cover their duties had been killed in the attack.

The remaining months and years of their tours of duty were nightmares. Not one of them spoke to the others of what had happened in the desert.

The little fakir, in the meantime, grew increasingly wealthy and demanding in his treatment of people around him. People in Cairo began to whisper about him conspiring with demons, and he escaped in the night just ahead of a mob that wanted to kill him. He went from one town to another and eventually reached Baghdad. There, he began his program again in its Chaldean community. He would tell them about a group of young American sailors and how they all became very wealthy following his advice. He would then show the picture he took of the sailors in Egypt, and then show news reports about them.

Several people complained to their priest, Father Yosip Berosus, about family members who went to the fakir. They told Berosus about the strange red pearl and said they feared something demonic was involved. Berosus was a quiet, holy man, and was greatly troubled by these stories.

He read widely, and talk of a red pearl niggled in his brain. He researched it, and eventually learned of stories of an evil red pearl stolen by Marco Polo, and that men throughout European history were often connected to the pearl, including Adolph Hitler. When evidence of demonic possession began to appear among his parishioners, he knew he had to get the pearl away from the fakir by whatever means necessary.

He went to visit the Egyptian under pretense of wanting to have his future told. As soon as the fakir brought out the bronze, Berosus attacked him. The fakir would not give up the bronze, and when a blow from the priest caused him to hit his head on his stone hearth, the fakir died. Berosus was horrified by what he had done. He took the bronze, the pearl, and the photo of the American sailors it had made wealthy, and fled Baghdad.

He devoted his life to prayer, to penance for the death he had caused, and to learning how to stop the evil of the pearl.

The demons inside the pearl constantly attacked him. At times they mocked him and said he was wasting his life as a priest, and then attempted to seduce him with visions of pleasures of the flesh if he would simply release the pearl from the container. At other times, they said he was an evil murderer who would spend eternity in Hell for killing the fakir and that the only way to avoid damnation was to give the pearl to someone who would use it 'properly'—as the demons wished it to be used—in other words, to do evil. The more they attacked, the more steadfast he became. They posed a danger not only to his soul, but to anyone he came into contact with. They attacked his fellow priests and bishops, causing several to go astray. Berosus went into hiding, spending his days in prayer to overcome the temptations the demons threw at him, and to keep their attention on him rather than on others.

He learned that the owner of the pearl had control over the demons, but also, the demons could look into the owner's mind and find his weak spot, then go after it, again and again, to get him to commit outrageous acts against others. A constant battle of wills ensued.

Berosus wrote to the seven Americans in the fakir's photo, asking if they had found a way to combat the demons, but none of them answered him. He continued to struggle alone until, worn out and dying, he passed the pearl to the only man he could find that might believe how dangerous it was.

The Americans who received his long, rambling letter, written in poor English, and easy to dismiss as being from a crazy crank, had all become successful beyond their wildest dreams. They chose to believe that success came about because of their hard work and superior intellect—traits which none of them possessed before their strange time in the desert.

Only one, Hank Bennett, was troubled by it. And another, Stuart Eliot, had no idea what the priest was talking about.

Then, ten years ago, Stuart Eliot, owner of a mining operation called Powermore Industries, had an accident in one of those mines that nearly killed him. During the time he had no heartbeat and wasn't breathing, a black fox came to him and told him it was ready to receive him. With that, everything that had taken place while he was on that bizarre shore leave in Cairo came back to him.

He remembered the priest's letter and immediately contacted the men who had been on leave with him. He believed he was going crazy, and wanted them to assure him that none of his memories were true —that the priest's letter was a sick joke, and the words of a fox a horrible nightmare. All refused to speak to him except Hank Bennett.

Bennett, too, had been plagued by memories of that time, and learning that a black fox came for Stuart Eliot at the time of death, threw him into a panic. He and Stuart spent whatever it took to find out all they could about the pearl's history and learned relatively quickly what it had taken Father Berosus decades to discover.

Also, since Stuart was a geologist who once owned several rare earth element mines, he realized that the 'special earth' that neutralized the demons in northern China and Inner Mongolia had to be the rare earth elements—the metallic, chemically similar scandium, yttrium and lanthanide series of elements—so prevalent in those areas.

Stuart knew that good quantities of the elements were also found in Idaho. He and Bennett sold everything and went there, searching until they found a rugged area, high in the mountains, where the landscape had reddish brown earth with glints of crystalline metals in it—rare earth metals. They hoped that there, surrounded by rare earth elements, and cut off from temptations, that they would be out of reach of the demons, and when the end came for them, they would be spared eternal damnation.

They re-read Berosus' letter and realized he had to be somehow keeping the demons in check.

They learned the "Year of the Rat" referred to the Chinese zodiac, and its second occurrence from the year they were in the desert, the time they should have all returned to the desert creatures, was 1999. They also discovered that rats were favorite foods of foxes.

They tried to contact Berosus, fearing what might happen when he died. They couldn't find him until Bennett found an article in a Florence newspaper with Berosus photo in it, and sent a private investigator to see what he could learn.

They heard that the priest was dead, and the pearl was missing.

And then the deaths of the American sailors began …

CHAPTER 43

"I've never heard such nonsense in my entire life" Renata folded her arms and gave them all a harsh glare. "Demons? Seriously? I know all of you like old tales, obscure history, and the paranormal. I even went along with your story about Marco Polo and a red pearl because it was all basically harmless. But this is ridiculous. And it's getting more and more dangerous. We really need to leave before something bad happens."

Michael glanced at Kira. Her expression was also filled with disgust and skepticism. Jianjun met his eye and raised his eyebrows.

"Listen," Stuart said, ignoring Renata's outburst, "I know you're good people and want to find out who killed Kira's father and the others, but you can't. Believe me, if you want to live, forget all about the red pearl, and everything else you've been dealing with. Michael, if you have the pearl, give it to me and Hank. We're part of the problem, and we're the ones who need to fix it."

"Are you saying," Kira eyed him coldly, "because you surrounded yourselves with the rare earth elements, the demons left you alone? Why didn't you warn the other men who died?"

"We tried!" Stuart cried. "They wouldn't listen."

"In that case," she continued, "why, when you left the safety of those elements, didn't the demons kill you?"

"I don't know," Hank said. "Perhaps they were more interested, at that point, in Doctor Rempart, and wondering what he was up to. I suspect, however, their attention will come back to Stuart and me. That's why we're here."

"Where is your place in Idaho?" Michael asked. The phone number given to him by the two men who pursued him in Italy—the two killed as they left the Florence police station—had an Idaho area code. He couldn't help but suspect the two had been talking to Stuart and Hank.

Stuart explained the location. Michael knew the area, its remoteness, and harsh terrain—a place with no cell towers or phone lines.

"We want to bring the pearl there among the REEs," Stuart continued. "If you give it to us, you'll end all this, Doctor Rempart. Hank and I know that our five comrades died because of the demons. They're furious that we've all lived past the second Year of the Rat, and they're making up for lost time, killing us in ways that cause the most pain and anguish—mental as well as physical. And now your lives are in danger. We know how to neutralize them so they won't do harm to anyone."

"Stu's right," Hank said. "With the pearl, we can stop them."

The demon that attacked him asked Michael to give her the pearl, and now these two, with their dark auras, did the same. His jaw tightened. "Father Berosus visited me the night of his death and told me what needed to be done. He held off death to tell me. I won't walk away from his request."

"When your name came up," Hank said, "I did some research on you. The time you vanished in Idaho was never explained, but I suspect something supernatural happened. Stu and I heard a lot about those disappearances, since we live in the area. I suspect that's why Father Berosus went to you—because you believe in demons."

"Do I?"

"You know that where the spiritual exists, there are both good and bad spirits, and the bad ones must be controlled," Hank insisted. "Why else does the Catholic Church need more exorcists now than at any other time in the so-called 'modern' era? The fewer people believe in evil, the more the devil gets away with it. People like Doctor Holt excuse evil as 'maladjusted behavior.' It's the ultimate maladjusted behavior in my opinion. People used to believe in evil, they knew Satan, or Lucifer, was real. But now, when faced with the evil, we rationalize it away. That means the devil always wins."

"Or, humanity wins," Kira said, her voice tinged with anger, "because we don't make up excuses for what's wrong with the world and society by blaming it on the devil. We find out what's wrong in the here-and-now and do something about it. What do you expect us to do? Pray? Someone is out there killing the men in this photo, and I'm not about to cry 'the devil made them do it' and then go and hide! I'm going to find him—the very human 'him'—and put him behind bars for the rest of his earthly life. As for what happens when that life is over, I don't give a shit."

"That's the usual attitude." Hank sneered at her. "It's the reason I gave up and simply dropped out. You, Kira Holt, have confirmed that I'm right about everything I believe is wrong with modern society."

"Glad to be of service." Kira scowled right back at him. "Society has its faults, but there's nothing supernatural about murder. I know what I'm seeing is quite unbelievable, but I'm still convinced that once this is over, we will have found a rational answer. Something not demonic." She looked at Jianjun. "I'm sorry."

"I used to be that way," Hank said. "And then seven of us survived a week in the desert. Our survival had to do with those foxes—they took us in, succored us, and then possessed us. Possession is *real.* And it has nothing to do with your religious faith or lack thereof. We were all average guys in everything, and when we returned to the US, our deployment over, all of us became unbelievably successful. Not just simply successful, but the best in fields the fakir told us about. Seeing, my dear Ms. Holt, is believing."

By late night, the storm had grown worse. Polk went out to keep the first watch while the others blew out the candles and lay down. Sleeping bags and air mattresses had been brought in from the cars, so everyone was relatively comfortable. The Uyghurs used the pillows, carpets, and extra blankets.

The wind grew loud, at times sounding like screams. Michael felt everyone's restlessness. A sense that something horrible was about to happen, that something supernatural and ugly crept ever nearer, filled him.

Eventually, despite the noise of the storm and a constant, nagging worry, he heard the steady breathing of sleepers, and he slept as well.

He abruptly awoke the next morning and sat up. Kira was putting on her shoes. "Sorry," she whispered. "Girl bladder."

The one lone light bulb was on, and the low table was laden with a tea pot and cups, plus a soup tureen and bowls.

"Did you see who brought in the food and tea?" Michael asked.

She shook her head. The others began waking now as well.

"Where the hell did that food come from?" Hank demanded, eying all of them suspiciously.

"It also happened when I was here alone," Michael said. "A monk brought me food, but he never spoke."

"How the hell did he get past Taft?" Hank roared. Taft had the last shift and was still outside.

"I'll ask him," Kira said and went to the door. Once she opened it, she could hardly pull it closed against the strong wind of the storm.

The whistle of the wind was so loud they scarcely heard Kira's scream. Jianjun and Michael glanced at each other, then ran outside. They were held back momentarily by the raging storm, but pushed forward.

Kira grabbed onto Jianjun. "The bodyguard …" She pointed towards the side of the building.

Taft lay in a fetal position, his skin charred and blackened as if he had died in a fire, while his eyes and mouth were open wide in a silent scream. The others had followed Michael and Jianjun, and now gaped in shock and horror. Even the Uyghurs were there. Dilnar huddled near Michael until her brother pulled her away.

"How can he look like that?" Kira cried, close to hysteria. "There was no fire. Not here, not anywhere near us!"

"How can this have happened, and we didn't hear anything?" Stuart asked.

Hank, Michael and Polk carried Taft's body to the porch and looked him over while Carter clutched the rifle, his eyes constantly moving as he searched for danger.

"No stab wounds, gunshot, no obvious head trauma," Hank said. He sniffed the semi-automatic rifle. "He never fired his weapon."

"Why was he on the side of the building?" Polk asked. "When I kept watch, I sat near the door. With him off to one side, in this storm, anyone could have snuck into the building from the opposite side and he wouldn't have seen them."

"Someone like whoever brought us food," Stuart said. "What if that person is both feeding us and killing us?"

"He looks like he was screaming," Kira said softly. She was shaking, and Jianjun put a supportive arm around her. "That was the way my father looked."

"Maybe from the pain of the fire," Hank murmured.

"What fire?" Jianjun remarked. "There wasn't one."

"Spontaneous combustion?" Stuart asked. But no one answered.

"We are interlopers here, trespassers, and we are not welcome," Hank said. "We need to keep going. Let's move on. Don't touch the food."

A crow shrieked, its shrill voice startling them. Eventually everyone went back into the church except Carter, who insisted he would keep watch at the door as well as over his fallen comrade's body.

"I think we should leave this place and continue along the Silk Road," Hank said. "If this is the Nestorian monastery Father Berosus told Michael to find, I'm just not seeing it. I wouldn't leave the pearl here. Anyone could steal it, like Polo did, and we'd be in danger all over again."

"I agree," Stuart said.

Kira held up her hand in a gesture of 'stop.' "Before we go rushing off, why would the monk tell Michael to come here if this isn't the right place?"

"For one thing," Renata said, "there are no Nestorian monks in Kyrgyzstan, so whoever talked to Michael was an imposter. And lying."

"Exactly," Hank said. "This place is worthless."

Michael's uneasiness grew as he listened to all of them. Sirom had been right to send him here, so why did these others insist on leaving? "The rain is coming down harder than ever. I wonder if anyone can leave here for any reason."

"You just want to keep us here. Let's load the SUV and go," Stuart said. "I'll get Carter to help us." He opened the door and stepped onto the porch, then came back inside. "Where is Carter?"

Michael felt everyone's anxiety and despair at those words. He hurried outside, the others following. The courtyard was empty. The rain came down in sheets now, pooling on the hard clay soil. It covered the toes of his boots.

"He's got to be out here somewhere," Hank shouted.

Polk headed towards the gate. But before he reached it, it slammed shut. Michael helped him pull it open, but it stuck fast. "I'm going over it," Polk said.

Michael nodded. "Me, too."

They climbed over the gate and shoved while Jianjun and Hank pulled. Finally, it opened.

"Damn storm," Polk muttered. Michael watched others nod, even as they looked over their shoulders.

"I still don't see Carter," Polk shouted above the roar of the storm and the constant pelting of the rain. It fell with an almost human-like fury. Michael's boots sank deep in the soil with each step he took. It seemed to want to hold him and not let go.

"I see him!" Hank yelled. "He's in the SUV."

They all followed, but then Hank slowed down. Right behind him, Michael saw that Carter wasn't moving, and sat at an awkward angle.

Hank yanked the door open. Carter's forehead lay against the steering wheel, his arms oddly twisted and bent. Wires used to start a car without a key hung loose under the dash. Everyone crowded near.

"What the hell!" Hank yelled over the sound of heavy rainfall.

"It looks like he was trying to run away," Stuart shouted back. "Desperately trying."

"As if he was being chased," Jianjun added, "and tried to hotwire the car."

"He wouldn't do that!" Polk insisted.

"But he did!" Hank said. "Just didn't get very far."

No one moved as Hank's words sunk in.

When Hank and Polk checked Carter for obvious signs of what had killed him, they discovered that all the bones in his hands and arms had been broken.

As Polk started to pull him from the SUV, he found that Carter's legs and ankles flopped bizarrely. Those bones, too, had been snapped. "Man, this is all so fucked up."

Stuart turned away and threw up.

Michael helped Hank and Polk carry Carter's broken body back to the porch where they placed him beside Taft.

"Shouldn't we bury them?" Kira asked softly.

"No," Jianjun said. "It's better for us if the Chinese government sees them with as little interference from us as possible. We don't want them to think we did this."

"Let's get out of here, then." She leaned against him. "I can't take it."

"Me, neither." Jianjun glanced at Michael, Hank and Stuart.

"I agree," Stuart said.

"Me, too," Hank muttered.

Michael nodded, although he wondered if they actually could leave.

The Uyghur performers clapped their hands and smiled, also ready and eager to leave this strange place. Everyone picked up their belongings and went to the vehicles, Hank and Michael were in the drivers' seats. The Uyghurs went with Hank since his SUV now had room to spare.

Michael's van was the first to start, but he drove only a couple of inches when the front two tires hit a rut of some sort and dipped low. The tires spun, but couldn't climb out of the rut. He got out of the vehicle to look for wood or rocks to put under the tires to help them grip the road. The water now reached over his ankles. He had never seen rain water rise that quickly.

Hank was having no better luck. He walked over to Michael. "The ground's too wet and muddy. The more I try to get the SUV to move, the deeper into the mud I go."

"Same here. Looks like we have no choice but to wait until the storm passes."

He gave word to the others, and they reluctantly left the vehicles, slogging through the deep rainwater back to the monastery.

Hank took some tools out of his SUV, handed them to Stuart, and then grabbed a few more. "If I'm staying in that old church, I want to know what's behind the locked door in the back of it. Someone—probably some group—has killed two well-trained former Army Rangers. I'm not taking any chances."

The others agreed. Renata, Jianjun and Kira picked up more blankets, candles, and batteries, while Michael was glad to see that Hank's SUV held a tarp. As the others headed for the church, Michael covered Carter and Taft's bodies with the tarp. He then also went inside.

Hank and Polk had already pried open the door in the back of the church. It led to a small, completely empty room. As Michael suspected, a back door to the outside courtyard was on the far wall. It had been nailed shut, as was a tiny window beside it. They decided to leave them closed.

Michael felt a small, soft hand clasp his. It was Dilnar's. "I'm scared," she whispered, gazing up at him with dark, almond-shaped eyes.

Kira looked over the sacristy. "How can this be a monastery if there's no place for anyone to live?"

Jianjun answered. "Quarters for monks probably were built out of wood and very plain. Any such building from Polo's time wouldn't have lasted more than a couple of centuries, if that."

"No other monastery is in the area," Michael said, "so this must be it. It also explains why we're stuck here, and can't leave."

"No, that's because of rain," Kira began when a crash sounded.

Michael pushed Dilnar against the wall, away from the open sacristy door. "Stay here," he said to her.

From the sacristy, he saw that someone had opened the front door to the church. Shots fired through the open door ricocheted through the main room.

Hank, Polk, and Michael darted out of the sacristy to the semi-automatic rifles Hank and the bodyguards had brought. Michael took the one Taft had used. The three of them fired a volley of rounds through the doorway.

When they stopped, all was again quiet.

They carefully approached the door, then swung it shut. When all remained quiet for about five minutes, those in the sacristy came back into the church's main room.

"Who's doing this?" Kira cried.

"Apparently, we aren't the only ones who know about the pearl," Hank said. "For all we know, it could well be soldiers or government mercenaries."

Jianjun caught Michael's eye and shook his head. "The government would have sent a larger force," Jianjun said. "And our few shots wouldn't have gotten them to run. It was the villagers. We scared them, and now they've come to kill us."

"He's right," Michael said. "If they were soldiers, they'd be in here by now, and we'd be dead or under arrest."

"I agree." Renata picked up her backpack. "That's why I'm going out there to talk to them, to explain."

"You can't," Michael said. "They're scared. They won't listen."

"You forget, I speak their language and I've studied their customs all my life. I'm safer with them than here with all of you! You're crazy —each and every one of you. Demons? Philosopher's stones? It's all nonsense. The only rational answer is that one of you killed the two bodyguards. One of you is a murderer, and I'm not sticking around to find out which it is. I've had enough."

"Renata, please." Michael reached for her, but she pushed him away, and then hurried to the wall beside the main door. Dilnar ran to Michael's side.

"You aren't going to stop me," Renata said with disgust. "Don't even try."

"At least take a weapon." Michael held out the rifle. "Have some means to protect yourself if they refuse to listen."

"That will only make things worse."

"Please, Renata." Michael wracked his brain, trying to think of how to get through to her. "They aren't rational. They're afraid."

"But not of me. They'll listen." She placed her hand on the doorknob and then quickly slipped outside.

Michael ran towards her, but Dilnar grabbed his arm and refused to let go. "Please, no. They'll kill you."

"She's right," Jianjun said. "Don't go."

Michael stepped out of the doorway, but the door remained open. He heard Renata shouting something in Uyghur. Her voice became fainter. A male voice shouted in reply, and then all was quiet.

"Shut the door, Michael," Hank said. "She made it; they listened to her."

Michael hoped Hank was right. Reluctantly, he shut the door, and then walked over to the low table, and sat by it. Despair at the thought of Renata weighed down his shoulders.

Out of the silence, he heard a single shot. He shut his eyes and bowed his head. After that he heard nothing except the steady pounding of rain.

CHAPTER 44

The group sat in the church around the small table, listening to the storm. No one spoke. Jianjun and Kira sat side-by-side, then Hank, Stuart, Michael, Dilnar, Az'har, and Paziliya. Polk stood by the window looking out, his rifle propped beside him against the wall.

Thoughts of Renata, her brilliance, her enthusiasm, sharing the room in Tashkent, seeing her so desirable and full of life pushed away everything else from Michael's mind. He hoped he was wrong about the meaning of the gunshot, but he doubted it.

He considered the possibility of them leaving their cars and walking away on foot, back to the main road, and then walking or trying to hitch a ride to Khotan. If the villagers spotted them, however, they would try to kill them. Few things made men as irrational as fear of demons.

But if they stayed, would they be picked off one-by-one as the bodyguards had been? He simply didn't know. The hour was late, but no one felt sleepy. The people no longer with them—Taft, Carter, and Renata—weighed too heavily on everyone's minds.

"You know," Jianjun mused, "all that's going on here is oddly familiar. I realized it when I listened to Hank and Stuart's story along with the creepy Chinese word, *yaojing*. A *yaojing* can be a plain old everyday demon, or it can mean a seductive female demon, a Chinese version of a succubus."

A succubus, Michael thought, could explain what he had encountered as Irina. "What do you mean that it's familiar?"

"There's a well-known Chinese story called *Fengshen Yanyi.* It's translated as *Investiture of the Gods,* although I don't know what 'investiture' means."

"It's a ceremony to give an honor or a rank to someone," Kira explained.

"Ah! Okay, that fits. Anyway, it's a horrible story, centuries old. Lots of torture and mutilation, kinky sex, you name it. Real ugly stuff. These days, you can find it as an *anime* and also as a really popular TV series in China."

"I've watched that story on TV," Az'har said. "It's good. It's what you Americans would call cool." He smiled broadly and his sisters giggled.

"Renata once mentioned the story to me," Michael said softly, struck again at the senselessness of her death. "She never explained it."

"So," Kira said, facing Jianjun, "are you going to tell us the story or just tease us about it?"

"Especially the kinky sex part," Hank said, then guffawed. No one joined him.

"What's interesting about it," Jianjun said, "is that for years, probably centuries, people thought it was pure fantasy. But now, there's some thought that it contains a lot of history—except the part about demons, of course. Anyway, it's the story of the last emperor of the Shang dynasty, King Zhou Xin, who lived more than a thousand years before Christ, long before Buddha, and even Lao Tzu."

Jianjun told them the story of the king who insulted a goddess and how she sent three demons—a Thousand Year Vixen, a Nine-Headed Pheasant, and a Jade Pipa to destroy him and his dynasty. Jianjun didn't give them graphic detail about the horrible tortures dreamed up by the fox-demon who came to be called Daji, but he didn't need to. Their imaginations filled in the blanks. "Daji was so cruel," Jianjun concluded, "that not even the goddess Nüwa could stomach her or her two fellow demons, so she put them in a pearl and banished them to somewhere around what we call Inner Mongolia, which was considered the outer darkness to the Chinese people. There they remained for all eternity. And that, as far as I know, is the end of the story."

The listeners remained quiet as they pondered all he had said.

"We came across the story in our studies of the pearl," Stuart said. "Some say the pearl Marco Polo stole is the one the goddess put the three demons in."

"It does fit," Michael agreed.

"It's just an old fantasy," Hank insisted. "I'm sure there are lots of similar ones in every culture."

"Well, I've never come across any story like that in my studies. It would be a Freudian psychiatrist's wet dream to analyze," Kira said with a nervous chuckle. "I wonder if any of us will be able to sleep tonight."

"It's just a TV show," Az'har told her.

"Is it?" Paziliya murmured, her eyes wide.

As night fell, and the constant rain continued, nerves grew increasingly short. Everyone made sure they were always in each other's sight, even to use the outhouse. Food was now down to a few power bars and the soup left in the church that morning.

Finally, hungry, they ate the cold soup and drank the cold tea, saving their power bars for an emergency.

Eventually, everyone settled down to sleep, deciding that Jianjun, then Michael, then Polk, would keep watch. They rigged up a string from the porch indoors and attached it to whatever metal they could get their hands on. If anything at all happened outside, the watcher could pull the string and alert everyone inside.

Michael woke up before he needed to, aware of Kira's tossing and turning in her sleep. Thoughts of fox-demons from Jianjun's story and how a fox tried to bite her in Florence played in his mind. He put on his heavy jacket and went outside to relieve Jianjun. "Any problems?" he asked.

"No. You don't need to be here yet," Jianjun said. "You can get a little more sleep."

He sat beside Jianjun on the porch. "It's okay. Besides, Kira's tossing and turning—a nightmare, I suspect. Things seem to have progressed between you two. You should go to her."

Jianjun sucked in his breath, but didn't answer.

Michael waited, then said, "You never complain, but I get the feeling things aren't great at home."

Jianjun nodded. "True, and I'll admit that I really like Kira. A lot. But I'm not fooling myself. If it wasn't for this crazy situation, she wouldn't look twice at me."

Michael didn't like his friend putting himself down. "You can't be sure of that."

"Yeah. I can. But it's nice to be someone's hero for once in my life." He gave a wry smile.

Michael gripped Jianjun's shoulder. "Don't go selling yourself short. Get in there, put your arms around her, and let her know you'll keep her safe."

Jianjun grinned. "If I'm getting advice about my love life from you, bro, I'm really in a sorry state."

"So true," Michael said with a chuckle as Jianjun went back inside.

Not five minutes later, Dilnar came out, carrying a pillow and a blanket. "I saw Jianjun come in, and knew you were alone out here," she said. "It's not safe."

"You shouldn't be here," he said.

She placed the pillow beside him and sat. "I want to help."

"Your brother will be angry."

"No, he will say I'm brave, guarding him and my sister as they sleep." She yawned, lay her head on the pillow then turned on her side, her back against his hip and leg, and shut her eyes. "My eyes are tired, but I'm listening for danger."

"I'm sure you are," Michael whispered.

He knew better than to trust her, but at the same time, he didn't mind her company, even if she was already asleep.

About an hour later, he was startled by the sound of the church door opening.

Stuart, coatless and barefoot, walked out the door, across the porch and out into the night. He was sleep walking or under control of some evil force. Michael watched with almost a sense of awe as Stuart headed out the gate.

Michael quietly woke Dilnar. "Go inside," he whispered.

"What?" she reached for him.

He helped her sit up, but saw how sleepy she was. "Go inside." With that, he quietly left her and followed Stuart, his skin prickling. He heard a strange sound, one that wasn't the wind or the rain which had lessened a bit, but sounded like footsteps. Was that foolish girl following him out here? He turned to order her inside, but she wasn't there. No one was. Moonlight shone through a break in the clouds.

When he turned back, Stuart's pace had quickened. A ghostly mist, rolling and roiling in the wind, floated towards Stuart.

"Stuart!" Michael tried to run, but the wind held him back even as it swallowed his voice. "Stuart, stop!"

Stuart's step slowed.

"Come back here!" Michael shouted. He somehow managed to move forward, but his feet stuck to the mud with each step as if he were wading through molasses.

A figure approached the sleep-walker. It was the Chinese woman Michael had seen in Kashgar—the one who so strangely stared at him across the market square. Now, she moved closer to Stuart. Her teeth turned to fangs and her fingers into talons.

"Stuart! Wake up!" Michael yelled as loud and forcefully as he could.

The woman vanished.

Stuart's eyes opened, and he stumbled backwards until he fell in the mud. He sat there, dazed, until Michael reached him and helped him stand. "You were walking in your sleep. You need to get back inside, you're freezing out here."

"I saw *her.*" Stuart's voice quaked in fear as his fingers gripped Michael's arms. "I saw Daji. She's here."

CHAPTER 45

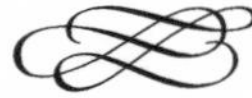

A SCREAM RIPPED through the church.

Everyone immediately sat up. None of them slept well or deeply after waking in the middle of the night when Michael and Stuart returned to the church. Michael told of Stuart's sleepwalking and that Stuart claimed he saw "Daji"—the name of the demon in Jianjun's tale.

"It was a nightmare," Kira had exclaimed, and glowered at Jianjun. "Sleepwalking and a nightmare caused by a certain someone's scary tale." Despite her statement, the others decided that, from that time forward, no one should venture outside alone, and that Polk would take his watch indoors, seated at a window.

"Where's Polk?" Michael asked.

Everyone, including Stuart and the Uyghur performers, went out to look for him. The storm had again grown fierce. All made sure they stayed in sight of at least one other person.

Some twenty minutes later, Az'har and his sisters called out. Michael was first to reach them. Polk lay at the bottom of a rain-soaked pit, face down in the water. Snakes, each a foot long with black and yellow bands, crawled over him. Everyone had been near that spot on previous days, and no pit had been there.

Michael saw Az'har's arm around Paziliya, but Dilnar stood alone.

She was shaking like a leaf, her face tear-stained and etched with horror. He went to her side. "It's all right," he said. "We'll protect you."

She wiped her eyes. "I know," she whispered. "I know you will."

"Good God!" Jianjun cried when he reached the pit. "That's one of the tortures from *Fengshen Yanyi*, the book I told you about."

"It's the work of the demons," Hank said. "They've gotten rid of the men I hired to defend us."

"What if we're next?" Stuart's eyes were round with fear.

"I can't take it," Kira whispered. "Whatever is behind this is horrible. If that means they're demons, fine. I'll believe it, if that'll make them stop. I don't care anymore. I just want it to stop!" All pretense of the rational psychologist was gone, and she folded her arms, rocking slightly.

"I agree," Hank said. "I'm getting the hell out of here, whatever it takes."

"Me, too," Stuart said.

As they headed towards the vehicles, the others joined them. Kira, as one of the lightest of the group, got into Michael's van and started it. She slowly stepped on the gas while everyone else pushed, even the Uyghur performers who still looked in shock from finding Polk's body. But the truck scarcely budged. It was as if something was holding it back, pushing in the opposite direction. They packed gravel under the tires, but it still wouldn't move. The more the wheels spun, the deeper the ruts grew. The same happened when they tried to free Hank's truck from the mud.

Dejected, they went back to the church. Hank lit the candles on the low table. The Uyghurs, as if sensing the mood of the group, took out their instruments and played a slow, haunting tune. No one said aloud what they all knew—that something demonic held them there.

"Why don't we send the three of them down to the village to buy food," Hank suggested, nodding towards the musicians. "They're Uyghurs. The villagers won't hurt them."

"How can you say that? The villagers saw them with us," Michael said. "They're in as much danger as we are."

"We've got to try something!" Hank yelled. "We can't just sit here and starve. We've got weapons. Let's use them!"

"Are you crazy?" Jianjun scoffed. "We can't hold off a whole village."

"Stop," Kira said. "It does no good to argue with each other."

Michael leaned back against the church wall and listened to the music. It was the only bit of comfort in this otherwise miserable spot. From time to time, Dilnar put down her instrument and danced, at other times Paziliya did, and once both together while Az'har alone played. The dances were slow, delicate, seductive, and all of them watched. But then the incessant pounding of the rain on the roof and the thundering of the wind through the eaves grew so loud, they drowned out the music, and the Uyghurs stopped their performance.

Outdoors, the midday sky had turned dark. With that darkness, Michael felt a creeping uneasiness and dread descend over him, a dread that seemed to come from some deep, ancestral terror. He felt alone in an unknown world, a place held by the dwellers of the mist, a place where demons lurked.

"They're here," Hank whispered. "I know that they are, and as much as I believe I have protected myself from them, they know me. I can feel them."

"Don't let them pull your mind away from this world," Michael said. "Control your thoughts. If you give in to them, it'll be all over for you. This place, all that's happening is not a part of our usual world. When a man in the village, Hajji, described this monastery to me, what he described is not what we see here. This world is illusion, but that doesn't make it any less deadly."

"How do you know this?" Stuart asked.

"How else did a Nestorian monk find me in the freezing mountains of Kyrgyzstan? How did I find a monastery which no longer exists? Why did monks feed and welcome me when I arrived here? The monks are trying to help secure the philosopher's stone. That's the only explanation. But the demons want it as well. Brother Sirom didn't make a mistake sending us here," Michael said. "He knew this is the spot where our confrontation must happen. But you're correct to say the demons are already with us."

"God, I hope not," Jianjun murmured.

"I had hoped for some sign, something that would tell me where to put the stone, a sign that would tell me it was safe to leave it here," Michael said. "But there's nothing. I believe that's why we have to confront the demons ourselves."

"Confront them?" Hank shouted. "You're crazy! We've spent our lives trying to stay clear of them."

"But, as you said, they're here now," Michael said. "You know it as well as I do."

"What I know is this," Hank said, drawing a handgun and pointing it at Michael. "Give me the pearl. I'm leaving here if I have to walk. I'm heading to a place I know I'll be safe."

Stuart picked up one of the rifles and stood beside Hank, pointed the rifle at Michael and the others.

"Hank, Stu—don't be crazy," Jianjun shouted.

Michael looked at the two men holding firearms on him. He should have known. Their auras were black now.

"We want the stone," Stuart yelled. "Give it over, or we'll shoot and take it anyway!"

Michael faced Stuart. Something bothered him, but he had no choice except to play it out. "So he'll turn you into a killer, too, is that it?"

Stuart looked shocked. "What are you saying?"

"You got more than you bargained for in all this, didn't you, Stu?" Michael asked. "But so did the men who were following me in Florence and Rome, and then ended up dead. Why did you kill them, Hank?"

Stuart gaped at Hank.

"He's wrong!" Hank bellowed. "I don't know what the hell he's talking about. I haven't killed anybody!"

"Your private eyes, or whatever they were, are dead, Hank," Michael said calmly. "They were shot as soon as they left the police station."

"What? Nonsense! No! I …" He looked at Stuart, his eyes wide, questioning. "Stu?"

Stuart swallowed hard, lifting the rifle a bit higher, as if to better aim it.

"What did you do, Stuart?"

Stuart ran his tongue over dry lips. "They were learning too much. They would have kept the stone for themselves. Who knows what damage they'd have done. So I paid someone to stop them." He faced Michael. "All we want is the philosopher's stone. Nothing more. We've studied alchemy for ten years. The old Egyptian fakir said there was a way to save us from the demons, but when he grew angry, he refused to do it. With our studies, we learned how."

Michael looked at both men with disgust. "You know it's about more than that."

"It was step one." The rifle in Stuart's hands shook violently.

"Shut up, Stu," Hank said.

"No, they should understand that we would use the stone to grant to us the ultimate desire of all alchemists—immortality. But that meant we would do good things. That's all we ever wanted. We never wanted to hurt anyone."

"No? Then why did your people attack us in Kyrgyzstan?" Michael asked. "It was clear they were no highway bandits."

"We paid them to rob you, and get the pearl," Hank said. "Nothing more. We thought it would be easy, but when you and your guides shot at them, we came up with a different plan. We 'saved' your friends from the second attack"—he nodded at Kira and Jianjun —"knowing that, with them, we'd find you. And we did."

From the corner of his eye, Michael saw that Jianjun was slowly inching closer to Stuart. "I want to go back to why you two are still alive. Are you demons now, or simply doing their dirty work—killing people, hunting me? I doubt you're demons because it seems they can't attack the owner of the pearl which tells me the demons are using you to do it for them. The question is why?"

"We're our own boss," Stuart cried, sounding on the verge of hysteria. "We fight the demons."

"Sure you do." Michael smirked. "That's why you killed two men in Florence, and you delivered your bodyguards to the demons to kill in bizarre ways, which seems to be a specialty of theirs."

"It's not true," Stuart cried. He was on the verge of tears. "We never meant for anyone to die."

Hank raised his gun. "And no one else needs to die. Not if you give us the stone. But if you don't ..."

Jianjun was closing in on Stuart, so Michael concentrated on Hank. "All right! This has gone far enough. And you're right. The pearl isn't worth us dying. I'll give it to you, if you let us go."

Hank raised his chin. "Fine."

"It's in my pocket." Michael put his hand in his pocket and curled his fingers into a fist, then held it out to Hank.

Hank looked suspicious as he cautiously reached for the pearl, his gaze fixed on Michael's hand. "Here. Take it." Michael thrust forward his hand as he spoke and at the same time delivered a Shaolin kick to Hank's stomach. Hank doubled over, his gun going off into the crumbling floor. Michael grabbed Hank's wrist and twisted, causing Hank to flip, head over heels, onto the ground. He dropped the gun, and Michael swooped down to pick it up.

As Stuart's attention turned for a split second towards Hank and Michael, Jianjun spun towards him, grabbed his arm then twisted around so that his back was to Stuart's chest and Stuart's elbow lay atop his shoulder. He then pulled downward on Stuart's arm, using all his strength and weight to hyperextend and then crack the elbow. Stuart screamed, high and loud, and dropped to the floor, shrieking and clutching his arm. Jianjun picked up his gun.

"Good job," Michael said. "Let's tie them up."

"No!" A woman's voice ordered.

Michael and the others looked towards the door to the church to see who had cried out.

The door lay open, and two beautiful women in short, black dresses and four-inch heels strolled into the church. Vibrant green eyes latched on to Hank and Stuart.

"No!" Hank crawled towards the back of the church.

Stuart remained petrified, still on his knees, cradling his broken elbow. The woman with long, wavy auburn hair reached him. She pointed from him to a far wall.

Michael tried to speak, to move, but he, Jianjun, Kira, and the Uyghurs seemed frozen in place, as if time stood still except for the female demons and their prey.

"It's my turn," Stuart whispered, sounding resigned. "Like the others." With tears streaming from his eyes, he stood and faced the beautiful redhead. She nodded. Still crying, he bent from the waist and ran hard at a wall. At the last second, still bent, he leaped, keeping his hands and arms down so that his head took the full force of the blow. The room resounded with a loud snap as the bulk of his weight caused his head to hit the wall so hard that his neck snapped. He fell to the floor dead as blood flowed from the crushed bone and lacerations on his skull.

Hank watched in horror. He faced the blonde woman standing over him. "No, no, no! You can't do this!"

"Can't I?" she said dismissively. "You knew this time would come. You made a deal. You enjoyed the good and now don't want to pay the price. Deals are not made to be broken." With that, she held out a dagger, its hilt crested with old-style Chinese characters.

"Please, no …" The sound from his lips was more of a wail than a word.

The sounds of war filled the church, gunfire, the putt-putt of helicopter blades, and the blast of a ship's whistle. Horrifying, ugly screams and cries of pain rang in all their heads.

"I can't …" Hank cried as he took the dagger in both hands.

Michael struggled, trying to shout out, to move towards Hank, to do anything to stop the trance Hank seemed to be in. But nothing worked.

Hank was beyond hearing, beyond reason. He held the dagger straight outward, pointed at his chest, and then plunged it in below the ribcage, angled upward so it struck his heart. Blood spewed from his body, hitting the wall, the ceiling and floor, raining down on him as he fell onto his back, mortally wounded, the hilt of the blade protruding from his chest.

The two women, their tasks completed, turned into black foxes.

Michael, who had been straining to reach Hank, nearly fell to the floor when whatever force had been holding him back suddenly let go. He gripped the gun he had gotten from Hank and fired at a fox. The bullet went right through the demon and didn't hurt it.

The foxes began to walk towards him. He fired again, to no avail.

"Those women," Kira gasped, scarcely able to speak. "One of them fits the description of the person who brought a birthday gift to Gene Oliveros' daughter. The gift that had a bomb that killed his whole family!"

"Run!" Jianjun cried. He grabbed Kira's arm and headed out the door, the Uyghurs behind him, and Michael following.

They knew their vehicles were useless in the rain and ran downhill. "We'll need to stay on the hillside as long as possible," Michael called. "Skirt the road, but try to stay out of sight of any villagers who might be on it."

Between the dark and the rain, they found it difficult to see where they were going, and the footing was treacherous. Wet mud under Michael's feet gave way and began to slide. Soon, the mud above him, where the others stood, also slid, and all of them tumbled and rolled down the hill until they came to a spot where the ground leveled off.

Michael sat up, glad he hadn't been hurt. Jianjun was near him. They looked for Kira and the Uyghur performers.

The four had disappeared.

CHAPTER 46

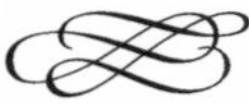

MICHAEL AND JIANJUN searched all around, but could find no sign of Kira or the musicians.

"What the fuck happened to them?" Jianjun shouted, scared and worried. "It wasn't that much of a slide. Even if they didn't get caught up in it, they should be here. I was holding Kira's hand. I know I had her as the mud started to slip. One minute she was with me and then gone."

"We were getting away," Michael said. "The demons stopped us."

"Again." Jianjun walked in circles, desperately searching, hoping against hope. "They want us back at the monastery."

Michael met his gaze and nodded.

"Damn!" Jianjun drew in his breath.

It took a lot longer to make their way up the hill to the monastery than it had going down it. The building looked deserted. No light shone.

They entered.

Hank and Stuart's bloodied bodies lay on the floor. A faint glow came from under the door of the sacristy. They walked back there and opened the door.

The middle of the room now had a staircase heading downward.

The staircase was lit as was the floor below. "What the hell?" Jianjun cried.

Michael plunged down the stairs, Jianjun on his heels. They reached a large basement, as large as the church above it. Its walls were wood framed, the floor thick shards of wood and sawdust.

In the center stood a tall, thick iron pole that glowed red hot. Daji's instrument of torture—her *paolou.* The heat from it was almost unbearable.

The three Uyghurs stood on the far side of the basement, and at their feet lay Kira, her eyes shut.

"Kira!" Jianjun started to run towards her, but Michael grabbed his arm, holding him back.

"Her mind was too weak to fight them," Dilnar said. "The demons have her now."

"So I see," Michael said. "Finally, I meet you as well."

Dilnar smiled warmly at him. "Michael, I knew you would recognize me—and that you'd come to me." She removed the Uyghur headdress, dropped it to the floor, and stepped on it. Her hair was arranged in a traditional Chinese style, parted in the center and pulled back into a braided coil. Michael recognized the woman who had stared at him in Kashgar—and the monster who wanted to attack Stuart the night he sleepwalked outdoors.

She raised her chin and immediately took on a distinction and regal bearing that had not been present in the Uyghur performer.

"Daji." Michael whispered.

A slow smile spread over her face.

–I make wishes come true. My wishes.

Her voice wasn't a voice, but something in his head.

"You are the one who will be destroyed," Michael said.

"You're so funny," she said sweetly. "You would never do that. You know I'm the only one who comforted you. Remember the peace you felt when I was near? Whenever I touched you? I can do that, and more." She moved closer. "Dilnar, you saw as little more than a child. But I'm much a woman." Her voice changed to the one he would never forget. "Or, if you prefer, I'll be *her* for you. For all eternity, you'll be with her. With me. No longer alone. No longer lonely."

"Go to hell," he said.

She ignored his words and glanced at the two remaining Uyghurs.

—My kinsmen, the Nine-Headed Pheasant. Az'har took off his Muslim hat and gave a bow.

—And the Jade Pipa. Paziliya also bowed and then removed her headdress.

Daji's cold gaze slid over Michael, Jianjun and Kira, then the demon who had been Dilnar held out her hand.

—Give me the philosopher's stone or I will use my most terrible creation on your friends. The iron pole sears the flesh quite crisply as the body's internal organs slowly cook. Death is agonizingly slow, and in the end, welcomed.

Jianjun looked confused, but called out, "Michael, fight her. You've got to fight her. No matter what she says."

"You must be proud, Daji," Michael said with utter disgust, "to be the creator of something so monstrous."

The demon laughed.

"Tell us first," Michael said, knowing Daji's arrogance meant she loved talking about herself, "how you came to free yourself from the captivity that the Goddess Nüwa placed you in."

Daji smirked at his request.

"Please," Michael said. "I would like to hear it."

—Tell him.

—Yes. Tell him our story. We would like to hear it once again.

—As you wish.

After the Goddess Nüwa gave the red pearl, encased in a bronze vessel, to the warriors who defeated King Zhou Xin, it remained buried in the northern lands for over two thousand years. And then, one day, a slovenly, unimportant Mongolian warlord captured a Chinese nobleman and his family. The nobleman exchanged a secret of the Chinese people for his family's life. He told the warlord how to find a red pearl that afforded power over demons. The warlord believed him and searched for the pearl. He found it, but it appeared powerless. He killed the nobleman and his family for their decep-

tion, and then left the area. Once away from the special elements, however, the demons revived and bestowed their power on the warlord who had saved them.

His name was Genghis Khan and with their help, he conquered most of the known world. After his death, his body was returned to Mongolia, the pearl with him. For a while, the demons' power was again diminished. But one day, a handsome young man stole the pearl and carried it to the Western world. There, the demons discovered many new playthings. In Egypt, when the 'pearl' was pressed to the foreheads of American sailors, the demons turned them, and found yet another continent for their fun. The entire world, one could say, became their oyster.

At her quip, demonic laughter filled Michael's head.

"Wait, you 'turned' the sailors?" Michael asked. "What do you mean?"

—They are the children of the Thousand Year Vixen—the most powerful of the Nüwa's demons—those foxes who have chosen to join the vixen forever.

Michael shook his head at the folly of men who think they can overcome the evil they accept in the face of temptation. "If they're your children, why did you kill them?"

—Why do you think they are dead.?

At that, all seven sailors—Daniel Holt, Gene Oliveros, the senator, hedge fund manager, newspaper publisher, Hank, and Stuart—appeared and slowly descended the stairs. Their faces and bodies bore ghastly scars and mutilations from the way they had died.

"Oh, my God," Jianjun whispered, and Michael knew he, too, could somehow see these dead, these monsters.

—Here is our audience.

The Jade Pipa picked up Kira and walked her towards the *paolou*.

"No!" Michael and Jianjun cried. Jianjun reached Kira and tried to pull her free, but the Pheasant demon held him back.

—Only one thing can save her.

"Stop. I'll trade you. Me for Kira and Jianjun," Michael said.

Daji looked at him coldly, lifted an eyebrow, and said nothing. The other two demons moved closer to the *paolou* with their captive.

"All right," Michael said. "You win."

He took out his key ring. On it was a fob in the shape of a cheap plastic soccer ball—the sort of thing many men in Italy carry around in honor of their favorite pastime. He placed it on the ground, then used the butt of the gun that he still carried to give it a hard rap. The hollow plastic shell split along its glued seam, and out rolled a small red orb.

Michael picked it up between his thumb and forefinger. "Here it is. Now let them go."

—But we have set up the paolou.

—We want to use it.

—My sisters are unhappy. We have two things you want, but you only have one item to trade. Give us the pearl and you can have the girl, but we keep your friend—the traitor to his people.

"Do you hear them?" Michael asked Jianjun.

"Yes, but I don't know how."

He nodded. The demons were influencing his mind, but they, in turn, were controlled by the philosopher's stone, which he possessed. And through it, somehow, he could influence what others saw and heard, even if other worldly—just as he caused those around him to see this monastery as an erect building, rather than as a flattened ruin.

"I will trade as you wish," Michael said, "but my friend needs a chance. Let me give him this"—he picked a sliver of sawdust up off the floor—"to protect himself."

The demons laughed so hard Michael thought his head would explode.

Michael placed the sliver on Jianjun's palm. "Take this *phurba,*" he said. "You know the *phurba*. You remember hearing about it when we were on a dig in Nepal. It's from Tibet. It kills demons. Use it!"

The demons all but screamed with laughter at Michael and his friend.

"Do it!" Michael ordered.

In Jianjun's hand Michael suddenly saw a magnificent, three-sided, silver Tibetan dagger. Without hesitation, Jianjun jabbed the *phurba* into the Pheasant demon's side, then he spun towards the Jade Pipa who held Kira and drove the blade into its heart. He pulled Kira from its arms as it fell. The demons howled in pain and fury as they writhed on the ground from the magic of the *phurba*.

Michael picked up the *phurba* and stepped towards Daji. She backed away as she, too, clearly saw the dagger. But then she waved her arm, starting a fire between her and Michael.

Michael jumped back from the flames. He helped Jianjun run with Kira towards the stairs, hoping to climb up them to escape. But when as they reached them, the stairs began to burn as well.

—Where will you go now?

Daji and the seven sailors around her all laughed with delight at Michael and Jianjun's fear. They also pointed and laughed at the Jade Pipa and Pheasant's moans and cries of pain.

Michael took the red pearl from his pocket and clutched it, desperately trying to think what he could do. Then it struck him. The monks. They wanted him here; they welcomed the pearl—and him—and they should know how to stop the demons. Michael pushed Jianjun and Kira behind him, knowing the demons couldn't directly attack him, and they would have to get past him to reach them. He filled his mind with the vision of the monks kneeling before an unseen altar. "Help us!"

Daji spun towards the demon who had been Hank.

—Hank Bennett, take him, and hold him against the paolou until he gives up the pearl. Do it now!

The Hank-demon walked through the fire and grabbed Michael. Michael was strong, but the demon's strength was greater as it dragged him closer to the *paolou*. Still, Michael wouldn't let go of the stone, and kept concentrating on the monks.

Jianjun charged the Hank-demon and stabbed him with the *phurba*, but it had no effect. "Help us, Hank," Jianjun pleaded. "The man you once were, the good man, is still inside you. Don't let that *thing* win!"

The Hank-demon stiffened and stopped moving. Its torso bore the scars of Hank's death, of the way he had stabbed himself in the heart, but now his form seemed to pulsate, as if going between its demon self and something else, something that still bore a semblance of humanity.

"Please!" Jianjun cried. "Don't let Daji do this to you, Hank! You're strong—you've tried to be a good man, even when the demons became too strong for you to fight."

The Hank-demon swung his arm, lifting Jianjun off his feet and throwing him hard against a wall. He hit it and fell to the floor. The Hank-demon looked from Jianjun to Michael, then to the other sailors, and finally his gaze rested on Stuart who had been his friend. A vision of Hank—of a man suffering and eternally damned—appeared in the body of the demon, but then vanished as the demon took over again. "The man you've been all these years is still alive," Michael said, struggling to physically hold the monster back, but knowing he was failing. "Is this what you fought for, planned for, all those years? To let Daji do this to you now?"

Hank and the demon pulsated, as first one emerged, then the other. It was almost like looking through a strobe light as he moved from one form to the other. "Come and help us," Michael whispered, calling to the monks as he clutched the pearl, praying for a miracle to help them get away from these demons.

Suddenly, the Hank-demon spun around and lunged at Daji, swinging her around and shoving her towards the *paolou.*

She was too strong for him and pushed back.

Michael jumped to Hank's side. Together, they shoved Daji backwards. But then, Daji vanished and in her place stood Irina. Michael drew back, his movements frozen. His heart ached just looking at her face. She reached for him. "Help me, Michael," she whispered. "Please help me."

"Damn you! You'll never be her." He shoved Daji even harder towards the *paolou*.

Irina vanished as Daji's screams pierced through Michael's head. She tried to run, but Hank's fury got the upper hand, and he pushed her against the red hot pole. She screamed in rage while he yelled that she took his life from him, took away the man he once was. She fought, but his demonic strength coupled with his human fury was too much for her to overcome.

Their fight caused sparks and embers from the fire to fly about the dry wood cellar, starting many small fires that quickly spread and sucked the oxygen from the room.

Michael stumbled backwards, away from the *paolou* while Hank continued to hold Daji down. He went to Kira and saw that she was still unconscious. Jianjun reached them both.

Michael opened his hand and stared at the philosopher's stone. He dropped to his knees, physically, mentally and emotionally exhausted. "Where are the monks you kept here waiting for someone to return? I need them. We need them." He looked towards the *paolou.* Hank's body, not the demon's lay dead on the ground before it.

Daji was with the Pheasant and Jade Pipa. They held each other, all weakened from the torments inflicted on them. The demons could suffer but not die.

Around them, six sailors writhed and burned in the fire, suffering, as was the fitting result of their fate. Six, not seven. Hank wasn't among them, and Michael could only hope that meant that Hank's final actions had saved him from eternity among the damned. He turned his head, unable to look at them suffer. They were once good, young men who made a terrible mistake and now would pay forever because of it. Michael was sickened by everything around him, by everything demonic. The fires grew, and he and his friends could hardly breathe. "You brought us here, damn you!" he called to the monks. "Help us!"

Something in the wall behind them, one of the few areas not in flames, looked different to him. He crawled towards it, and as he did, he saw it was a door. Jianjun was coughing hard, struggling to breathe. Michael went back and picked up Kira, knowing Jianjun would somehow find the strength to follow. Once through the doorway the air was clear. He saw a circular staircase that went downward. He glanced at the demons, the fire, and had no choice. Jianjun stumbled towards him and Kira. Michael nodded at him and then plunged down the stairs. Jianjun followed.

They descended a long way, ending in a square chamber lit by candles. The walls of the chamber were strange—reddish-brown in color, with glints of a crystalline metal in them. He remembered Stuart's words about rare earth metals.

Alchemical symbols drawn in white paint covered those walls. They reminded Michael of the tomb he had opened in Mongolia belonging to an alchemist known as Lady Hsieh—symbols like these appeared on items in her casket. And all at once memories came to him of seeing similar symbols in another place. His father's study.

The only object in the room was a tiny metal chest, no more than four inches on all sides, with a hinged lid and a simple hook latch. Michael took a step towards it when he heard Jianjun whisper, "God, no!"

He turned.

The three demons walked down the staircase and into the room. They now looked like wraiths, almost translucent, and in shades of white and gray.

"Father Berosus told me if I look at the pearl, it will look back at me and read my mind," Michael said. "It will know I'm the one with the power over it." With that, he held out his hand, the philosopher's stone cupped in his open palm, and stared at it.

"You demons," he continued, "are made powerless by rare earth elements, and the walls here are covered with them. They are making you increasingly weak." Simply by saying that, he could feel the strength of the demons lessening.

The fight, now, was for their minds. He allowed his eyes to travel over the wall symbols, and then to the demons. "You are too weak to leave this place. The only way is to go back into the pearl."

The three demons held onto each other, as if finding more strength that way.

Michael felt the pull of their demonic power fighting against him. He felt his hold slipping.

"Enter the pearl," he commanded. "And I'll walk you out of this room."

The room quaked. A rainbow of colors shot out from the stone, and with it a loud terrible scream filled not only his mind, but the entire room. Jianjun pressed Kira's head to his chest, holding his head to hers, trying to cover her ears as well as his own.

Michael remained where he stood as the stone seemed to grow larger.

Furious, the demons rushed at him as if to attack, but then swirled around him so that they appeared to be a gray-black churning mist. Their movement caused a low rumble in the room. Michael held his hand higher, even as the mist buffeted his body, and the rumble grew to a loud roar, causing the walls to shudder.

"Enter the pearl!" His voice was louder this time, and as he stared at the alchemical symbols, they began to make sense to him. As if from some innate part of his soul, some collective unconscious memory, he knew their meaning. *Do it!* he ordered, no longer saying the words, but speaking from his mind.

Strange lumps appeared on his hands, arms, and face, as if something was being drawn under his skin and fighting to break free.

Jianjun held Kira tighter, bending over her to protect her if the demons escaped Michael's control. Then, as quickly as it began, the noise in the room stopped. Michael's skin was no longer contorted, and the pearl shrank back to its past size.

Michael stared at the stone. "Got you."

"Michael," Jianjun whispered. "Kira's breathing is stronger. Her eyes ... she's opened them."

She lifted her hand to his face, then gripped his shoulder as he helped her sit up.

Michael nodded, grateful she had survived.

"You now know the full measure of your power," said a voice behind him. The monk who had brought him food appeared from nowhere. "I suspect you knew much of this before, because you appear to already be an alchemist. But I warn you, the path you are now on will destroy you, as surely as it has me and my brothers, and as it did the sailors. The Nestorians knew the dangers of the philosopher's stone and its demons and built this room to house the stone. They kept it in that small box, created from the metals the demons most fear." He pointed to the metal chest.

Michael picked it up. "This, then, is the demons' coffin." He opened the chest and was about to place the stone inside when he stopped. He felt its pull. He knew what it could do, and he had enjoyed having its power.

He looked up at the monk, and with that, the meaning of the monk's words struck him. He placed the stone inside the chest and then shut and secured the lid. He took a deep, quavering breath. "It's done." He glanced up at the monk. "Now, explain to me who you are, and why you're here."

"I was the bungler, the idiot monk, who showed the philosopher's stone to Marco Polo." The monk hung his head a moment. "I am Brother Qinom. I was proud, too proud, of the faith the mother of Kublai Khan put our monastery to hold the red pearl. She asked us to take it far from her son, so we filled ten wagons with soil from the area near Xanadu, and traveled to this hilltop. We dug this room and lined the walls with the rare earth soil, and stored the pearl here, then built the monastery above it.

"Some years later, three Venetians, a father, his brother and his son, Marco, came to see what it was that had caused so much consternation among the family of Kublai Khan. I brought the box up to the monastery to show them and even showed them how to open the Shang dynasty bronze that held it. They looked at the pearl and laughed about it, saying it wasn't even a real pearl. They were far more interested in the very old bronze it was kept in. They brought good food and quantities of drink for me and the other monks. They were jolly men, who spoke a surprisingly good mix of Chinese and Mongolian. We had many laughs.

"In the morning, when we woke up, the men, the bronze, and the pearl were gone. We searched for them, but they had many hours start, and fast horses, while we had none. Because I was the one in charge of the pearl, the one who lost it, I have been condemned to remain here until the pearl was returned. My fellow monks were also condemned since they did not prevent this catastrophe from happening, but they only join me now and then to pray. We have waited centuries for this day, for the pearl's return."

"This area was once remote, but it's not any longer," Michael said. "The Chinese government is moving more and more people into the Xinjiang province. I can easily imagine them coming here to bulldoze and clear what's left of the monastery. Also, the villagers are now curious about this place, I'm sure, thanks to our presence. If someone levels the monastery, they could discover this chamber. If that happens, and they find the pearl, they'll unleash the demons on an unsuspecting world once more."

The monk nodded, then said, "Then, I pass the responsibility on to you. My work is done. *Consummatum est.*" He bowed his head and collapsed into dust.

"We should get out of here," Jianjun said, helping Kira to her feet.

Michael shook his head as if coming out of a trance. "Yes, you're right." He looked around the room, at the alchemical symbols on the walls, and finally at the chest in his hand, the pearl safely inside it. "It was all about possession, demonic possession. But the question now is, with the philosopher's stone, who possesses whom?"

"Boss," Jianjun said, "I don't ..."

"Don't worry about it." Michael held up the chest. "They're trapped. For the moment, at least."

Michael, Jianjun and Kira went up the stairs, and when they reached the top, they saw that there was no cellar; there was no fire.

Before them stretched a crumbling, blackened ruin—much as the villagers had described the building all along. But among the ruins they saw the bodies of Hank, Stuart, the three bodyguards, and then, some distance away, Renata Corbi.

CHAPTER 47

NOT ONLY HAD the rain stopped, but the ground was dry as if it had never rained at all. The three got into the rented van and drove practically nonstop some nine-hundred miles to Ürümqi on the opposite side of the Taklamakan Desert. It had an international airport used by many foreigners. Michael hoped people from the village would be too scared to go up to the monastery before the three of them were safely out of the country. Once the villagers did go up there, he suspected they might bury the bodies and not say anything that would cause the attention of the Chinese government to rain down on them. The deaths would also very likely confirm what they already believed—that *yaojing* haunted the area.

At the airport, Jianjun asked, "Are we going try to get to Inner Mongolia, boss?"

"I don't want to take the chance of being stopped by government officials. I want the pearl out of China as soon as possible, so I'll head west, Ürümqi to Moscow to Seattle, and then make my way to Idaho." He looked from Jianjun to Kira, at how much they had grown to care about each other. "You and Kira will be safe taking a more direct route to Beijing and then to Los Angeles."

"No, boss. I'm going with you," Jianjun said. He faced Kira and took both her hands, his gaze more than sad, and his voice soft. "It's best that you don't go with us."

Dismay and surprise filled her face, but then, slowly, it changed to understanding. "You're right. Go with Michael, help him protect the pearl. I could use some time alone, to try to understand all this, and process it in my own way."

"It won't be easy," Jianjun said, tucking a wayward lock of hair behind her ear. "You once told me about your mother, your regret about the past. Maybe it's time to look for her."

She nodded. "I think I've got a lot of searching to do ... of many kinds. But I'll be fine."

He studied her a long moment. "I wish ..." he began.

"I know," she said. "So do I. But sometimes things aren't meant to be. I'll be sure to follow your exploits with Michael in the news. I suspect they won't end here."

She put her arms around him, and they kissed then held each other tight before she let him go. Alone, she walked away.

Michael and Jianjun had no problems as they flew to Seattle, and from there, took a small local flight to Missoula, Montana. Kira had texted Jianjun and Michael that she arrived safely in Los Angeles where, as suspected, all the deaths had been attributed to accidents or suicides, no one was investigating anything any longer, and the entire matter had been neatly swept under the rug. Jianjun texted her back a long message with some of the words held in his heart and ended with a goodbye.

Once in Missoula, Michael rented a four-wheel-drive jeep and bought the supplies they needed to carry out their plan.

Michael got in the driver's side. "I've been thinking," he said.

"Uh oh," Jianjun muttered, getting in beside him.

"Seriously. How often does one come across a philosopher's stone? Charlotte Reed deserves to see this. She helped us, after all."

"And you deserve to keep it, perhaps?" Jianjun asked. "To learn to use it? Maybe to test it out a time, or two?"

"It's in the name of science," Michael said. And there's Irina, he told himself. What if, to help her, he needed the stone? How could he not keep it?

"You've seen what it can do," Jianjun said softly. "You know all the people the demons killed just in these few weeks. Leaving it 'in the world' so to speak, even if you think you can control it, is simply too dangerous. For you … and your friends." Jianjun studied him before adding, "Even for Irina Petrescu."

Michael put his hands on the steering wheel as he pondered Jianjun's words. Then, he nodded.

They drove along Highway 12 in Idaho to a place called Lowell, and from there, headed south east into the mountains, past the point where a fire road became so rugged the four-wheel-drive jeep could scarcely make it, and even past the point where the road vanished altogether.

Once they could drive no further, they carried their supplies deep into the mountains for another day until they found an area with a number of reddish-brown rocks with embedded metals, similar to the walls of the room deep under the monastery. They didn't see Hank or Stuart's homes and didn't look for them.

Neither slept well that night and rose early to watch the sunrise. Not long before they had been to an area called the "top of the world" in the T'ian Shan mountains, but the feeling here was every bit as desolate, every bit as lonely. They began to dig. About eight feet down, they stopped.

"Okay, boss," Jianjun said as he climbed out. "It's time."

Michael watched his friend. At moments like this, he wondered which of them was the boss. Jianjun was right, but still, as he placed the pearl and its metal box onto the floor of the pit they had dug, every fiber of his body told him he needed to keep the stone with him, to keep it close, to use its power. To become a proper alchemist.

But his mind said otherwise.

The Thousand-Year Vixen couldn't be killed, but deep in earth filled with elements that left her too weak to be harmful, she could no longer destroy anyone ... as long as the rare earth elements worked the way Stuart and Hank thought they did. But he could think of no place safer.

And he wouldn't be tempted any longer by the philosopher's stone. Or so he hoped.

He climbed out of the pit. He and Jianjun shoveled the soil on top of the pearl, and as he did, he heard Daji's voice in his head raining vile curses on him and his progeny until the end of time.

Michael and Jianjun spent another day cleaning up the area to make sure no one would notice anything wrong and inadvertently start digging.

When they returned to Missoula, Jianjun rented a car to drive home to Vancouver, and Michael turned in the jeep for a passenger car to head down the highway to Salmon City, Idaho. He planned to spend a little time with his old friends, Sheriff Jake Sullivan and Charlotte Reed.

"I guess I'm all set to leave again." Jianjun held the rental car keys in hand and eyed Michael with a worried expression that said he wondered what strange situation Michael would get involved in the minute his back was turned.

"I'll be fine," Michael said. "I'm just going to Salmon."

"And then back to Italy?"

"I don't know," he replied. "I don't know what my future holds. But enough of that, are you sure you don't want to simply take a plane home? It's a long drive."

"I'm sure. I need time to think about all that's happened." Jianjun dropped his gaze to the ground, then up to the mountains that framed the city.

"But you are going home?" Michael was worried about his friend. This trip had aged Jianjun—or, if not aged, it had matured him. Love, he guessed, could do that to a man.

"I am, yes. I'll go back to my wife, my loving, charming wife, who my father insisted I marry because of who her family is, not because of anything to do with me. It's going to be harder than ever." He shook his head and met Michael's gaze. "Sometimes Chinese customs and family honor are a bitch!"

Michael put his arm around his friend's shoulders as they walked to Jianjun's rental car. "I'll do my best to find a dig site somewhere that interests me, and then I'll give you a call."

"It can be none too soon, boss!" Jianjun said with a wan smile.

Jianjun got into the car and drove off, leaving Michael alone once more.

Michael got into his rental car for the drive to Salmon City, but before leaving, he called Magda's phone number. He wanted to be sure Irina was safe. He received a message telling him that number was no longer in service.

He was disappointed, but not surprised.

He would spend some time with his friends, and then he would visit his father. Only by resolving all that lay unfinished between them would he ever find peace in his life. And perhaps, someday, find the woman he once loved. He wasn't the lovesick boy he had been years ago, and he greatly doubted that seeing the "real" Irina would be anything like the way the demon made him believe he still felt about her. Too many years had passed, and they were two very different people now.

He recognized that he could never live a conventional life, not after all he had experienced because of his connection to things normal people never saw or experienced. He had no idea where his life would lead, but he couldn't shake the sense that there was something more for him to do. At the same time, the strong feeling filled him that nothing truly important in life could be left hanging—that when a meaningful event was left unresolved, it ate at you and festered into something far worse than it might have been otherwise.

Before he could go forward, he needed to find a resolution to his past, one way or the other.

And he must start with his father.

Two weeks later, high in the mountains of central Idaho, in a barren, roadless area far from any civilization, a thin, gray, wraith-like hand jutted upward from deep under the ground. The hand broke through the dank soil and reached for the sunlight, then spread its fingers wide, slightly rotating back and forth, and enjoying the feel, once again, of warmth.

—*We must find a way.*

—*We always do.*

—*And the world will be ours.*

—*Again.*

NOTE FROM THE AUTHOR

For those who would like to read more about Marco Polo's journey to Asia, *Marco Polo, From Venice to Xanadu* by Laurence Bergreen is a very readable history. Also, two books by John Man, *Xanadu, Marco Polo and Europe's discovery of the East,* and *Marco Polo, the Journey that Changed the World* are a mixture of travel writing and history, giving a rich personal account of the author following Polo's footsteps across Asia.

A 16th century Chinese novel called, *Fengshen Yanyi,* (usually translated as *Investiture of the Gods*) recounts of the last days of the Shang dynasty and the war that resulted in the overthrow of King Zhou Xin. The novel is quite lengthy, about a hundred chapters, and a great deal of it involves the battles that led to the establishment of the Chou dynasty, and the brave men and women who died in the battles. Few translations have been published. Perhaps the most readable and accessible, *Tales of the Teahouse Retold: Investiture of the Gods* by Katherine Liang Chew, covers the first part of the Chinese tale.

Almost unknown in the West, the story recently has been captured in two Chinese television series, and forms the basis for at least two Japanese video games, a Japanese *manga* (graphic novel) and *anime* (film).

There is no "red pearl" in the original story.

PLUS ...

Don't miss hearing about the next archeologist Michael Rempart adventure and all of Joanne's new books by signing up for her mailing list at www.joannepence.com.

For your enjoyment, here's chapter one of **Ancient Illusions***, the next book in the "Ancient Secrets" series:*

CHAPTER ONE

Nightmare, the most awful form of dream ... You feel afraid without knowing why. Then you have the impression that something is acting upon you ... you wish to escape, to get away from the influence that is making you afraid. Then you find it not easy to escape...

—Lafcadio Hearn

Cape Cod, Massachusetts

Michael Rempart parked his rental car along the road on the ocean side of Cape Cod. The sky over the Atlantic was dark with clouds as a storm rolled in.

From this location he could see Wintersgate on a bleak rise near the water's edge. A few stands of firs stood nearby, their limbs bent and stretching away from the ocean. The massive house was gray and forbidding with a high stone turret on one corner, as if the long-ago builder couldn't decide between a grand manor or a castle, and ended up with a structure that was neither. Instead, it was monstrous and unsettling.

Sixteen years had passed since Michael last walked the floors of his family home. Sixteen years, during which he gained renown as an archaeologist, and traveled over much of the world, but had never ventured back to Cape Cod. "You aren't welcome here," were his father's last words to him. There was nothing welcoming here; the place itself was threatening.

Now, he stood with shoulders hunched against the biting wind. Forty-two years old, he was tall, with a rangy build and a tan from time spent working remote dig sites. Solitary, with few friends, his coworkers felt he actively discouraged camaraderie. Even on digs where people often grew close, they stayed away as if an unseen barrier lay between them.

He had been that way most of his life, and he attributed it to his upbringing behind the morose walls of Wintersgate. That was why this sudden compulsion to return there made no sense to him. He had no idea why he would want to face the father he had spent his earliest years fearing, and his later years loathing. But he did. He struggled to ignore the feeling. And then his nightmares began.

In every one, he was back at Wintersgate facing his father, his all too present personal demons, and trying to find answers to the questions that had haunted him throughout his life.

In the end, he gave in. And now he was here.

The wind grew fierce as he got into the rental. He ran his hands through wavy, jet-black hair. No sense putting off the inevitable, he told himself. Still, as he started the car for the drive to Wintersgate, he felt a tightness in his chest and a quickening of his pulse over what he was about to face.

William Claude Rempart was at work, as usual, in his laboratory on the second floor of Wintersgate. Shelves with flasks and bottles of minerals, chemicals, reference books, and botched experiments, each carefully labeled, covered the room.

He moved slowly. His hands quivered with age as he gathered the chemicals he needed and placed them on one side of the lab table. Last of all, he picked up a philosopher's stone, the prime agent of alchemy, and rubbed the stone with his thumb, feeling its warmth, its power. Those ignorant fools who knew nothing about alchemy would think he was caressing a chunk of reddish pink rock. Poor sots, he thought. In his hand, he held the key to life.

William Claude was an alchemist, a position past ages called a sorcerer or a wizard. He knew to be an alchemist meant doing more than mixing chemicals together. Any idiot could do that. It required the ability to imbue one's creation with a life-force, an ability few people possessed. He believed it was a powerful family trait transmitted from one generation to the next.

Not that William Claude cared one whit about family. He cared about himself, and the aging happening to him. He looked at the sunken flesh of his hands, the sagging skin and brown age marks. His face's wrinkled skin felt soft and thin, while his shoulders had become stooped. Each day he found it increasingly difficult to stand as straight and tall as he once had. He was eighty-eight years old, which made it imperative he learn to perfect the alchemy he had worked on all his life.

Most people thought the goal of alchemy was to create gold. They were wrong.

Alchemists not only wanted to create gold, the perfect metal that would not rot, but to develop the perfect *man*, one that would not age. In other words, one who would be immortal.

His thoughts were interrupted by the sound of rain hitting the windows as a streak of lightning flashed across the sky. Thunder soon followed.

He placed the philosopher's stone on a solid gold plate on the worktable. He had already prepared beakers of chemicals, and they were in varying stages of development. He picked up the latest vial he had been working on when a stabbing headache struck. He gripped the edge of the table with one hand, his eyes squeezed shut until the pain began to recede. But then another bolt hit like a knife slashing into his temple, and he fell to his knees.

He dropped the vial and a pool of blue liquid puddled before him. In it, he saw his son, Michael. His only living child. He gasped for breath against the pain.

"Michael," he whispered, touching the liquid with his fingertips. He pulled himself to his feet and tried to reach Michael's thoughts with his mind. As always, he failed. But strangely, although he couldn't penetrate Michael's mind, William Claude knew his son was near.

"Finally, it must be working." He was so pleased he almost smiled.

William Claude's mind raced as he unlocked the cabinet door and removed a gold-filled elixir. He poured out a tablespoon of potion and drank it. Then he sat as it slowly warmed, enriched, and rejuvenated him. He had waited sixteen years for Michael to come home.

Now, he could put his plan in place.

Continue with **Ancient Illusions** *wherever fine e-books and print books are sold.*

ABOUT THE AUTHOR

Joanne Pence was born and raised in northern California. She has been an award-winning, *USA Today* best-selling author of mysteries for many years, but she has also written historical fiction, contemporary romance, romantic suspense, a fantasy, and supernatural suspense. All of her books are now available as ebooks and in print, and many are also offered in special large print editions. Joanne hopes you'll enjoy her books, which present a variety of times, places, and reading experiences, from mysterious to thrilling, emotional to lightly humorous, as well as powerful tales of times long past.

Visit her at www.joannepence.com and be sure to sign up for Joanne's mailing list to hear about new books.

The Rebecca Mayfield Mysteries

Rebecca is a by-the-book detective, who walks the straight and narrow in her work, and in her life. Richie, on the other hand, is not at all by-the-book. But opposites can and do attract, and there are few mystery two-somes quite as opposite as Rebecca and Richie.

ONE O'CLOCK HUSTLE – North American Book Award winner in Mystery

TWO O'CLOCK HEIST

THREE O'CLOCK SÉANCE

FOUR O'CLOCK SIZZLE

FIVE O'CLOCK TWIST

SIX O'CLOCK SILENCE

Plus a Christmas Novella: The Thirteenth Santa

The Angie & Friends Food & Spirits Mysteries

Angie Amalfi and Homicide Inspector Paavo Smith are soon to be married in this latest mystery series. Crime and calories plus a new "twist" in Angie's life in the form of a ghostly family inhabiting the house she and Paavo buy, create a mystery series with a "spirited" sense of fun and adventure.

COOKING SPIRITS

ADD A PINCH OF MURDER

COOK'S BIG DAY

MURDER BY DEVIL'S FOOD

Plus a Christmas mystery-fantasy: COOK'S CURIOUS CHRISTMAS

And a cookbook: COOK'S DESSERT COOKBOOK

The early "Angie Amalfi mystery series" began when Angie first met San Francisco Homicide Inspector Paavo Smith. Here are those mysteries in the order written:

SOMETHING'S COOKING

TOO MANY COOKS

COOKING UP TROUBLE

COOKING MOST DEADLY

COOK'S NIGHT OUT

COOKS OVERBOARD

A COOK IN TIME

TO CATCH A COOK

BELL, COOK, AND CANDLE

IF COOKS COULD KILL

TWO COOKS A-KILLING

COURTING DISASTER

RED HOT MURDER

THE DA VINCI COOK

Supernatural Suspense

Ancient Echoes

Top Idaho Fiction Book Award Winner

Over two hundred years ago, a covert expedition shadowing Lewis and Clark disappeared in the wilderness of Central Idaho. Now, seven anthropology students and their professor vanish in the same area. The key to finding them lies in an ancient secret, one that men throughout history have sought to unveil.

Michael Rempart is a brilliant archeologist with a colorful and controversial career, but he is plagued by a sense of the supernatural and a spiritual intuitiveness. Joining Michael are a CIA consultant on paranormal phenomena, a washed-up local sheriff, and a former scholar of Egyptology. All must overcome their personal demons as they attempt to save the students and learn the expedition's terrible secret....

Ancient Shadows

One by one, a horror film director, a judge, and a newspaper publisher meet brutal deaths. A link exists between them, and the deaths have only begun ....

Archeologist Michael Rempart finds himself pitted against ancient demons and modern conspirators when a dying priest gives him a powerful artifact—a pearl said to have granted Genghis Khan the power, eight centuries ago, to lead his Mongol warriors across the steppes to the gates of Vienna.

The artifact has set off centuries of war and destruction as it conjures demons to play upon men's strongest ambitions and cruelest desires. Michael realizes the so-called pearl is a philosopher's stone, the prime agent of alchemy. As much as he would like to ignore the artifact, when he sees horrific deaths and experiences, first-hand, diabolical possession and affliction, he has no choice but to act, to follow a path along the Old Silk Road to a land that time forgot, and to somehow find a place that may no longer exist in the world as he knows it.

Ancient Illusions

A long-lost diary, a rare book of ghost stories, and unrelenting nightmares combine to send archeologist Michael Rempart on a forbidden journey into the occult and his own past.

When Michael returns to his family home after more than a decade-long absence, he is rocked by the emotion and intensity of the memories it awakens. His father is reclusive, secretive, and obsessed with alchemy and its secrets—secrets that Michael possesses. He believes the way to end this sudden onslaught of nightmares is to confront his disturbing past.

But he soon learns he isn't the only one under attack. Others in his life are also being tormented by demonic nightmares that turn into a deadly reality. Forces from this world and other realms promise madness and death unless they obtain the powerful, ancient secrets in Michael's possession. Their violence creates an urgency Michael cannot ignore. The key to defeating them seems to lie in a land of dreams inhabited by ghosts … and demons.

From the windswept shores of Cape Cod to a mystical land where samurai and daimyo once walked, Michael must find a way to stop not only the demons, but his own father. Yet, doing so, he fears may unleash an ancient evil upon the world that he will be powerless to contain.

Historical, Contemporary & Fantasy Romance

Dance with a Gunfighter

Gabriella Devere wants vengeance. She grows up quickly when she witnesses the murder of her family by a gang of outlaws, and vows to make them pay for their crime. When the law won't help her, she takes matters into her own hands.

Jess McLowry left his war-torn Southern home to head West, where he hired out his gun. When he learns what happened to Gabriella's family, and what she plans, he knows a young woman like her will have no chance against the outlaws, and vows to save her the way he couldn't save his own family.

But the price of vengeance is high and Gabriella's willingness to sacrifice everything ultimately leads to the book's deadly and startling conclusion.

Willa Cather Literary Award finalist for Best Historical Novel.

The Dragon's Lady

Turn-of-the-century San Francisco comes to life in this romance of star-crossed lovers whose love is forbidden by both society and the laws of the time.

Ruth Greer, wealthy daughter of a shipping magnate, finds a young boy who has run away from his home in Chinatown—an area of gambling parlors, opium dens, and sing-song girls, as well as families trying to eke out a living. It is also home to the infamous and deadly "hatchet men" of Chinese lore.

There, Ruth meets Li Han-lin, a handsome, enigmatic leader of one such tong, and discovers he is neither as frightening cruel, or wanton as reputation would have her believe. As Ruth's fascination with the lawless area grows, she finds herself pulled deeper into its intrigue and dangers, particularly those surrounding Han-lin. But the two are from completely different worlds, and when both worlds are shattered by the Great Earthquake and Fire of 1906 that destroyed most of San Francisco, they face their ultimate test.

Seems Like Old Times

When Lee Reynolds, nationally known television news anchor, returns to the small town where she was born to sell her now-vacant childhood home, little does she expect to find that her first love has moved back to town. Nor does she expect that her feelings for him are still so strong.

Tony Santos had been a major league baseball player, but now finds his days of glory gone. He's gone back home to raise his young son as a single dad.

Both Tony and Lee have changed a lot. Yet, being with him, she finds that in her heart, it seems like old times...

The Ghost of Squire House

For decades, the home built by reclusive artist, Paul Squire, has stood empty on a windswept cliff overlooking the ocean. Those who attempted to live in the home soon fled in terror. Jennifer Barrett knows nothing of the history of the house she inherited. All she knows is she's glad for the chance to make a new life for herself.

It's Paul Squire's duty to rid his home of intruders, but something about this latest newcomer's vulnerable status ... and resemblance of someone from his past ... dulls his resolve. Jennifer would like to find a real flesh-and-blood man to liven her days and nights—someone to share her life with—but living in the artist's house, studying his paintings, she is surprised at how close she feels to him.

A compelling, prickly ghost with a tortured, guilt-ridden past, and a lonely heroine determined to start fresh, find themselves in a battle of wills and emotion in this ghostly fantasy of love, time, and chance.

Dangerous Journey

C.J. Perkins is trying to find her brother who went missing while on a Peace Corps assignment in Asia. All she knows is that the disappearance has something to do with a "White Dragon." Darius Kane, adventurer and bounty hunter, seems to be her only hope, and she practically shanghais him into helping her.

With a touch of the romantic adventure film Romancing the Stone, C.J. and Darius follow a trail that takes them through the narrow streets of Hong Kong, the backrooms of San Francisco's Chinatown, and the wild jungles of Borneo as they pursue both her brother and the White Dragon. The closer C.J. gets to them, the more danger she finds herself in—and it's not just danger of losing her life, but also of losing her heart.

Made in the USA
Coppell, TX
17 December 2019

13192624R00171